AF194412

The Portent And Other Stories

by

George MacDonald

Double 9
BOOKS

The Portent And Other Stories
by George MacDonald

Copyright © 2024

All Rights reserved.

No part of this publication may be reproduced,
stored in a retrieval system, or transmitted in any
form or by any means, electronic, mechanical,
photocopying or Otherwise, without the written
permission of the publisher.
The author/editor asserts the moral right to
be identified as the author/editor of this work.

ISBN: 978-93-67140-66-6

Published by

DOUBLE 9 BOOKS
2/13-B, Ansari Road
Daryaganj, New Delhi – 110002
info@double9books.com
www.double9books.com
Tel. 011-40042856

This book is under public domain

ABOUT THE AUTHOR

George MacDonald was a Scottish author, poet, and Christian Congregational clergyman. He established himself as a pioneering figure in modern fantasy writing and mentored fellow writer Lewis Carroll. In addition to his fairy stories, MacDonald wrote various works on Christian theology, including sermon collections. George MacDonald was born on December 10, 1824 in Huntly, Aberdeenshire, Scotland. His father, a farmer, descended from the Clan MacDonald of Glen Coe and was a direct descendant of one of the families killed in the 1692 massacre. MacDonald was raised in an exceptionally literary household: one of his maternal uncles was a renowned Celtic scholar, editor of the Gaelic Highland Dictionary, and collector of fairy stories and Celtic oral poetry. His paternal grandfather had helped to publish an edition of James Macpherson's Ossian, a contentious epic poem based on the Fenian Cycle of Celtic Mythology that contributed to the birth of European Romanticism. MacDonald's step-uncle was a Shakespeare scholar, while his paternal cousin was also a Celtic intellectual.

CONTENTS

DEDICATION

MY DEAR SIR, KENSINGTON, *May, 1864.*

Allow me, with the honour due to my father's friend, to inscribe this little volume with your name. The name of one friend is better than those of all the Muses.

And permit me to say a few words about the story.—It is a Romance. I am well aware that, with many readers, this epithet will be enough to ensure condemnation. But there ought to be a place for any story, which, although founded in the marvellous, is true to human nature and to itself. Truth to Humanity, and harmony within itself, are almost the sole unvarying essentials of a work of art. Even *The Rime of the Ancient Mariner*—than which what more marvellous?—is true in these respects. And Shakespere himself will allow any amount of the marvellous, provided this truth is observed. I hope my story is thus true; and therefore, while it claims some place, undeserving of being classed with what are commonly called *sensational novels.*

I am well aware that such tales are not of much account, at present; and greatly would I regret that they should ever become the fashion; of which, however, there is no danger. But, seeing so much of our life must be spent in dreaming, may there not be a still nook, shadowy, but not miasmatic, in some lowly region of literature, where, in the pauses of labour, a man may sit down, and dream such a day-dream as I now offer to your acceptance, and that of those who will judge the work, in part at least, by its purely literary claims? If I confined my pen to such results, you, at least, would have a right to blame me. But you, for one, will, I am sure, justify an author in dreaming *sometimes.*

In offering you a story, however, founded on *The Second Sight*, the belief in which was common to our ancestors, I owe you, at the same time, an apology. For the tone and colour of the story are so different from those naturally belonging to a Celtic tale, that you might well be inclined to refuse my request, simply on the ground that your pure Highland blood revolted from the degenerate embodiment given to the ancient belief. I can only say that my early education was not Celtic enough to enable me to do better in this respect. I beg that you will accept the offering with forgiveness, if you cannot with approbation.

Yours affectionately,

GEORGE MACDONALD.

Chapter I
My Boyhood

My father belonged to the widespread family of the Campbells, and possessed a small landed property in the north of Argyll. But although of long descent and high connection, he was no richer than many a farmer of a few hundred acres. For, with the exception of a narrow belt of arable land at its foot, a bare hill formed almost the whole of his possessions. The sheep ate over it, and no doubt found it good; I bounded and climbed all over it, and thought it a kingdom. From my very childhood, I had rejoiced in being alone. The sense of room about me had been one of my greatest delights. Hence, when my thoughts go back to those old years, it is not the house, nor the family room, nor that in which I slept, that first of all rises before my inward vision, but that desolate hill, the top of which was only a wide expanse of moorland, rugged with height and hollow, and dangerous with deep, dark pools, but in many portions purple with large-belled heather, and crowded with cranberry and blaeberry plants. Most of all, I loved it in the still autumn morning, outstretched in stillness, high uplifted towards the heaven. On every stalk hung the dew in tiny drops, which, while the rising sun was low, sparkled and burned with the hues of all the gems. Here and there a bird gave a cry; no other sound awoke the silence. I never see the statue of the Roman youth, praying with outstretched arms, and open, empty, level palms, as waiting to receive and hold the blessing of the gods, but that outstretched barren heath rises before me, as if it meant the same thing as the statue—or were, at least, the fit room in the middle space of which to set the praying and expectant youth.

There was one spot upon the hill, half-way between the valley and the moorland, which was my favourite haunt. This part of the hill was covered with great blocks of stone, of all shapes and sizes—here crowded together, like the slain where the battle had been fiercest; there parting asunder from spaces of delicate green—of softest grass. In the centre of one of these green spots, on a steep part of the hill, were three huge rocks—two projecting out of the hill, rather than standing up from it, and one, likewise projecting from the hill, but lying across the tops of the two, so as to form a little cave, the back of which was the side of the hill. This was my refuge, my home within a home, my study—and, in the hot noons, often my sleeping chamber, and my house of dreams. If the wind blew cold on the hillside, a hollow of lulling warmth was there, scooped as it were out of the body of the blast, which, sweeping around, whistled keen and thin through the cracks and crannies of the rocky chaos that lay all about; in which confusion of rocks the wind plunged, and flowed, and eddied, and withdrew, as the sea-waves on the cliffy shores or the unknown rugged bottoms. Here I would often lie, as the sun went down, and watch the silent growth of another sea, which the stormy ocean of the wind could not disturb—the sea of the darkness. First it would begin to gather in the bottom of hollow places. Deep valleys, and all little pits on the hill-sides, were well-springs where it gathered, and whence it seemed to overflow, till it had buried the earth beneath its mass, and, rising high into the heavens, swept over the faces of the stars, washed the blinding day from them, and let them shine, down through the waters of the dark, to the eyes of men below. I would lie till nothing but the stars and the dim outlines of hills against the sky was to be seen, and then rise and go home, as sure of my path as if I had been descending a dark staircase in my father's house.

On the opposite side the valley, another hill lay parallel to mine; and behind it, at some miles' distance, a great mountain. As often as, in my hermit's cave, I lifted my eyes from the volume I was reading, I saw this mountain before me. Very different was its character from that of the hill on which I was seated. It was a mighty thing, a chieftain of the race, seamed and scarred, featured with chasms and precipices and over-leaning rocks, themselves huge as hills; here blackened with shade, there overspread with glory; interlaced with the silvery lines of falling streams, which, hurrying from heaven to earth, cared not how they went, so it were downwards. Fearful stories were told of the gulfs, sullen waters, and dizzy heights upon that terror-haunted mountain. In storms the wind roared like thunder in its caverns and along the jagged sides of its cliffs, but at other times that uplifted land-uplifted, yet secret and full of dismay—lay silent as a cloud on the horizon.

I had a certain peculiarity of constitution, which I have some reason to believe I inherit. It seems to have its root in an unusual delicacy of hearing, which often conveys to me sounds inaudible to those about me. This I have had many opportunities of proving. It has likewise, however, brought me sounds which I could never trace back to their origin; though they may have arisen from some natural operation which I had not perseverance or mental acuteness sufficient to discover. From this, or, it may be, from some deeper cause with which this is connected, arose a certain kind of fearfulness associated with the sense of hearing, of which I have never heard a corresponding instance. Full as my mind was of the wild and sometimes fearful tales of a Highland nursery, fear never entered my mind by the eyes, nor, when I brooded over tales of terror, and fancied new and yet more frightful embodiments of horror, did I shudder at any imaginable spectacle, or tremble lest the fancy should become fact, and from behind the whin-bush or the elder-hedge should glide forth the tall swaying form of the Boneless. When alone in bed, I used to lie awake, and look out into the room, peopling it with the forms of all the persons who had died within the scope of my memory and acquaintance. These fancied forms were vividly present to my imagination. I pictured them pale, with dark circles around their hollow eyes, visible by a light which glimmered within them; not the light of life, but a pale, greenish phosphorescence, generated by the decay of the brain inside. Their garments were white and trailing, but torn and soiled, as by trying often in vain to get up out of the buried coffin. But so far from being terrified by these imaginings, I used to delight in them; and in the long winter evenings, when I did not happen to have any book that interested me sufficiently, I used even to look forward with expectation to the hour when, laying myself straight upon my back, as if my bed were my coffin, I could call up from underground all who had passed away, and see how they fared, yea, what progress they had made towards final dissolution of form—but all the time, with my fingers pushed hard into my ears, lest the faintest sound should invade the silent citadel of my soul. If inadvertently I removed one of my fingers, the agony of terror I instantly experienced is indescribable. I can compare it to nothing but the rushing in upon my brain of a whole churchyard of spectres. The very possibility of hearing a sound, in such a mood, and at such a time, was almost enough to paralyse me. So I could scare myself in broad daylight, on the open hillside, by imagining unintelligible sounds; and my imagination was both original and fertile in the invention of such. But my mind was too active to be often subjected to such influences. Indeed life would have been hardly endurable had these moods been of more than occasional occurrence. As I grew older, I almost outgrew them. Yet sometimes one awful dread would seize me—that, perhaps, the prophetic power manifest in the gift of second sight, which, according to the testimony of my old nurse, had belonged to several of my ancestors, had been in my case transformed in kind without losing its nature, transferring its abode from the sight to the hearing, whence resulted its keenness, and my fear and suffering.

Chapter II
The Second Hearing

One summer evening, I had lingered longer than usual in my rocky retreat: I had lain half dreaming in the mouth of my cave, till the shadows of evening had fallen, and the gloaming had deepened half-way towards the night. But the night had no more terrors for me than the day. Indeed, in such regions there is a solitariness for which there seems a peculiar sense, and upon which the shadows of night sink with a strange relief, hiding from the eye the wide space which yet they throw more open to the imagination. When I lifted my head, only a star here and there caught my eye; but, looking intently into the depths of blue-grey, I saw that they were crowded with twinkles. The mountain rose before me, a huge mass of gloom; but its several peaks stood out against the sky with a clear, pure, sharp outline, and looked nearer to me than the bulk from which they rose heaven-wards. One star trembled and throbbed upon the very tip of the loftiest, the central peak, which seemed the spire of a mighty temple where the light was worshipped—crowned, therefore, in the darkness, with the emblem of the day. I was lying, as I have said, with this fancy still in my thought, when suddenly I heard, clear, though faint and far away, the sound as of the iron-shod hoofs of a horse, in furious gallop along an uneven rocky surface. It was more like a distant echo than an original sound. It seemed to come from the face of the mountain, where no horse, I knew, could go at that speed, even if its rider courted certain destruction. There was a peculiarity, too, in the sound—a certain tinkle, or clank, which I fancied myself able, by auricular analysis, to distinguish from the body of the sound. Supposing the sound to be caused by the feet of a horse, the peculiarity was just such as would result from one of the shoes being loose. A terror—strange even to my experience—seized me, and I hastened home. The sounds gradually died away as I descended the hill. Could they have been an echo from some precipice of the mountain? I knew of no road lying so that, if a horse were galloping upon it, the sounds would be reflected from the mountain to me.

The next day, in one of my rambles, I found myself near the cottage of my old foster-mother, who was distantly related to us, and was a trusted servant in the family at the time I was born. On the death of my mother, which took place almost immediately after my birth, she had taken the entire charge of me, and had brought me up, though with difficulty; for she used to tell me, I should never be either *folk* or *fairy*. For some years she had lived alone in a cottage, at the bottom of a deep green circular hollow, upon which, in walking over a healthy table-land, one came with a sudden surprise. I was her frequent visitor. She was a tall, thin, aged woman, with eager eyes, and well-defined clear-cut features. Her voice was harsh, but with an undertone of great tenderness. She was scrupulously careful in her attire, which was rather above her station. Altogether, she had much the bearing of a gentle-woman. Her devotion to me was quite motherly. Never having had any family of her own, although she had been the wife of one of my father's shepherds, she expended the whole maternity of her nature upon me. She was always my first resource in any perplexity, for I was sure of all the help she could give me. And as she had much influence with my father, who was rather severe in his notions, I had had occasion to beg her interference. No necessity of this sort, however, had led to my visit on the present occasion.

I ran down the side of the basin, and entered the little cottage. Nurse was seated on a chair by the wall, with her usual knitting, a stocking, in one hand; but her hands were motionless, and her eyes wide open and fixed. I knew that the neighbours stood rather in awe of her, on the ground that she had the second sight; but, although she often told us frightful enough stories, she had never alluded to such a gift as being in her possession. Now I concluded at once that she was *seeing*. I was confirmed in this conclusion when, seeming to come to herself suddenly, she covered her head with her plaid, and sobbed audibly, in spite of her efforts to command herself. But I did not dare to ask her any questions, nor did she attempt any excuse for her behaviour. After a few moments, she unveiled herself, rose, and welcomed me with her usual kindness; then got me some refreshment, and began to question me about matters at home. After a pause, she said suddenly: "When are you going to get your commission, Duncan, do you know?" I replied that I had heard nothing of it; that I did not think my father had influence or money enough to procure me one, and that I feared I should have no such good chance of distinguishing myself. She did not answer, but nodded her head three times, slowly and with compressed lips—apparently as much as to say, "I know better."

Just as I was leaving her, it occurred to me to mention that I had heard an odd sound the night before. She turned towards me, and looked at me fixedly. "What was it like, Duncan, my dear?"

"Like a horse galloping with a loose shoe," I replied.

"Duncan, Duncan, my darling!" she said, in a low, trembling voice, but with passionate earnestness, "you did not hear it? Tell me that you did not hear it! You only want to frighten poor old nurse: some one has been telling you the story!"

It was my turn to be frightened now; for the matter became at once associated with my fears as to the possible nature of my auricular peculiarities. I assured her that nothing was farther from my intention than to frighten her; that, on the contrary, she had rather alarmed me; and I begged her to explain. But she sat down white and trembling, and did not speak. Presently, however, she rose again, and saying, "I have known it happen sometimes without anything very bad following," began to put away the basin and plate I had been using, as if she would compel herself to be calm before me. I renewed my entreaties for an explanation, but without avail. She begged me to be content for a few days, as she was quite unable to tell the story at present. She promised, however, of her own accord, that before I left home she would tell me all she knew.

The next day a letter arrived announcing the death of a distant relation, through whose influence my father had had a lingering hope of obtaining an appointment for me. There was nothing left but to look out for a situation as tutor.

Chapter III
My Old Nurses Story

I was now almost nineteen. I had completed the usual curriculum of study at one of the Scotch universities; and, possessed of a fair knowledge of mathematics and physics, and what I considered rather more than a good foundation for classical and metaphysical acquirement, I resolved to apply for the first suitable situation that offered. But I was spared the trouble. A certain Lord Hilton, an English nobleman, residing in one of the midland counties, having heard that one of my father's sons was desirous of such a situation, wrote to him, offering me the post of tutor to his two boys, of the ages of ten and twelve. He had been partly educated at a Scotch university; and this, it may be, had prejudiced him in favour of a Scotch tutor; while an ancient alliance of the families by marriage was supposed by my nurse to be the reason of his offering me the situation. Of this connection, however, my father said nothing to me, and it went for nothing in my anticipations. I was to receive a hundred pounds a year, and to hold in the family the position of a gentleman, which might mean anything or nothing, according to the disposition of the heads of the family. Preparations for my departure were immediately commenced. I set out one evening for the cottage of my old nurse, to bid her good-bye for many months, probably years. I was to leave the next day for Edinburgh, on my way to London, whence I had to repair by coach to my new abode—almost to me like the land beyond the grave, so little did I know about it, and so wide was the separation between it and my home. The evening was sultry when I began my walk, and before I arrived at its end, the clouds rising from all quarters of the horizon, and especially gathering around the peaks of the mountain, betokened the near approach of a thunderstorm. This was a great delight to me. Gladly would I take leave of my home with the memory of a last night of tumultuous magnificence; followed, probably, by a day of weeping rain, well suited to the mood of my own heart in bidding farewell to the best of parents and the dearest of homes. Besides, in common with most Scotchmen who are young and hardy enough to be unable to realise the existence of coughs and rheumatic fevers, it was a positive pleasure to me to be out in rain, hail, or snow.

"I am come to bid you good-bye, Margaret; and to hear the story which you promised to tell me before I left home: I go to-morrow."

"Do you go so soon, my darling? Well, it will be an awful night to tell it in; but, as I promised, I suppose I must."

At the moment, two or three great drops of rain, the first of the storm, fell down the wide chimney, exploding in the clear turf-fire.

"Yes, indeed you must," I replied.

After a short pause, she commenced. Of course she spoke in Gaelic; and I translate from my recollection of the Gaelic; but rather from the impression left upon my mind, than from any recollection of the words. She drew her chair near the fire, which we had reason to fear would soon be put out by the falling rain, and began.

"How old the story is, I do not know. It has come down through many generations. My grandmother told it to me as I tell it to you; and her mother and my mother sat beside, never interrupting, but nodding their heads at every turn. Almost it ought to begin like the fairy tales, *Once upon a time,*—it took place so long ago; but it is too dreadful and too true to tell like a fairy tale.—There were two brothers, sons of the chief of our clan, but as different in appearance and disposition as two men could be. The elder was fair-haired and strong, much given to hunting and fishing; fighting too, upon occasion, I dare say, when they made a foray upon the Saxon, to get back a mouthful of their own. But he was gentleness itself to every one about him, and the very soul of honour in all his doings. The younger was very dark in complexion, and tall and slender compared to his brother. He was very fond of book-learning, which, they say, was an uncommon taste in those times. He did not care for any sports or bodily exercises but one; and that, too, was unusual in these parts. It was horsemanship. He was a fierce rider, and as much at home in the saddle as in his study-chair. You may think that, so long ago, there was not much fit room for riding hereabouts; but, fit or not fit, he rode. From his reading and riding, the neighbours looked doubtfully upon him, and whispered about the black art. He usually bestrode a great powerful black horse, without a white hair on him; and people said it was either the devil himself, or a demon-horse from the devil's own stud. What favoured this notion was, that, in or out of the stable, the brute would let no other than his master go near him. Indeed, no one would venture, after he had killed two men, and grievously maimed a third, tearing him with his teeth and hoofs like a wild beast. But to his master he was obedient as a hound, and would even tremble in his presence sometimes.

"The youth's temper corresponded to his habits. He was both gloomy and passionate. Prone to anger, he had never been known to forgive. Debarred from anything on which he had set his heart, he would have gone mad with longing if he had not gone mad with rage. His soul was like the

night around us now, dark, and sultry, and silent, but lighted up by the red levin of wrath and torn by the bellowings of thunder-passion. He must have his will: hell might have his soul. Imagine, then, the rage and malice in his heart, when he suddenly became aware that an orphan girl, distantly related to them, who had lived with them for nearly two years, and whom he had loved for almost all that period, was loved by his elder brother, and loved him in return. He flung his right hand above his head, swore a terrible oath that if he might not, his brother should not, rushed out of the house, and galloped off among the hills.

"The orphan was a beautiful girl, tall, pale, and slender, with plentiful dark hair, which, when released from the snood, rippled down below her knees. Her appearance formed a strong contrast with that of her favoured lover, while there was some resemblance between her and the younger brother. This fact seemed, to his fierce selfishness, ground for a prior claim.

"It may appear strange that a man like him should not have had instant recourse to his superior and hidden knowledge, by means of which he might have got rid of his rival with far more of certainty and less of risk; but I presume that, for the moment, his passion overwhelmed his consciousness of skill. Yet I do not suppose that he foresaw the mode in which his hatred was about to operate. At the moment when he learned their mutual attachment, probably through a domestic, the lady was on her way to meet her lover as he returned from the day's sport. The appointed place was on the edge of a deep, rocky ravine, down in whose dark bosom brawled and foamed a little mountain torrent. You know the place, Duncan, my dear, I dare say."

(Here she gave me a minute description of the spot, with directions how to find it.)

"Whether any one saw what I am about to relate, or whether it was put together afterwards, I cannot tell. The story is like an old tree—so old that it has lost the marks of its growth. But this is how my grandmother told it to me.—An evil chance led him in the right direction. The lovers, startled by the sound of the approaching horse, parted in opposite directions along a narrow mountain-path on the edge of the ravine. Into this path he struck at a point near where the lovers had met, but to opposite sides of which they had now receded; so that he was between them on the path. Turning his horse up the course of the stream, he soon came in sight of his brother on the ledge before him. With a suppressed scream of rage, he rode head-long at him, and ere he had time to make the least defence, hurled him over the precipice. The helplessness of the strong man was uttered in one single despairing cry as he shot into the abyss. Then all was still. The sound of his

fall could not reach the edge of the gulf. Divining in a moment that the lady, whose name was Elsie, must have fled in the opposite direction, he reined his steed on his haunches. He could touch the precipice with his bridle-hand half outstretched; his sword-hand half outstretched would have dropped a stone to the bottom of the ravine. There was no room to wheel. One desperate practicability alone remained. Turning his horse's head towards the edge, he compelled him, by means of the powerful bit, to rear till he stood almost erect; and so, his body swaying over the gulf, with quivering and straining muscles, to turn on his hind-legs. Having completed the half-circle, he let him drop, and urged him furiously in the opposite direction. It must have been by the devil's own care that he was able to continue his gallop along that ledge of rock.

"He soon caught sight of the maiden. She was leaning, half fainting, against the precipice. She had heard her lover's last cry, and although it had conveyed no suggestion of his voice to her ear, she trembled from head to foot, and her limbs would bear her no farther. He checked his speed, rode gently up to her, lifted her unresisting, laid her across the shoulders of his horse, and, riding carefully till he reached a more open path, dashed again wildly along the mountain-side. The lady's long hair was shaken loose, and dropped trailing on the ground. The horse trampled upon it, and stumbled, half dragging her from the saddle-bow. He caught her, lifted her up, and looked at her face. She was dead. I suppose he went mad. He laid her again across the saddle before him, and rode on, reckless whither. Horse, and man, and maiden were found the next day, lying at the foot of a cliff, dashed to pieces. It was observed that a hind-shoe of the horse was loose and broken. Whether this had been the cause of his fall, could not be told; but ever when he races, as race he will, till the day of doom, along that mountain-side, his gallop is mingled with the clank of the loose and broken shoe. For, like the sin, the punishment is awful: he shall carry about for ages the phantom-body of the girl, knowing that her soul is away, sitting with the soul of his brother, down in the deep ravine, or scaling with him the topmost crags of the towering mountain-peaks. There are some who, from time to time, see the doomed man careering along the face of the mountain, with the lady hanging across the steed; and they say it always betokens a storm, such as this which is now raving around us."

I had not noticed till now, so absorbed had I been in her tale, that the storm had risen to a very ecstasy of fury.

"They say, likewise, that the lady's hair is still growing; for, every time they see her, it is longer than before; and that now such is its length and the head-long speed of the horse, that it floats and streams out behind, like one of those curved clouds, like a comet's tail, far up in the sky; only the cloud

is white, and the hair dark as night. And they say it will go on growing till the Last Day, when the horse will falter and her hair will gather in; and the horse will fall, and the hair will twist, and twine, and wreathe itself like a mist of threads about him, and blind him to everything but her. Then the body will rise up within it, face to face with him, animated by a fiend, who, twining her arms around him, will drag him down to the bottomless pit."

I may mention something which now occurred, and which had a strange effect on my old nurse. It illustrates the assertion that we see around us only what is within us: marvellous things enough will show themselves to the marvellous mood.—During a short lull in the storm, just as she had finished her story, we heard the sound of iron-shod hoofs approaching the cottage. There was no bridle-way into the glen. A knock came to the door, and, on opening it, we saw an old man seated on a horse, with a long slenderly-filled sack lying across the saddle before him. He said he had lost the path in the storm, and, seeing the light, had scrambled down to inquire his way. I perceived at once, from the scared and mysterious look of the old woman's eyes, that she was persuaded that this appearance had more than a little to do with the awful rider, the terrific storm, and myself who had heard the sound of the phantom-hoofs. As he ascended the hill, she looked after him, with wide and pale but unshrinking eyes; then turning in, shut and locked the door behind her, as by a natural instinct. After two or three of her significant nods, accompanied by the compression of her lips, she said:—

"He need not think to take me in, wizard as he is, with his disguises. I can see him through them all. Duncan, my dear, when you suspect anything, do not be too incredulous. This human demon is of course a wizard still, and knows how to make himself, as well as anything he touches, take a quite different appearance from the real one; only every appearance must bear some resemblance, however distant, to the natural form. That man you saw at the door was the phantom of which I have been telling you. What he is after now, of course, I cannot tell; but you must keep a bold heart, and a firm and wary foot, as you go home to-night."

I showed some surprise, I do not doubt; and, perhaps, some fear as well; but I only said, "How do you know him, Margaret?"

"I can hardly tell you," she replied; "but I do know him. I think he hates me. Often, of a wild night, when there is moonlight enough by fits, I see him tearing around this little valley, just on the top edge—all round; the lady's hair and the horses mane and tail driving far behind, and mingling, vaporous, with the stormy clouds. About he goes, in wild careering gallop; now lost as the moon goes in, then visible far round when she looks out again—an airy, pale-grey spectre, which few eyes but mine could see; for, as far as I am aware, no one of the family but myself has ever possessed the double gift of seeing and hearing both. In this case I hear no sound, except now and then a clank from the broken shoe. But I did not mean to tell you that I had ever seen him. I am not a bit afraid of him. He cannot do more than he may. His power is limited; else ill enough would he work, the miscreant."

"But," said I, "what has all this, terrible as it is, to do with the fright you took at my telling you that I had heard the sound of the broken shoe? Surely you are not afraid of only a storm?"

"No, my boy; I fear no storm. But the fact is, that that sound is seldom heard, and never, as far as I know, by any of the blood of that wicked man, without betokening some ill to one of the family, and most probably to the one who hears it—but I am not quite sure about that. Only some evil it does portend, although a long time may elapse before it shows itself; and I have a hope it may mean some one else than you."

"Do not wish that," I replied. "I know no one better able to bear it than I am; and I hope, whatever it may be, that I only shall have to meet it. It must surely be something serious to be so foretold—it can hardly be connected with my disappointment in being compelled to be a pedagogue instead of a soldier."

"Do not trouble yourself about that, Duncan," replied she. "A soldier you must be. The same day you told me of the clank of the broken horseshoe, I saw you return wounded from battle, and fall fainting from your horse in the street of a great city—only fainting, thank God. But I have particular reasons for being uneasy at your hearing that boding sound. Can you tell me the day and hour of your birth?"

"No," I replied. "It seems very odd when I think of it, but I really do not know even the day."

"Nor any one else; which is stranger still," she answered.

"How does that happen, nurse?"

"We were in terrible anxiety about your mother at the time. So ill was she, after you were just born, in a strange, unaccountable way, that you lay almost neglected for more than an hour. In the very act of giving birth to you, she seemed to the rest around her to be out of her mind, so wildly did she talk; but I knew better. I knew that she was fighting some evil power; and what power it was, I knew full well; for twice, during her pains, I heard the click of the horseshoe. But no one could help her. After her delivery, she lay as if in a trance, neither dead, nor at rest, but as if frozen to ice, and conscious of it all the while. Once more I heard the terrible sound of iron; and, at the moment, your mother started from her trance, screaming, 'My child! my child!' We suddenly became aware that no one had attended to the child, and rushed to the place where he lay wrapped in a blanket. Uncovering him, we found him black in the face, and spotted with dark spots upon the throat. I thought he was dead; but, with great and almost hopeless pains, we succeeded in making him breathe, and he gradually recovered. But his mother continued dreadfully exhausted. It seemed as if she had spent her life for her child's defence and birth. That was you, Duncan, my dear.

"I was in constant attendance upon her. About a week after your birth, as near as I can guess, just in the gloaming, I heard yet again the awful clank—only once. Nothing followed till about midnight. Your mother slept, and you lay asleep beside her. I sat by the bedside. A horror fell upon me suddenly, though I neither saw nor heard anything. Your mother started from her sleep with a cry, which sounded as if it came from far away, out of a dream, and did not belong to this world. My blood curdled with fear. She sat up in bed, with wide staring eyes and half-open rigid lips, and, feeble as she was, thrust her arms straight out before her with great force, her hands open and lifted up, with the palms outwards. The whole action was of one violently repelling another. She began to talk wildly as she had done before you were born, but, though I seemed to hear and understand it all at the time, I could not recall a word of it afterwards. It was as if I had listened to it when half asleep. I attempted to soothe her, putting my arms round her, but she seemed quite unconscious of my presence, and my arms seemed powerless upon the fixed muscles of hers. Not that I tried to constrain her, for I knew that a battle was going on of some kind or other, and my interference might do awful mischief. I only tried to comfort and encourage her. All the time, I was in a state of indescribable cold and suffering, whether more bodily or mental I could not tell. But at length I heard yet again the clank of the shoe A sudden peace seemed to fall upon my mind—or was it a warm, odorous wind that filled the room? Your mother dropped her arms, and turned feebly towards her baby. She saw that he slept a blessed sleep. She smiled like a glorified spirit, and fell back exhausted on the pillow. I went to the other side of the room to get a cordial. When I returned to the bedside, I saw at once that she was dead. Her face smiled still, with an expression of the uttermost bliss."

Nurse ceased, trembling as overcome by the recollection; and I was too much moved and awed to speak. At length, resuming the conversation, she said: "You see it is no wonder, Duncan, my dear, if, after all this, I should find, when I wanted to fix the date of your birth, that I could not determine the day or the hour when it took place. All was confusion in my poor brain.

But it was strange that no one else could, any more than I. One thing only I can tell you about it. As I carried you across the room to lay you down, for I assisted at your birth, I happened to look up to the window. Then I saw what I did not forget, although I did not think of it again till many days after,—a bright star was shining on the very tip of the thin crescent moon."

"Oh, then," said I, "it is possible to determine the day and the very hour when my birth took place."

"See the good of book-learning!" replied she. "When you work it out, just let me know, my dear, that I may remember it."

"That I will."

A silence of some moments followed. Margaret resumed:—

"I am afraid you will laugh at my foolish fancies, Duncan; but in thinking over all these things, as you may suppose I often do, lying awake in my lonely bed, the notion sometimes comes to me: What if my Duncan be the youth whom his wicked brother hurled into the ravine, come again in a new body, to live out his life on the earth, cut short by his brother's hatred? If so, his persecution of you, and of your mother for your sake, is easy to understand. And if so, you will never be able to rest till you find your fere, wherever she may have been born on the face of the earth. For born she must be, long ere now, for you to find. I misdoubt me much, however, if you will find her without great conflict and suffering between, for the Powers of Darkness will be against you; though I have good hope that you will overcome at last. You must forgive the fancies of a foolish old woman, my dear."

I will not try to describe the strange feelings, almost sensations, that arose in me while listening to these extraordinary utterances, lest it should be supposed I was ready to believe all that Margaret narrated or concluded. I could not help doubting her sanity; but no more could I help feeling very peculiarly moved by her narrative.

Few more words were spoken on either side, but after receiving renewed exhortations to carefulness on my way home, I said good-bye to dear old nurse, considerably comforted, I must confess, that I was not doomed to be a tutor all my days; for I never questioned the truth of that vision and its consequent prophecy.

I went out into the midst of the storm, into the alternating throbs of blackness and radiance; now the possessor of no more room than what my body filled, and now isolated in world-wide space. And the thunder seemed to follow me, bellowing after me as I went.

Absorbed in the story I had heard, I took my way, as I thought, homewards. The whole country was well known to me. I should have said, before that night, that I could have gone home blindfold. Whether the lightning bewildered me and made me take a false turn, I cannot tell; for the hardest thing to understand, in intellectual as well as moral mistakes, is—how we came to go wrong. But after wandering for some time, plunged in meditation, and with no warning whatever of the presence of inimical powers, a brilliant lightning-flash showed me that at least I was not near home. The light was prolonged for a second or two by a slight electric pulsation; and by that I distinguished a wide space of blackness on the ground in front of me. Once more wrapped in the folds of a thick darkness, I dared not move. Suddenly it occurred to me what the blackness was, and whither I had wandered. It was a huge quarry, of great depth, long disused, and half filled with water. I knew the place perfectly. A few more steps would have carried me over the brink. I stood still, waiting for the next flash, that I might be quite sure of the way I was about to take before I ventured to move. While I stood, I fancied I heard a single hollow plunge in the black water far below. When the lightning came, I turned, and took my path in another direction.

After walking for some time across the heath, I fell. The fall became a roll, and down a steep declivity I went, over and over, arriving at the bottom uninjured.

Another flash soon showed me where I was-in the hollow valley, within a couple of hundred yards from nurse's cottage. I made my way towards it. There was no light in it, except the feeblest glow from the embers of her peat fire. "She is in bed," I said to myself, "and I will not disturb her." Yet something drew me towards the little window. I looked in. At first I could see nothing. At length, as I kept gazing, I saw something, indistinct in the darkness, like an outstretched human form.

By this time the storm had lulled. The moon had been up for some time, but had been quite concealed by tempestuous clouds. Now, however, these had begun to break up; and, while I stood looking into the cottage, they scattered away from the face of the moon, and a faint vapoury gleam of her light, entering the cottage through a window opposite that at which I stood, fell directly on the face of my old nurse, as she lay on her back, outstretched upon chairs, pale as death, and with her eyes closed. The light fell nowhere but on her face. A stranger to her habits would have thought she was dead; but she had so much of the appearance she had had on a former occasion, that I concluded at once she was in one of her trances. But having often heard that persons in such a condition ought not to be disturbed, and feeling quite sure she knew best how to manage herself, I turned, though reluctantly, and left the lone cottage behind me in the night, with the death-like woman lying motionless in the midst of it.

I found my way home without any further difficulty, and went to bed, where I soon fell asleep, thoroughly wearied, more by the mental excitement I had been experiencing than by the amount of bodily exercise I had gone through.

My sleep was tormented with awful dreams; yet, strange to say, I awoke in the morning refreshed and fearless. The sun was shining through the chinks in my shutters, which had been closed because of the storm, and was making streaks and bands of golden brilliancy upon the wall. I had dressed and completed my preparations long before I heard the steps of the servant who came to call me.

What a wonderful thing waking is! The time of the ghostly moonshine passes by, and the great positive sunlight comes. A man who dreams, and knows that he is dreaming, thinks he knows what waking is; but knows it so little, that he mistakes, one after another, many a vague and dim change in his dream for an awaking. When the true waking comes at last, he is filled and overflowed with the power of its reality. So, likewise, one who, in the darkness, lies waiting for the light about to be struck, and trying to conceive, with all the force of his imagination, what the light will be like, is yet, when the reality flames up before him, seized as by a new and unexpected thing, different from and beyond all his imagining. He feels as if the darkness were cast to an infinite distance behind him. So shall it be with us when we wake from this dream of life into the truer life beyond, and find all our present notions of being, thrown back as into a dim, vapoury region of dreamland, where yet we thought we knew, and whence we looked forward into the present. This must be what Novalis means when he says: "Our life is not a dream; but it may become a dream, and perhaps ought to become one."

And so I looked back upon the strange history of my past; sometimes asking myself, — "Can it be that all this realty happened to the same *me*, who am now thinking about it in doubt and wonder?"

Chapter IV
Hilton Hall

As my father accompanied me to the door, where the gig, which was to carry me over the first stage of my journey, was in waiting, a large target of hide, well studded with brass nails, which had hung in the hall for time unknown—to me, at least—fell on the floor with a dull bang. My father started, but said nothing; and, as it seemed to me, rather pressed my departure than otherwise. I would have replaced the old piece of armour before I went, but he would not allow me to touch it, saying, with a grim smile,—

"Take that for an omen, my boy, that your armour must be worn over the conscience, and not over the body. Be a man, Duncan, my boy. Fear nothing, and do your duty."

A grasp of the hand was all the good-bye I could make; and I was soon rattling away to meet the coach *for Edinburgh and London. Seated on the top, I* was soon buried in a reverie, from which I was suddenly startled by the sound of tinkling iron. Could it be that my adversary was riding unseen alongside of the coach? Was that the clank of the ominous shoe? But I soon discovered the cause of the sound, and laughed at my own apprehensiveness. For I observed that the sound was repeated every time that we passed any trees by the wayside, and that it was the peculiar echo they gave of the loose chain and steel work about the harness. The sound was quite different from that thrown back by the houses on the road. I became perfectly familiar with it before the day was over.

I reached London in safety, and slept at the house of an old friend of my father, who treated me with great kindness, and seemed altogether to take a liking to me. Before I left he held out a hope of being able, some day or other, to procure for me what I so much desired—a commission in the army.

After spending a day or two with him, and seeing something of London, I climbed once more on the roof of a coach; and, late in the afternoon, was set down at the great gate of Hilton Hall. I walked up the broad avenue, through the final arch of which, as through a huge Gothic window, I saw the hall in the distance. Everything about me looked strange, rich, and lovely.

Accustomed to the scanty flowers and diminutive wood of my own country, what I now saw gave me a feeling of majestic plenty, which I can recall at will, but which I have never experienced again. Behind the trees which formed the avenue, I saw a shrubbery, composed entirely of flowering plants, almost all unknown to me. Issuing from the avenue, I found myself amid open, wide, lawny spaces, in which the flower-beds lay like islands of colour. A statue on a pedestal, the only white thing in the surrounding green, caught my eye. I had seen scarcely any sculpture; and this, attracting my attention by a favourite contrast of colour, retained it by its own beauty. It was a Dryad, or some nymph of the woods, who had just glided from the solitude of the trees behind, and had sprung upon the pedestal to look wonderingly around her. A few large brown leaves lay at her feet, borne thither by some eddying wind from the trees behind. As I gazed, filled with a new pleasure, a drop of rain upon my face made me look up. From a grey, fleecy cloud, with sun-whitened border, a light, gracious, plentiful rain was falling. A rainbow sprang across the sky, and the statue stood within the rainbow. At the same moment, from the base of the pedestal rose a figure in white, graceful as the Dryad above, and neither running, nor appearing to walk quickly, yet fleet as a ghost, glided past me at a few paces, distance, and, keeping in a straight line for the main entrance of the hall, entered by it and vanished.

I followed in the direction of the mansion, which was large, and of several styles and ages. One wing appeared especially ancient. It was neglected and out of repair, and had in consequence a desolate, almost sepulchral look, an expression heightened by the number of large cypresses which grew along its line. I went up to the central door and knocked. It was opened by a grave, elderly butler. I passed under its flat arch, as if into the midst of the waiting events of my story. For, as I glanced around the hall, my consciousness was suddenly saturated, if I may be allowed the expression, with the strange feeling—known to everyone, and yet so strange—that I had seen it before; that, in fact, I knew it perfectly. But what was yet more strange, and far more uncommon, was, that, although the feeling with regard to the hall faded and vanished instantly, and although I could not in the least surmise the appearance of any of the regions into which I was about to be ushered, I yet followed the butler with a kind of indefinable expectation of seeing something which I had seen before; and every room or passage in that mansion affected me, on entering it for the first time, with the same sensation of previous acquaintance which I had experienced with regard to the hall. This sensation, in every case, died away at once, leaving that portion such as it might be expected to look to one who had never before entered the place.

I was received by the housekeeper, a little, prim, benevolent old lady, with colourless face and antique head-dress, who led me to the room prepared for me. To my surprise, I found a large wood-fire burning on the hearth; but the feeling of the place revealed at once the necessity for it; and I scarcely needed to be informed that the room, which was upon the ground floor, and looked out upon a little solitary grass-grown and ivy-mantled court, had not been used for years, and therefore required to be thus prepared for an inmate. My bedroom was a few paces down a passage to the right.

Left alone, I proceeded to make a more critical survey of my room. Its look of ancient mystery was to me incomparably more attractive than any show of elegance or comfort could have been. It was large and low, panelled throughout in oak, black with age, and worm-eaten in many parts—otherwise entire. Both the windows looked into the little court or yard before mentioned. All the heavier furniture of the room was likewise of black oak, but the chairs and couches were covered with faded tapestry and tarnished gilding, apparently the superannuated members of the general household of seats. I could give an individual description of each, for every atom in that room, large enough for discernable shape or colour, seems branded into my brain. If I happen to have the least feverishness on me, the moment I fall asleep, I am in that room.

Chapter V
Lady Alice

When the bell rang for dinner, I managed to find my way to the drawing-room, where were assembled Lady Hilton, her only daughter, a girl of about thirteen, and the two boys, my pupils. Lady Hilton would have been pleasant, could she have been as natural as she wished to appear. She received me with some degree of kindness; but the half-cordiality of her manner towards me was evidently founded on the impassableness of the gulf between us. I knew at once that we should never be friends; that she would never come down from the lofty table-land upon which she walked; and that if, after being years in the house, I should happen to be dying, she would send the housekeeper to me. All right, no doubt; I only say that it was so. She introduced to me my pupils; fine, open-eyed, manly English boys, with something a little overbearing in their manner, which speedily disappeared in relation to me. Lord Hilton was not at home. Lady Hilton led the way to the dining-room; the elder boy gave his arm to his sister, and I was about to follow with the younger, when from one of the deep bay windows glided out, still in white, the same figure which had passed me upon the lawn. I started, and drew back. With a slight bow, she preceded me, and followed the others down the great staircase. Seated at table, I had leisure to make my observations upon them all; but most of my glances found their way to the lady who, twice that day, had affected me like an apparition. What is time, but the airy ocean in which ghosts come and go!

She was about twenty years of age; rather above the middle height, and rather slight in form; her complexion white rather than pale, her face being only less white than the deep marbly whiteness of her arms. Her eyes were large, and full of liquid night—a night throbbing with the light of invisible stars. Her hair seemed raven-black, and in quantity profuse. The expression of her face, however, generally partook more of vagueness than any other characteristic. Lady Hilton called her Lady Alice; and she never addressed Lady Hilton but in the same ceremonious style.

I afterwards learned from the old house-keeper, that Lady Alice's position in the family was a very peculiar one. Distantly connected with Lord Hilton's family on the mother's side, she was the daughter of the late

Lord Glendarroch, and step-daughter to Lady Hilton, who had become Lady Hilton within a year after Lord Glendarroch's death. Lady Alice, then quite a child, had accompanied her stepmother, to whom she was moderately attached, and who had been allowed to retain undisputed possession of her. She had no near relatives, else the fortune I afterwards found to be at her disposal would have aroused contending claims to the right of guardianship.

Although she was in many respects kindly treated by her stepmother, certain peculiarities tended to her isolation from the family pursuits and pleasures. Lady Alice had no accomplishments. She could neither spell her own language, nor even read it aloud. Yet she delighted in reading to herself, though, for the most part, books which Mrs. Wilson characterised as very odd. Her voice, when she spoke, had a quite indescribable music in it; yet she neither sang nor played. Her habitual motion was more like a rhythmical gliding than an ordinary walk, yet she could not dance. Mrs. Wilson hinted at other and more serious peculiarities, which she either could not, or would not describe; always shaking her head gravely and sadly, and becoming quite silent, when I pressed for further explanation; so that, at last, I gave up all attempts to arrive at an understanding of the mystery by her means. Not the less, however, I speculated on the subject.

One thing soon became evident to me: that she was considered not merely deficient as to the power of intellectual acquirement, but in a quite abnormal intellectual condition. Of this, however, I could myself see no sign. The peculiarity, almost oddity, of some of her remarks, was evidently not only misunderstood, but, with relation to her mental state, misinterpreted. Such remarks Lady Hilton generally answered only by an elongation of the lips intended to represent a smile. To me, they appeared to indicate a nature closely allied to genius, if not identical with it-a power of regarding things from an original point of view, which perhaps was the more unfettered in its operation from the fact that she was incapable of looking at them in the ordinary common-place way. It seemed to me, sometimes, as if her point of observation was outside of the sphere within which the thing observed took place; and as if what she said, had a relation, occasionally, to things and thoughts and mental conditions familiar to her, but at which not even a definite guess could be made by me. I am compelled to acknowledge, however, that with such utterances as these mingled now and then others, silly enough for any drawing-room young lady; which seemed again to be accepted by the family as proofs that she was not *altogether* out of her right mind. She was gentle and kind to the children, as they were still called; and they seemed reasonably fond of her.

There was something to me exceedingly touching in the solitariness of this girl; for no one spoke to her as if she were like other people, or as if any heartiness were possible between them. Perhaps no one could have felt quite at home with her but a mother, whose heart had been one with hers from a season long anterior to the development of any repulsive oddity. But her position was one of peculiar isolation, for no one really approached her individual being; and that she should be unaware of this loneliness, seemed to me saddest of all. I soon found, however, that the most distant attempt on my part to show her attention, was either received with absolute indifference, or coldly repelled without the slightest acknowledgment.

But I return to the first night of my sojourn at Hilton Hall.

Chapter VI
My Quarters

After making arrangements for commencing work in the morning, I took my leave, and retired to my own room, intent upon carrying out with more minuteness the survey I had already commenced: several cupboards in the wall, and one or two doors, apparently of closets, had especially attracted my attention. Strange was its look as I entered—as of a room hollowed out of the past, for a memorial of dead times. The fire had sunk low, and lay smouldering beneath the white ashes, like the life of the world beneath the snow, or the heart of a man beneath cold and grey thoughts. I lighted the candles which stood upon the table, but the room, instead of being brightened looked blacker than before, for the light revealed its essential blackness.

As I cast my eyes around me, standing with my back to the hearth (on which, for mere companionship's sake, I had just heaped fresh wood), a thrill ran suddenly throughout my frame. I felt as if, did it last a moment longer, I should become aware of another presence in the room; but, happily for me, it ceased before it had reached that point; and I, recovering my courage, remained ignorant of the cause of my fear, if there were any, other than the nature of the room itself. With a candle in my hand, I proceeded to open the various cupboards and closets. At first I found nothing remarkable about any of them. The latter were quite empty, except the last I came to, which had a piece of very old elaborate tapestry hanging at the back of it. Lifting this up, I saw what seemed at first to be panels, corresponding to those which formed the room; but on looking more closely, I discovered that this back of the closet was, or had been, a door. There was nothing unusual in this, especially in such an old house; but the discovery roused in me a strong desire to know what lay behind the old door. I found that it was secured only by an ordinary bolt, from which the handle had been removed. Soothing my conscience with the reflection that I had a right to know what sort of place had communication with my room, I succeeded, by the help of my deer-knife, in forcing back the rusty bolt; and though, from the stiffness of the hinges, I dreaded a crack, they yielded at last with only a creak.

The opening door revealed a large hall, empty utterly, save of dust and cobwebs, which festooned it in all quarters, and gave it an appearance of unutterable desolation. The now familiar feeling, that I had seen the place before, filled my mind the first moment, and passed away the next. A broad, right-angled staircase, with massive banisters, rose from the middle of the hall. This staircase could not have originally belonged to the ancient wing which I had observed on my first approach, being much more modern; but I was convinced, from the observations I had made as to the situation of my room, that I was bordering upon, if not within, the oldest portion of the pile. In sudden horror, lest I should hear a light footfall upon the awful stair, I withdrew hurriedly, and having secured both the doors, betook myself to my bedroom; in whose dingy four-post bed, with its carving and plumes reminding me of a hearse, I was soon ensconced amidst the snowiest linen, with the sweet and clean odour of lavender. In spite of novelty, antiquity, speculation, and dread, I was soon fast asleep; becoming thereby a fitter inhabitant of such regions, than when I moved about with restless and disturbing curiosity, through their ancient and death-like repose.

I made no use of my discovered door, although I always intended doing so; especially after, in talking about the building with Lady Hilton, I found that I was at perfect liberty to make what excursions I pleased into the deserted portions.

My pupils turned out to be teachable, and therefore my occupation was pleasant. Their sister frequently came to me for help, as there happened to be just then an interregnum of governesses: soon she settled into a regular pupil.

After a few weeks Lord Hilton returned. Though my room was so far from the great hall, I heard the clank of his spurs on its pavement. I trembled; for it sounded like the broken shoe. But I shook off the influence in a moment, heartily ashamed of its power over me. Soon I became familiar enough both with the sound and its cause; for his lordship rarely went anywhere except on horseback, and was booted and spurred from morning till night.

He received me with some appearance of interest, which immediately stiffened and froze. Beginning to shake hands with me as if he meant it, he instantly dropped my hand, as if it had stung him.

His nobility was of that sort which stands in constant need of repair. Like a weakly constitution, it required keeping up, and his lordship could not be said to neglect it; for he seemed to find his principal employment in administering continuous doses of obsequiousness to his own pride. His rank, like a coat made for some large ancestor, hung loose upon him: he was always trying to persuade himself that it was an excellent fit, but ever with an unacknowledged misgiving. This misgiving might have done him good, had he not met it with renewed efforts at looking that which he feared he was not. Yet this man was capable of the utmost persistency in carrying out any scheme he had once devised. Enough of him for the present: I seldom came into contact with him.

I scarcely ever saw Lady Alice, except at dinner, or by accidental meeting in the grounds and passages of the house; and then she took no notice of me whatever.

Chapter VII
The Library

One day, a week after his arrival, Lord Hilton gave a dinner-party to some of his neighbours and tenants. I entered the drawing-room rather late, and saw that, though there were many guests, not one was talking to Lady Alice. She appeared, however, altogether unconscious of neglect. Presently dinner was announced, and the company marshalled themselves, and took their way to the dining-room. Lady Alice was left unattended, the guests taking their cue from the behaviour of their entertainers. I ventured to go up to her, and offer her my arm. She made me a haughty bow, and passed on before me unaccompanied. I could not help feeling hurt at this, and I think she saw it; but it made no difference to her behaviour, except that she avoided everything that might occasion me the chance of offering my services.

Nor did I get any further with Lady Hilton. Her manner and smile remained precisely the same as on our first interview. She did not even show any interest in the fact that her daughter, Lady Lucy, had joined her brothers in the schoolroom. I had an uncomfortable feeling that the latter was like her mother, and was not to be trusted. Self-love is the foulest of all foul feeders, and will defile that it may devour. But I must not anticipate.

The neglected library was open to me at all hours; and in it I often took refuge from the dreariness of unsympathetic society. I was never admitted within the magic circle of the family interests and enjoyments. If there was such a circle, Lady Alice and I certainly stood outside of it; but whether even then it had any real inside to it, I doubted much. Nevertheless, as I have said, our common exclusion had not the effect of bringing us together as sharers of the same misfortune. In the library I found companions more to my need. But, even there, they were not easy to find; for the books were in great confusion. I could discover no catalogue, nor could I hear of the existence of such a useless luxury. One morning at breakfast, therefore, I asked Lord Hilton if I might arrange and catalogue the books during my leisure hours. He replied:—

"Do anything you like with them, Mr. Campbell, except destroy them."

Now I was in my element. I never had been by any means a book-worm; but the very outside of a book had a charm to me. It was a kind of sacrament—an outward and visible sign of an inward and spiritual grace; as, indeed, what on God's earth is not? So I set to work amongst the books, and soon became familiar with many titles at least, which had been perfectly unknown to me before. I found a perfect set of our poets-perfect according to the notion of the editor and the issue of the publisher, although it omitted both Chaucer and George Herbert. I began to nibble at that portion of the collection which belonged to the sixteenth century; but with little success. I found nothing, to my idea, but love poems without any love in them, and so I soon became weary. But I found in the library what I liked far better—many romances of a very marvellous sort, and plentiful interruption they gave to the formation of the catalogue. I likewise came upon a whole nest of the German classics which seemed to have kept their places undisturbed, in virtue of their unintelligibility. There must have been some well-read scholar in the family, and that not long before, to judge by the near approach of the line of this literature; happening to be a tolerable reader of German, I found in these volumes a mine of wealth inexhaustible. I learned from Mrs. Wilson that this scholar was a younger brother of Lord Hilton, who had died about twenty years before. He had led a retired, rather lonely life, was of a melancholy and brooding disposition, and was reported to have had an unfortunate love-story. This was one of many histories which she gave me. For the library being dusty as a catacomb, the private room of Old Time himself, I had often to betake myself to her for assistance. The good lady had far more regard than the owners of it for the library, and was delighted with the pains I was taking to re-arrange and clean it. She would allow no one to help me but herself; and to many a long-winded story, most of which I forgot as soon as I heard them, did I listen, or seem to listen, while she dusted the shelves and I the books.

One day I had sent a servant to ask Mrs. Wilson to come to me. I had taken down all the books from a hitherto undisturbed corner, and had seated myself on a heap of them, no doubt a very impersonation of the genius of the place; for while I waited for the housekeeper, I was consuming a morsel of an ancient metrical romance. After waiting for some time, I glanced towards the door, for I had begun to get impatient for the entrance of my helper. To my surprise, there stood Lady Alice, her eyes fixed upon me with an expression I could not comprehend. Her face instantly altered to its usual look of indifference, dashed with the least possible degree of scorn, as she turned and walked slowly away. I rose involuntarily. An old cavalry sword, which I had just taken down from the wall, and had placed leaning against the books from which I now rose, fell with a clash to the floor. I started; for it was a sound that always startled me; and stooping I lifted the weapon. But what was my surprise when I raised my head, to see once more the face of Lady Alice staring in at the door! yet not the same face, for it had changed in the moment that had passed. It was pale with fear—not fright; and her great black eyes were staring beyond me as if she saw something through the wall of the room. Once more her face altered to the former scornful indifference, and she vanished. Keen of hearing as I was, I had never yet heard the footstep of Lady Alice.

Chapter VIII
The Somnambulist

One night I was sitting in my room, devouring an old romance which I had brought from the library. It was late. The fire blazed bright; but the candles were nearly burnt out, and I grew sleepy over the volume, romance as it was.

Suddenly I found myself on my feet, listening with an agony of intention. Whether I had heard anything I could not tell; but I felt as if I had. Yes; I was sure of it. Far away, somewhere in the labyrinthine pile, I heard a faint cry. Driven by some secret impulse, I flew, without a moment's reflection, to the closet door, lifted the tapestry within, unfastened the second door, and stood in the great waste echoing hall, amid the touches, light and ghostly, of the cobwebs set afloat in the eddies occasioned by my sudden entrance.

A faded moonbeam fell on the floor, and filled the place with an ancient dream-light, which wrought strangely on my brain, and filled it, as if it, too, were but a deserted, sleepy house, haunted by old dreams and memories. Recollecting myself, I went back for a light; but the candles were both flickering in the sockets, and I was compelled to trust to the moon. I ascended the staircase. Old as it was, not a board creaked, not a banister shook—the whole felt solid as rock. Finding, at length, no more stair to ascend, I groped my way on; for here there was no direct light from the moon—only the light of the moonlit air. I was in some trepidation, I confess; for how should I find my way back? But the worst result likely to ensue was, that I should have to spend the night without knowing where; for with the first glimmer of morning, I should be able to return to my room. At length, after wandering into several rooms and out again, my hand fell on a latched door. I opened it, and entered a long corridor, with many windows on one side. Broad strips of moonlight lay slantingly across the narrow floor, divided by regular intervals of shade.

I started, and my heart swelled; for I saw a movement somewhere—I could neither tell where, nor of what: I was only aware of motion. I stood in the first shadow, and gazed, but saw nothing. I sped across the light to the next shadow, and stood again, looking with fearful fixedness of gaze towards the far end of the corridor. Suddenly a white form glimmered and vanished. I crossed to the next shadow. Again a glimmer and vanishing, but nearer. Nerving myself to the utmost, I ceased the stealthiness of my movements, and went forward, slowly and steadily. A tall form, apparently of a woman, dressed in a long white robe, appeared in one of the streams of light, threw its arms over its head, gave a wild cry—which, notwithstanding its wildness and force, had a muffled sound, as if many folds, either of matter or of space, intervened—and fell at full length along the moonlight. Amidst the thrill of agony which shook me at the cry, I rushed forward, and, kneeling beside the prostrate figure, discovered that, unearthly as was the scream which had preceded her fall, it was the Lady Alice. I saw the fact in a moment: the Lady Alice was a somnambulist. Startled by the noise of my advance, she had awaked; and the usual terror and fainting had followed. She was cold and motionless as death. What was to be done? If I called, the probability was that no one would hear me; or if any one should hear—but I need not follow the course of my thought, as I tried in vain to recover the poor girl. Suffice it to say, that both for her sake and my own, I could not face the chance of being found, in the dead of night, by common-minded domestics, in such a situation.

I was kneeling by her side, not knowing what to do, when a horror, as from the presence of death suddenly recognized, fell upon me. I thought she must be dead. But at the same moment, I hear, or seemed to hear, (how should I know which?) the rapid gallop of a horse, and the clank of a loose shoe.

In an agony of fear, I caught her up in my arms, and, carrying her on my arms, as one carries a sleeping child, hurried back through the corridor. Her hair, which was loose, trailed on the ground; and, as I fled, I trampled on it and stumbled. She moaned; and that instant the gallop ceased. I lifted her up across my shoulder, and carried her more easily. How I found my way to the stair I cannot tell: I know that I groped about for some time, like one in a dream with a ghost in his arms. At last I reached it, and descending, crossed the hall, and entered my room. There I placed Lady Alice upon an old couch, secured the doors, and began to breathe—and think. The first thing was to get her warm, for she was cold as the dead. I covered her with my plaid and my dressing-gown, pulled the couch before the fire, and considered what to do next.

Chapter IX
The First Waking

While I hesitated, Nature had her own way, and, with a deep-drawn sigh, Lady Alice opened her eyes. Never shall I forget the look of mingled bewilderment, alarm, and shame, with which her great eyes met mine. But, in a moment, this expression changed to that of anger. Her dark eyes flashed with light; and a cloud of roseate wrath grew in her face, till it glowed with the opaque red of a camellia. She had almost started from the couch, when, apparently discovering the unsuitableness of her dress, she checked her impetuosity, and remained leaning on her elbow. Overcome by her anger, her beauty, and my own confusion, I knelt before her, unable to speak, or to withdraw my eyes from hers. After a moment's pause, she began to question me like a queen, and I to reply like a culprit.

"How did I come here?"

"I carried you."

"Where did you find me, pray?"

Her lip curled with ten times the usual scorn.

"In the old house, in a long corridor."

"What right had you to be there?"

"I heard a cry, and could not help going."

"'Tis impossible.—I see. Some wretch told you, and you watched for me."

"I did not, Lady Alice."

She burst into tears, and fell back on the couch, with her face turned away. Then, anger reviving, she went on through her sobs:—

"Why did you not leave me where I fell? You had done enough to hurt me without bringing me here."

And again she fell a-weeping.

Now I found words.

"Lady Alice," I said, "how could I leave you lying in the moonlight? Before the sun rose, the terrible moon might have distorted your beautiful face."

"Be silent, sir. What have you to do with my face?"

"And the wind, Lady Alice, was blowing through the corridor windows, keen and cold as the moonlight. How could I leave you?"

"You could have called for help."

"Forgive me, Lady Alice, if I erred in thinking you would rather command the silence of a gentleman to whom an accident had revealed your secret, than be exposed to the domestics who would have gathered round us."

Again she half raised herself, and again her eyes flashed.

"A secret with *you*, sir!"

"But, besides, Lady Alice," I cried, springing to my feet, in distress at her hardness, "I heard the horse with the clanking shoe, and, in terror, I caught you up, and fled with you, almost before I knew what I did. And I hear it now—I hear it now!" I cried, as once more the ominous sound rang through my brain.

The angry glow faded from her face, and its paleness grew almost ghastly with dismay.

"Do *you* hear it?" she said, throwing back her covering, and rising from the couch. "I do not."

She stood listening with distended eyes, as if *they* were the gates by which such sounds entered.

"I do not hear it," she said again, after a pause. "It must be gone now." Then, turning to me, she laid her hand on my arm, and looked at me. Her black hair, disordered and entangled, wandered all over her white dress to her knees. Her face was paler than ever; and her eyes were so wide open that I could see the white all round the large dark iris.

"Did you hear it?" she said. "No one ever heard it before but me. I must forgive you—you could not help it. I will trust you, too. Take me to my room."

Without a word of reply, I wrapped my plaid about her. Then bethinking me of my chamber-candle, I lighted it, and opening the two doors, led her out of the room.

"How is this?" she asked. "Why do you take me this way? I do not know the place."

"This is the way I brought you in, Lady Alice," I answered. "I know no other way to the spot where I found you. And I can guide you no farther than there—hardly even so far, for I groped my way there for the first time this night or morning—whichever it may be."

"It is past midnight, but not morning yet," she replied, "I always know. But there must be another way from your room?"

"Yes, of course; but we should have to pass the housekeeper's door— she is always late."

"Are we near her room? I should know my way from there. I fear it would not surprise any of the household to see me. They would say—'It is only Lady Alice.' Yet I cannot tell you how I shrink from being seen. No—I will try the way you brought me—if you do not mind going back with me."

This conversation passed in low tone and hurried words. It was scarcely over before we found ourselves at the foot of the staircase. Lady Alice shivered, and drew the plaid close round her.

We ascended, and soon found the corridor; but when we got through it, she was rather bewildered. At length, after looking into several of the rooms, empty all, except for stray articles of ancient furniture, she exclaimed, as she entered one, and, taking the candle from my hand, held it above her head—

"Ah, yes! I am right at last. This is the haunted room. I know my way now."

I caught a darkling glimpse of a large room, apparently quite furnished; but how, except from the general feeling of antiquity and mustiness, I could not tell. Little did I think then what memories—old, now, like the ghosts that with them haunt the place—would ere long find their being and take their abode in that ancient room, to forsake it never more. In strange, half-waking moods, I seem to see the ghosts and the memories flitting together through the spectral moonlight, and weaving mystic dances in and out of the storied windows and the tapestried walls.

At the door of this room she said, "I must leave you here. I will put down the light a little further on, and you can come for it. I owe you many thanks. You will not be afraid of being left so near the haunted room?"

I assured her that at present I felt strong enough to meet all the ghosts in or out of Hades. Turning, she smiled a sad, sweet smile, then went on a few paces, and disappeared. The light, however, remained; and I found the candle, with my plaid, deposited at the foot of a short flight of steps, at right angles to the passage she left me in. I made my way back to my room, threw myself on the couch on which she had so lately lain, and neither went to bed nor slept that night. Before the morning, I had fully entered that phase of individual development commonly called *love*, of which the real nature is as great a mystery to me now, as it was at any period previous to its evolution in myself.

Chapter X
Love and Power

When the morning came, I began to doubt whether my wakefulness had not been part of my dream, and I had not dreamed the whole of my supposed adventures. There was no sign of a lady's presence left in the room.—How could there have been?—But throwing the plaid which covered me aside, my hand was caught by a single thread of something so fine that I could not see it till the light grew strong. I wound it round and round my finger, and doubted no longer.

At breakfast there was no Lady Alice—nor at dinner. I grew uneasy, but what could I do? I soon learned that she was ill; and a weary fortnight passed before I saw her again. Mrs. Wilson told me that she had caught cold, and was confined to her room. So I was ill at ease, not from love alone, but from anxiety as well. Every night I crept up through the deserted house to the stair where she had vanished, and there sat in the darkness or groped and peered about for some sign. But I saw no light even, and did not know where her room was. It might be far beyond this extremity of my knowledge; for I discovered no indication of the proximity of the inhabited portion of the house. Mrs. Wilson said there was nothing serious the matter; but this did not satisfy me, for I imagined something mysterious in the way in which she spoke.

As the days went on, and she did not appear, my soul began to droop within me; my intellect seemed about to desert me altogether. In vain I tried to read. Nothing could fix my attention. I read and re-read the same page; but although I understood every word as I read, I found when I came to a pause, that there lingered in my mind no palest notion of the idea. It was just what one experiences in attempting to read when half-asleep.

I tried Euclid, and fared a little better with that. But having now to initiate my boys into the mysteries of equations, I soon found that although I could manage a very simple one, yet when I attempted one more complex— one in which something bordering upon imagination was necessary to find out the object for which to appoint the symbol to handle it by—the necessary power of concentration was itself a missing factor.

But although my thoughts were thus beyond my control, my duties were not altogether irksome to me. I remembered that they kept me near her; and although I could not learn, I found that I could teach a little.

Perhaps it is foolish to dwell upon an individual variety of an almost universal stage in the fever of life; but one exception to these indications of mental paralysis I think worth mentioning.

I continued my work in the library, although it did not advance with the same steadiness as before. One day, in listless mood, I took up a volume, without knowing what it was, or what I sought. It opened at the *Amoretti* of Edmund Spenser. I was on the point of closing it again, when a line caught my eye. I read the sonnet; read another; found I could understand them perfectly; and that hour the poetry of the sixteenth century, hitherto a sealed fountain, became an open well of refreshment, and the strength that comes from sympathy. What if its second-rate writers were full of conceits and vagaries, the feelings are very indifferent to the mere intellectual forms around which the same feelings in others have gathered, if only by their means they hint at, and sometimes express themselves. Now I understood this old fantastic verse, and knew that the foam-bells on the torrent of passionate feeling are iris-hued. And what was more—it proved an intellectual nexus between my love and my studies, or at least a bridge by which I could pass from the one to the other.

That same day, I remember well, Mrs. Wilson told me that Lady Alice was much better. But as days passed, and still she did not make her appearance, my anxiety only changed its object, and I feared that it was from aversion to me that she did not join the family. But her name was never mentioned in my hearing by any of the other members of it; and her absence appeared to be to them a matter of no moment or interest.

One night, as I sat in my room, I found, as usual, that it was impossible to read; and throwing the book aside, relapsed into that sphere of thought which now filled my soul, and had for its centre the Lady Alice. I recalled her form as she lay on the couch, and brooded over the remembrance till a longing to see her, almost unbearable, arose within me.

"Would to heaven," I said to myself, "that will were power!"

In this concurrence of idleness, distraction, and vehement desire, I found all at once, without any foregone resolution, that I was concentrating and intensifying within me, until it rose almost to a command, the operative volition that Lady Alice should come to me. In a moment more I trembled at the sense of a new power which sprang into conscious being within me. I had had no prevision of its existence, when I gave way to such extravagant and apparently helpless wishes. I now actually awaited the fulfilment of my desire; but in a condition ill-fitted to receive it, for the effort had already exhausted me to such a degree, that every nerve was in a conscious tremor. Nor had I long to wait.

I heard no sound of approach: the closet-door folded back, and in glided, open-eyed, but sightless pale as death, and clad in white, ghostly-pure and saint-like, the Lady Alice. I shuddered from head to foot at what I had done. She was more terrible to me in that moment than any pale-eyed ghost could have been. For had I not exercised a kind of necromantic art, and roused without awaking the slumbering dead? She passed me, walking round the table at which I was seated, went to the couch, laid herself down with a maidenly care, turned a little on one side, with her face towards me, and gradually closed her eyes. In something deeper than sleep she lay, and yet not in death. I rose, and once more knelt beside her, but dared not touch her. In what far realms of life might the lovely soul be straying! What mysterious modes of being might now be the homely surroundings of her second life! Thoughts unutterable rose in me, culminated, and sank, like the stars of heaven, as I gazed on the present symbol of an absent life—a life that I loved by means of the symbol; a symbol that I loved because of the life. How long she lay thus, how long I gazed upon her thus, I do not know. Gradually, but without my being able to distinguish the gradations, her countenance altered to that of one who sleeps. But the change did not end there. A colour, faint as the blush in the centre of a white rose, tinged her lips, and deepened; then her cheek began to share in the hue, then her brow and her neck. The colour was that of the cloud which, the farthest from the sunset, yet acknowledges the rosy atmosphere. I watched, as it were, the dawn of a soul on the horizon of the visible. The first approaches of its far-off flight were manifest; and as I watched, I saw it come nearer and nearer, till its great, silent, speeding pinions were folded, and it looked forth, a calm, beautiful, infinite woman, from the face and form sleeping before me.

I knew that she was awake, some moments before she opened her eyes. When at last those depths of darkness disclosed themselves, slowly uplifting their white cloudy portals, the same consternation she had formerly manifested, accompanied by yet greater anger, followed.

"Yet again! Am I your slave, because I am weak?" She rose in the majesty of wrath, and moved towards the door.

"Lady Alice, I have not touched you. I am to blame, but not as you think. Could I help longing to see you? And if the longing passed, ere I was aware, into a will that you should come, and you obeyed it, forgive me."

I hid my face in my hands, overcome by conflicting emotions. A kind of stupor came over me. When I lifted my head, she was standing by the closet-door.

"I have waited," she said, "to make a request of you."

"Do not utter it, Lady Alice. I know what it is. I give you my word—my solemn promise, if you like—that I will never do it again." She thanked me, with a smile, and vanished.

Much to my surprise, she appeared at dinner next day. No notice was taken of her, except by the younger of my pupils, who called out,—

"Hallo, Alice! Are you down?"

She smiled and nodded, but did not speak. Everything went on as usual. There was no change in her behaviour, except in one point. I ventured the experiment of paying her some ordinary enough attention. She thanked me, without a trace of the scornful expression I all but expected to see upon her beautiful face. But when I addressed her about the weather, or something equally interesting, she made no reply; and Lady Hilton gave me a stare, as much as to say, "Don't you know it's of no use to talk to her?" Alice saw the look, and colouring to the eyes, rose, and left the room. When she had gone, Lady Hilton said to me,—

"Don't speak to her, Mr. Campbell—it distresses her. She is very peculiar, you know."

She could not hide the scorn and dislike with which she spoke; and I could not help saying to myself, "What a different thing scorn looks on *your* face, Lady Hilton!" for it made her positively and hatefully ugly for the moment—to my eyes, at least.

After this, Alice sat down with us at all our meals, and seemed tolerably well. But, in some indescribable way, she was quite a different person from the Lady Alice who had twice awaked in my presence. To use a phrase common in describing one of weak intellect—she never seemed to be all there. There was something automatical in her movements; and a sort of frozen indifference was the prevailing expression of her countenance. When she smiled, a sweet light shone in her eyes, and she looked for the moment like the Lady Alice of my nightly dreams. But, altogether, the Lady Alice of the night, and the Lady Alice of the day, were two distinct persons. I believed that the former was the real one.

What nights I had now, watching and striving lest unawares I should fall into the exercise of my new power! I allowed myself to think of her as much as I pleased in the daytime, or at least as much as I dared; for when occupied with my pupils, I dreaded lest any abstraction should even hint that I had a thought to conceal. I knew that I could not hurt her then; for that only in the night did she enter that state of existence in which my will could exercise authority over her. But at night—at night—when I knew she lay there, and might be lying here; when but a thought would bring her, and that thought was fluttering its wings, ready to spring awake out of the dreams of my heart—then the struggle was fearful. And what added force to the temptation was, that to call her to me in the night, seemed like calling the real immortal Alice forth from the tomb in which she wandered about all day. It was as painful to me to see her such in the day, as it was entracing to remember her such as I had seen her in the night. What matter if her true self came forth in anger against me? What was I? It was enough for my life, I said, to look on her, such as she really was. "Bring her yet once, and tell her all—tell her how madly, hopelessly you love her. She will forgive you at least," said a voice within me. But I heard it as the voice of the tempter, and kept down the thought which might have grown to the will.

Chapter XI
A New Pupil

One day, exactly three weeks after her last visit to my room, as I was sitting with my three pupils in the schoolroom, Lady Alice entered, and began to look on the bookshelves as if she wanted some volume. After a few moments, she turned, and, approaching the table, said to me, in an abrupt, yet hesitating way.

"Mr. Campbell, I cannot spell. How am I to learn?"

I thought for a moment, and replied: "Copy a passage every day, Lady Alice, from some favourite book. Then, if you allow me, I shall be most happy to point out any mistakes you may have made."

"Thank you, Mr. Campbell, I will; but I am afraid you will despise me, when you find how badly I spell."

"There is no fear of that," I rejoined. "It is a mere peculiarity. So long as one can *think* well, spelling is altogether secondary."

"Thank you; I will try," she said, and left the room. Next day, she brought me an old ballad, written tolerably, but in a school-girl's hand. She had copied the antique spelling, letter for letter.

"This is quite correct," I said; "but to copy such as this will not teach you properly; for it is very old, and consequently old-fashioned."

"Is it old? Don't we spell like that now? You see I do not know anything about it. You must set me a task, then."

This I undertook with more pleasure than I dared to show. Every day she brought me the appointed exercise, written with a steadily improving hand. To my surprise, I never found a single error in the spelling. Of course, when, advancing a step in the process, I made her write from my dictation, she did make blunders, but not so many as I had expected; and she seldom repeated one after correction.

This new association gave me many opportunities of doing more for her than merely teaching her to spell. We talked about what she copied; and I had to explain. I also told her about the writers. Soon she expressed a desire to know something of figures. We commenced arithmetic. I proposed geometry along with it, and found the latter especially fitted to her powers. One by one we included several other necessary branches; and ere long I had four around the schoolroom table—equally my pupils. Whether the attempts previously made to instruct her had been insufficient or misdirected, or whether her intellectual powers had commenced a fresh growth, I could not tell; but I leaned to the latter conclusion, especially after I began to observe that her peculiar remarks had become modified in form, though without losing any of their originality. The unearthliness of her beauty likewise disappeared, a slight colour displacing the almost marbly whiteness of her cheek.

Long before Lady Alice had made this progress, my nightly struggles began to diminish in violence. They had now entirely ceased. The temptation had left me. I felt certain that for weeks she had never walked in her sleep. She was beyond my power, and I was glad of it.

I was, of course, most careful of my behaviour during all this period. I strove to pay Lady Alice no more attention than I paid to the rest of my pupils; and I cannot help thinking that I succeeded. But now and then, in the midst of some instruction I was giving Lady Alice, I caught the eye of Lady Lucy, a sharp, common-minded girl, fixed upon one or the other of us, with an inquisitive vulgar expression, which I did not like. This made me more careful still. I watched my tones, to keep them even, and free from any expression of the feeling of which my heart was full. Sometimes, however, I could not help revealing the gratification I felt when she made some marvellous remark—marvellous, I mean, in relation to her other attainments; such a remark as a child will sometimes make, showing that he has already mastered, through his earnest simplicity, some question that has for ages perplexed the wise and the prudent. On one of these occasions, I found the cat eyes of Lady Lucy glittering on me. I turned away; not, I fear, without showing some displeasure.

Whether it was from Lady Lucy's evil report, or that the change in Lady Alice's habits and appearance had attracted the attention of Lady Hilton, I cannot tell; but one morning she appeared at the door of the study, and called her. Lady Alice rose and went, with a slight gesture of impatience. In a few minutes she returned, looking angry and determined, and resumed her seat. But whatever it was that had passed between them, it had destroyed that quiet flow of the feelings which was necessary to the working of her thoughts. In vain she tried: she could do nothing correctly. At last she burst into tears and left the room. I was almost beside myself with distress and apprehension. She did not return that day.

Next morning she entered at the usual hour, looking composed, but paler than of late, and showing signs of recent weeping. When we were all seated, and had just commenced our work, I happened to look up, and caught her eyes intently fixed on me. They dropped instantly, but without any appearance of confusion. She went on with her arithmetic, and succeeded tolerably. But this respite was to be of short duration. Lady Hilton again entered, and called her. She rose angrily, and my quick ear caught the half-uttered words, "That woman will make an idiot of me again!" She did not return; and never from that hour resumed her place in the schoolroom.

The time passed heavily. At dinner she looked proud and constrained; and spoke only in monosyllables.

For two days I scarcely saw her. But the third day, as I was busy in the library alone, she entered.

"Can I help you, Mr. Campbell?" she said.

I glanced involuntarily towards the door.

"Lady Hilton is not at home," she replied to my look, while a curl of indignation contended with a sweet tremor of shame for the possession of her lip.—"Let me help you."

"You will help me best if you sing that ballad I heard you singing just before you came in. I never heard you sing before."

"Didn't you? I don't think I ever did sing before."

"Sing it again, will you, please?"

"It is only two verses. My old Scotch nurse used to sing it when I was a little girl-oh, so long ago! I didn't know I could sing it."

She began without more ado, standing in the middle of the room, with her back towards the door.

> *Annie was dowie, an' Willie was wae:*
> *What can be the matter wi' siccan a twae?*
> *For Annie was bonnie's the first o' the day,*
> *And Willie was strang an' honest an' gay.*
>
> *Oh! the tane had a daddy was poor an' was proud;*
> *An' the tither a minnie that cared for the gowd.*
> *They lo'ed are anither, an' said their say—*
> *But the daddy an' minnie hae pairtit the twae.*

Just as she finished the song, I saw the sharp eyes of Lady Lucy peeping in at the door.

"Lady Lucy is watching at the door, Lady Alice," I said.

"I don't care," she answered; but turned with a flush on her face, and stepped noiselessly to the door.

"There is no one there," she said, returning.

"There was, though," I answered.

"They want to drive me mad," she cried, and hurried from the room.

The next day but one, she came again with the same request. But she had not been a minute in the library before Lady Hilton came to the door and called her in angry tones.

"Presently," replied Alice, and remained where she was.

"Do go, Lady Alice," I said. "They will send me away if you refuse."

She blushed scarlet, and went without another word.

She came no more to the library.

Chapter XII
Confession

Day followed day, the one the child of the other. Alice's old paleness and unearthly look began to reappear; and, strange to tell, my midnight temptation revived. After a time she ceased to dine with us again, and for days I never saw her. It was the old story of suffering with me, only more intense than before. The day was dreary, and the night stormy. "Call her," said my heart; but my conscience resisted.

I was lying on the floor of my room one midnight, with my face to the ground, when suddenly I heard a low, sweet, strange voice singing somewhere. The moment I became aware that I heard it I felt as if I had been listening to it unconsciously for some minutes past. I lay still, either charmed to stillness, or fearful of breaking the spell. As I lay, I was lapt in the folds of a waking dream.

I was in bed in a castle, on the seashore; the wind came from the sea in chill *eerie soughs*, and the waves fell with a threatful tone upon the beach, muttering many maledictions as they rushed up, and whispering cruel portents as they drew back, hissing and gurgling, through the million narrow ways of the pebbly ramparts; and I knew that a maiden in white was standing in the cold wind, by the angry sea, singing. I had a kind of dreamy belief in my dream; but, overpowered by the spell of the music, I still lay and listened. Keener and stronger, under the impulses of my will, grew the power of my hearing. At last I could distinguish the words. The ballad was *Annie of Lochroyan*; and Lady Alice was singing it. The words I heard were these:—

> *Oh, gin I had a bonnie ship,*
> *And men to sail wi' me,*
> *It's I wad gang to my true love,*
> *Sin' he winna come to me.*
>
> *Lang stood she at her true love's door,*
> *And lang tirled at the pin;*

At length up gat his fause mother,
Says, "Wha's that wad be in?"

Love Gregory started frae his sleep,
And to his mother did say:
"I dreamed a dream this night, mither,
That maks my heart right wae.

"I dreamed that Annie of Lochroyan,
The flower of a' her kin,
Was standing mournin' at my door,
But nane wad let her in."

I sprang to my feet, and opened the hidden door. There she stood, white, asleep, with closed eyes, singing like a bird, only with a heartful of sad meaning in every tone. I stepped aside, without speaking, and she passed me into the room. I closed the door, and followed her. She lay already upon the couch, still and restful—already covered with my plaid. I sat down beside her, waiting; and gazed upon her in wonderment. That she was possessed of very superior intellectual powers, whatever might be the cause of their having lain dormant so long, I had already fully convinced myself; but I was not prepared to find art as well as intellect. I had already heard her sing the little song of two verses, which she had learned from her nurse. But here was a song, of her own making as to the music, so true and so potent, that, before I knew anything of the words, it had surrounded me with a dream of the place in which the scene of the ballad was laid. It did not then occur to me that, perhaps, our idiosyncrasies were such as not to require even the music of the ballad for the production of *rapport* between our minds, the brain of the one generating in the brain of the other the vision present to itself.

I sat and thought:—Some obstruction in the gateways, outward, prevented her, in her waking hours, from uttering herself at all. This obstruction, damming back upon their sources the out-goings of life, threw her into this abnormal sleep. In it the impulse to utterance, still unsatisfied, so wrought within her unable, yet compliant form, that she could not rest, but rose and walked. And now, a fresh surge from the sea of her unknown being, unrepressed by the *hitherto* of the objects of sense, had burst the gates and bars, swept the obstructions from its channel, and poured from her in melodious song.

The first green lobes, at least, of these thoughts, appeared above the soil of my mind, while I sat and gazed on the sleeping girl. And now I had once more the delight of watching a spirit-dawn, a soul-rise, in that lovely form. The light flushing of its pallid sky was, as before, the first sign. I dreaded the flash of lovely flame, and the outburst of regnant anger, ere I should have time to say that I was not to blame. But when, at length, the full dawn, the slow sunrise came, it was with all the gentleness of a cloudy summer morn. Never did a more celestial rosy red hang about the skirts of the level sun, than deepened and glowed upon her face, when, opening her eyes, she saw me beside her. She covered her face with her hands; and instead of the words of indignant reproach which I dreaded to hear, she murmured behind the snowy screen: "I am glad you have broken your promise."

My heart gave a bound and was still. I grew faint with delight. "No," I said; "I have not broken my promise, Lady Alice; I have struggled nearly to madness to keep it—and I have kept it."

"I have come then of myself. Worse and worse! But it is their fault."

Tears now found their way through the repressing fingers. I could not endure to see her weep. I knelt beside her, and, while she still covered her face with her hands, I said—I do not know what I said. They were wild, and, doubtless, foolish words in themselves, but they must have been wise and true in their meaning. When I ceased, I knew that I had ceased only by the great silence around me. I was still looking at her hands. Slowly she withdrew them. It was as when the sun breaks forth on a cloudy day. The winter was over and gone; the time of the singing of birds had come. She smiled on me through her tears, and heart met heart in the light of that smile.

She rose to go at once, and I begged for no delay. I only stood with clasped hands, gazing at her. She turned at the door, and said;

"I daresay I shall come again; I am afraid I cannot help it; only mind you do not wake me."

Before I could reply, I was alone; and I felt that I must not follow her.

Chapter XIII
Questioning

I laid myself on the couch she had left, but not to sleep. A new pulse of life, stronger than I could bear, was throbbing within me. I dreaded a fever, lest I should talk in it, and drop the clue to my secret treasure. But the light of the morning stilled me, and a bath in ice-cold water made me strong again. Yet I felt all that day as if I were dying a delicious death, and going to a yet more exquisite life. As far as I might, however, I repressed all indications of my delight; and endeavoured, for the sake both of duty and of prudence, to be as attentive to my pupils and their studies as it was possible for man to be. This helped to keep me in my right mind. But, more than all my efforts at composure, the pain which, as far as my experience goes, invariably accompanies, and sometimes even usurps, the place of the pleasure which gave it birth, was efficacious in keeping me sane.

Night came, but brought no Lady Alice. It was a week before I saw her again. Her heart had been stilled, and she was able to sleep aright.

But seven nights after, she did come. I waited her awaking, possessed with one painful thought, which I longed to impart to her. She awoke with a smile, covered her face for a moment, but only for a moment, and then sat up. I stood before her; and the first words I spoke were:

"Lady Alice, ought I not to go?"

"No," she replied at once. "I can claim some compensation from them for the wrong they have been doing me. Do you know in what relation I stand to Lord and Lady Hilton? They are but my stepmother and her husband."

"I know that."

"Well, I have a fortune of my own, about which I never thought or cared—till—till—within the last few weeks. Lord Hilton is my guardian. Whether they made me the stupid creature I *was*, I do not know; but I believe they have represented me as far worse than I was, to keep people from making my acquaintance. They prevented my going on with my lessons, because they saw I was getting to understand things, and grow like other people; and that would not suit their purposes. It would be false delicacy in you to leave me to them, when you can make up to me for their injustice. Their behaviour to me takes away any right they had over me, and frees you from any obligation, because I am yours.—Am I not?"

Once more she covered her face with her hands. I could answer only by withdrawing one of them, which I *was* now emboldened to keep in my own.

I was very willingly persuaded to what was so much my own desire. But whether the reasoning was quite just or not, I am not yet sure. Perhaps it might be so for her, and yet not for me: I do not know; I am a poor casuist.

She resumed, laying her other hand upon mine:—

"It would be to tell the soul which you have called forth, to go back into its dark moaning cavern, and never more come out to the light of day."

How could I resist this?

A long pause ensued.

"It is strange," she said, at length, "to feel, when I lie down at night, that I may awake in your presence, without knowing how. It is strange, too, that, although I should be utterly ashamed to come wittingly, I feel no confusion when I find myself here. When I feel myself coming awake, I lie for a little while with my eyes closed, wondering and hoping, and afraid to open them, lest I should find myself only in my own chamber; shrinking a little, too—just a little—from the first glance into your face."

"But when you awake, do you know nothing of what has taken place in your sleep?"

"Nothing whatever."

"Have you no vague sensations, no haunting shadows, no dim ghostly moods, seeming to belong to that condition, left?"

"None whatever."

She rose, said "Good-night," and left me.

Chapter XIV
Jealousy

Again seven days passed before she revisited me. Indeed, her visits had always an interval of seven days, or a multiple of seven, between.

Since the last, a maddening jealousy had seized me. For, returning from those unknown regions into which her soul had wandered away, and where she had stayed for hours, did she not sometimes awake with a smile? How could I be sure that she did not lead two distinct existences?—that she had not some loving spirit, or man, who, like her, had for a time left the body behind—who was all in all to her in that region, and whom she forgot when she forsook it, as she forgot me when she entered it? It was a thought I could not brook. But I put aside its persistency as well as I could, till she should come again. For this I waited. I could not now endure the thought of compelling the attendance of her unconscious form; of making her body, like a living cage, transport to my presence the unresisting soul. I shrank from it as a true man would shrink from kissing the lips of a sleeping woman whom he loved, not knowing that she loved him in return.

It may well be said that to follow such a doubt was to inquire too curiously; but once the thought had begun, and grown, and been born, how was I to slay the monster, and be free of its hated presence? Was its truth not a possibility?—Yet how could even she help me, for she knew nothing of the matter? How could she vouch for the unknown? What news can the serene face of the moon, ever the same to us, give of the hidden half of herself turned ever towards what seems to us but the blind abysmal darkness, which yet has its own light and its own life? All I could hope for was to see her, to tell her, to be comforted at least by her smile.

My saving angel glided blind into my room, lay down upon her bier, and awaited the resurrection. I sat and awaited mine, panting to untwine from my heart the cold death-worm that twisted around it, yet picturing to myself the glow of love on the averted face of the beautiful spirit—averted from me, and bending on a radiant companion all the light withdrawn from the lovely form beside me. That light began to return. "She is coming, she is coming," I said within me. "Back from its glowing south travels the sun of my spring, the glory of my summer." Floating slowly up from the infinite depths of her being, came the conscious woman; up—up from the realms of stillness lying deeper than the plummet of self-knowledge can sound; up from the formless, up into the known, up into the material, up to the windows that look forth on the embodied mysteries around. Her eyelids rose. One look of love all but slew my fear. When I told her my grief, she answered with a smile of pity, yet half of disdain at the thought.

"If ever I find it so, I will kill myself there, that I may go to my Hades with you. But if I am dreaming of another, how is it that I always rise in my vision and come to you? You will go crazy if you fancy such foolish things," she added, with a smile of reproof.

The spectral thought vanished, and I was free.

"Shall I tell you," she resumed, covering her face with her hands, "why I behaved so proudly to you, from the very first day you entered the house? It was because, when I passed you on the lawn, before ever you entered the house, I felt a strange, undefinable attraction towards you, which continued, although I could not account for it and would not yield to it. I was heartily annoyed at it. But you see it was of no use—here I am. That was what made me so fierce, too, when I first found myself in your room."

It was indeed long before she came to my room again.

Chapter XV
The Chamber of Ghosts

But now she returned once more into the usual routine of the family. I fear I was unable to repress all signs of agitation when, next day, she entered the dining-room, after we were seated, and took her customary place at the table. Her behaviour was much the same as before; but her face was very different. There was light in it now, and signs of mental movement. The smooth forehead would be occasionally wrinkled, and she would fall into moods which were evidently not of inanity, but of abstracted thought. She took especial care that our eyes should not meet. If by chance they did, instead of sinking hers, she kept them steady, and opened them wider, as if she was fixing them on nothing at all, or she raised them still higher, as if she was looking at something above me, before she allowed them to fall. But the change in her altogether was such that it must have attracted the notice and roused the speculation of Lady Hilton at least. For me, so well did she act her part, that I was thrown into perplexity by it. And when day after day passed, and the longing to speak to her grew, and remained unsatisfied, new doubts arose. Perhaps she was tired of me. Perhaps her new studies filled her mind with the clear, gladsome morning light of the pure intellect, which always throws doubt and distrust and a kind of negation upon the moonlight of passion, mysterious, and mingled ever with faint shadows of pain. I walked as in an unresting sleep. Utterly as I loved her, I was yet alarmed and distressed to find how entirely my being had grown dependent upon her love; how little of individual, self-existing, self-upholding life, I seemed to have left; how little I cared for anything, save as I could associate it with her.

I was sitting late one night in my room. I had all but given up hope of her coming. I had, perhaps, deprived her of the somnambulic power. I was brooding over this possibility, when all at once I felt as if I were looking into the haunted room. It seemed to be lighted by the moon, shining through the stained windows. The feeling came and went suddenly, as such visions of places generally do; but this had an indescribable something about it more clear and real than such resurrections of the past, whether willed or unwilled, commonly possess; and a great longing seized me to look into the room once more. I rose with a sense of yielding to the irresistible, left the room, groped my way through the hall and up the oak staircase—I had never thought of taking a light with me—and entered the corridor. No sooner had I entered it, than the thought sprang up in my mind—"What if she should be there!" My heart stood still for a moment, like a wounded deer, and then bounded on, with a pang in every bound. The corridor was night itself, with a dim, bluish-grey light from the windows, sufficing to mark their own spaces. I stole through it, and, without erring once, went straight to the haunted chamber. The door stood half open. I entered, and was bewildered by the dim, mysterious, dreamy loveliness upon which I gazed. The moon shone full upon the windows, and a thousand coloured lights and shadows crossed and intertwined upon the walls and floor, all so soft, and mingling, and undefined, that the brain was filled as with a flickering dance of ghostly rainbows. But I had little time to think of these; for out of the only dark corner in the room came a white figure, flitting across the chaos of lights, bedewed, besprinkled, bespattered, as she passed, with their multitudinous colours. I was speechless, motionless, with something far beyond joy. With a low moan of delight, Lady Alice sank into my arms. Then, looking up, with a light laugh—"The scales are turned, dear," she said. "You are in my power now; I brought you here. I thought I could, and I tried, for I wanted so much to see you—and you are come." She led me across the room to the place where she had been seated, and we sat side by side.

"I thought you had forgotten me," I said, "or had grown tired of me."

"Did you? That was unkind. You have made my heart so still, that, body and soul, I sleep at night."

"Then shall I never see you more?"

"We can meet here. This is the best place. No one dares come near the haunted room at night. We might even venture in the evening. Look, now, from where we are sitting, across the air, between the windows and the shadows on the floor. Do you see nothing moving?"

I looked, but could see nothing. She resumed:—

"I almost fancy, sometimes, that what old stories say about this room may be true. I could fancy now that I see dim transparent forms in ancient armour, and in strange antique dresses, men and women, moving about, meeting, speaking, embracing, parting, coming and going. But I was never afraid of such beings. I am sure these would not, could not hurt us."

If the room was not really what it was well fitted to be—a rendezvous for the ghosts of the past—then either my imagination, becoming more active as she spoke, began to operate upon my brain, or her fancies were mysteriously communicated to me; for I was persuaded that I saw such dim undefined forms as she described, of a substance only denser than the moonlight, flitting, and floating about, between the windows and the illuminated floor. Could they have been coloured shadows thrown from the stained glass upon the fine dust with which the slightest motion in such an old and neglected room must fill its atmosphere? I did not think of that then, however.

"I could persuade myself that I, too, see them," I replied. "I cannot say that I am afraid of such beings any more than you—if only they will not speak."

"Ah!" she replied, with a lengthened, meaning utterance, expressing sympathy with what I said; "I know what you mean. I, too, am afraid of hearing things. And that reminds me, I have never yet asked you about the galloping horse. I too hear sometimes the sound of a loose horse-shoe. It always betokens some evil to me; but I do not know what it means. Do you?"

"Do you know," I rejoined, "that there is a connection between your family and mine, somewhere far back in their histories?"

"No! Is there? How glad I am! Then perhaps you and I are related, and that is how we are so much alike, and have power over each other, and hear the same things."

"Yes. I suppose that is how."

"But can you account for that sound which we both hear?"

"I will tell you what my old foster-mother told me," I replied. And I began by narrating when and where I had first heard the sound; and then gave her, as nearly as I could, the legend which nurse had recounted to me. I did not tell her its association with the events of my birth, for I feared exciting her imagination too much. She listened to it very quietly, however, and when I came to a close, only said:

"Of course, we cannot tell how much of it is true, but there may be something in it. I have never heard anything of the sort, and I, too, have an old nurse. She is with me still. You shall see her some day."

She rose to go.

"Will you meet me here again soon?" I said.

"As soon as you wish," she answered.

"Then to-morrow, at midnight?"

"Yes."

And we parted at the door of the haunted chamber. I watched the flickering with which her whiteness just set the darkness in motion, and nothing more, seeming to see it long after I knew she must have turned aside and descended the steps leading towards her own room. Then I turned and groped my way back to mine.

We often met after this in the haunted room. Indeed my spirit haunted it all day and all night long. And when we met amid the shadows, we were wrapped in the mantle of love, and from its folds looked out fearless on the ghostly world about us. Ghosts or none, they never annoyed us. Our love was a talisman, yea, an elixir of life, which made us equal to the twice-born,—the disembodied dead. And they were as a wall of fear about us, to keep far off the unfriendly foot and the prying eye.

In the griefs that followed, I often thought with myself that I would gladly die for a thousand years, might I then awake for one night in the haunted chamber, a ghost, among the ghosts who crowded its stained moonbeams, and see my dead Alice smiling across the glimmering rays, and beckoning me to the old nook, she, too, having come awake out of the sleep of death, in the dream of the haunted chamber. "Might we but sit there," I said, "through the night, as of old, and love and comfort each other, till the moon go down, and the pale dawn, which is the night of the ghosts, begin to arise, then gladly would I go to sleep for another thousand years, in the hope that when I next became conscious of life, it might be in another such ghostly night, in the chamber of the ghosts."

Chapter XVI
The Clanking Shoe

Time passed. We began to feel very secure in that room, watched as it was by the sleepless sentry, Fear. One night I ventured to take a light with me.

"How nice to have a candle!" she said as I entered. "I hope they are all in bed, though. It will drive some of them into fits if they see the light."

"I wanted to show you something I found in the library to-day."

"What is it?"

I opened a book, and showed her a paper inside it, with some verses written on it.

"Whose writing is that?" I asked.

"Yours, of course. As if I did not know your writing!"

"Will you look at the date?"

"*Seventeen hundred and ninety-three.'* You are making game of me, Duncan. But the paper does look yellow and old."

"I found it as you see it, in that book. It belonged to Lord Hilton's brother. The verses are a translation of part of the poem beside which they lie—one by Von Salis, who died shortly before that date at the bottom. I will read them to you, and then show you something else that is strange about them. The poem is called *Psyche's Sorrow*. Psyche means the soul, Alice."

"I remember. You told me about her before, you know."

> "*Psyche's sighing all her prison darkens;*
> *She is moaning for the far-off stars;*
> *Fearing, hoping, every sound she hearkens—*
> *Fate may now be breaking at her bars.*
>
> *Bound, fast bound, are Psyche's airy pinions:*
> *High her heart, her mourning soft and low—*
> *Knowing that in sultry pain's dominions*

Grow the palms that crown the victor's brow;

That the empty hand the wreath encloses;
Earth's cold winds but make the spirit brave;
Knowing that the briars bear the roses,
Golden flowers the waste deserted grave.

In the cypress-shade her myrtle groweth;
Much she loves, because she much hath borne;
Love-led, through the darksome way she goeth—
On to meet him in the breaking morn.

She can bear—"

"Here the translation ceases, you see; and then follows the date, with the words in German underneath it—'How weary I am!' Now what is strange, Alice, is, that this date is the very month and year in which I was born."

She did not reply to this with anything beyond a mere assent. Her mind was fixed on the poem itself. She began to talk about it, and I was surprised to find how thoroughly she entered into it and understood it. She seemed to have crowded the growth of a lifetime into the last few months. At length I told her how unhappy I had felt for some time, at remaining in Lord Hilton's house, as matters now were.

"Then you must go," she said, quite quietly.

This troubled me.

"You do not mind it?"

"No. I shall be very glad."

"Will you go with me?" I asked, perplexed.

"Of course I will."

I did not know what to say to this, for I had no money, and of course I should have none of my salary. She divined at once the cause of my hesitation.

"I have a diamond bracelet in my room," she said, with a smile, "and a few guineas besides."

"How shall we get away?"

"Nothing is easier. My old nurse, whom I mentioned to you before, lives at the lodge gate."

"Oh! I know her very well," I interrupted. "But she's not Scotch?"

"Indeed she is. But she has been with our family almost all her life. I often go to see her, and sometimes stay all night with her. You can get a carriage ready in the village, and neither of us will be missed before morning."

I looked at her in renewed surprise at the decision of her invention. She covered her face, as she seldom did now, but went on:

"We can go to London, where you will easily find something to do. Men always can there. And when I come of age—"

"Alice, how old are you?" I interrupted.

"Nineteen," she answered. "By the way," she resumed, "when I think of it—how odd!—that"—pointing to the date on the paper—"is the very month in which I too was born."

I was too much surprised to interrupt her, and she continued:

"I never think of my age without recalling one thing about my birth, which nurse often refers to. She was going up the stair to my mother's room, when she happened to notice a bright star, not far from the new moon. As she crossed the room with me in her arms, just after I was born, she saw the same star almost on the tip of the opposite horn. My mother died a week after. Who knows how different I might have been if she had lived!"

It was long before I spoke. The awful and mysterious thoughts roused in my mind by the revelations of the day held me silent. At length I said, half thinking aloud:

"Then you and I, Alice, were born the same hour, and our mothers died together."

Receiving no answer, I looked at her. She was fast asleep, and breathing gentle, full breaths. She had been sitting for some time with her head lying on my shoulder and my arm around her. I could not bear to wake her.

We had been in this position perhaps for half an hour, when suddenly a cold shiver ran through me, and all at once I became aware of the far-off gallop of a horse. It drew nearer. On and on it came—nearer and nearer. Then came the clank of the broken shoe!

At the same moment, Alice started from her sleep and, springing to her feet, stood an instant listening. Then crying out, in an agonised whisper,— "The horse with the clanking shoe!" she flung her arms around me. Her face was white as the spectral moon which, the moment I put the candle out, looked in through a clear pane beside us; and she gazed fearfully, yet wildly-defiant, towards the door. We clung to each other. We heard the sound come nearer and nearer, till it thundered right up to the very door of the room, terribly loud. It ceased. But the door was flung open, and Lord Hilton entered, followed by servants with lights.

I have but a very confused remembrance of what followed. I heard a vile word from the lips of Lord Hilton; I felt my fingers on his throat; I received a blow on the head; and I seem to remember a cry of agony from Alice as I fell. What happened next I do not know.

When I came to myself, I was lying on a wide moor, with the night wind blowing about me. I presume that I had wandered thither in a state of unconsciousness, after being turned out of the Hall, and that I had at last fainted from loss of blood. I was unable to move for a long time. At length the morning broke, and I found myself not far from the Hall. I crept back, a mile or two, to the gates, and having succeeded in rousing Alice's old nurse, was taken in with many lamentations, and put to bed in the lodge. I had a violent fever; and it was all the poor woman could do to keep my presence a secret from the family at the Hall.

When I began to mend, my first question was about Alice. I learned, though with some difficulty—for my kind attendant was evidently unwilling to tell me all the truth—that Alice, too, had been very ill; and that, a week before, they had removed her. But she either would not or could not tell me where they had taken her. I believe she could not. Nor do I know for certain to this day.

Mrs. Blakesley offered me the loan of some of her savings to get me to London. I received it with gratitude, and as soon as I was fit to travel, made my way thither. Afraid for my reason, if I had no employment to keep my thoughts from brooding on my helplessness, and so increasing my despair, and determined likewise that my failure should not make me burdensome to any one else, I enlisted in the Scotch Greys, before letting any of my friends know where I was. Through the help of one already mentioned in my story, I soon obtained a commission. From the field of Waterloo, I rode into Brussels with a broken arm and a sabre-cut in the head.

As we passed along one of the streets, through all the clang of iron-shod hoofs on the stones around me, I heard the ominous clank. At the same moment, I heard a cry. It was the voice of my Alice. I looked up. At a barred window I saw her face; but it was terribly changed. I dropped from my horse. As soon as I was able to move from the hospital, I went to the place, and found it was a lunatic asylum. I was permitted to see the inmates, but discovered no one resembling her. I do not now believe that she was ever there. But I may be wrong. Nor will I trouble my reader with the theories on which I sought to account for the vision. They will occur to himself readily enough.

For years and years I know not whether she was alive or dead. I sought her far and near. I wandered over England, France, and Germany, hopelessly searching; listening at *tables-d'hôte*; lurking about mad-houses; haunting theatres and churches; often, in wild regions, begging my way from house to house; I did not find her.

Once I visited Hilton Hall. I found it all but deserted. I learned that Mrs. Wilson was dead, and that there were only two or three servants in the place. I managed to get into the house unseen, and made my way to the haunted chamber. My feelings were not so keen as I had anticipated, for they had been dulled by long suffering. But again I saw the moon shine through those windows of stained glass. Again her beams were crowded with ghosts. She was not amongst them. "My lost love!" I cried; and then, rebuking myself, "No; she is not lost. They say that Time and Space exist not, save in our thoughts. If so, then that which has been, is, and the Past can never cease. She is mine, and I shall find her—what matters it where, or when, or how? Till then, my soul is but a moon-lighted chamber of ghosts; and I sit within, the dreariest of them all. When she enters, it will be a home of love. And I wait—I wait."

I sat and brooded over the Past, till I fell asleep in the phantom-peopled night. And all the night long they were about me—the men and women of the long past. And I was one of them. I wandered in my dreams over the whole house, habited in a long old-fashioned gown, searching for one who was Alice, and yet would be some one else. From room to room I wandered till weary, and could not find her. At last, I gave up the search, and, retreating to the library, shut myself in. There, taking down from the shelf the volume of Von Salis, I tried hard to go on with the translation of *Pysche's Sorrow*, from the point where the student had left it, thinking it, all the time, my own unfinished work.

When I woke in the morning, the chamber of ghosts, in which I had fallen asleep, had vanished. The sun shone in through the windows of the library; and on its dusty table lay Von Salis, open at *Pysche's Trauer*. The sheet of paper with the translation on it, was not there. I hastened to leave the house, and effected my escape before the servants were astir.

Sometimes I condensed my whole being into a single intensity of will—that she should come to me; and sustained it, until I fainted with the effort. She did not come. I desisted altogether at last, for I bethought me that, whether dead or alive, it must cause her torture not to be able to obey it.

Sometimes I questioned my own sanity. But the thought of the loss of my reason did not in itself trouble me much. What tortured me almost to the madness it supposed was the possible fact, which a return to my right mind might reveal—that there never had been a Lady Alice. What if I died, and awoke from my madness, and found a clear blue air of life, a joyous world of sunshine, a divine wealth of delight around and in me—but no Lady Alice—she having vanished with all the other phantoms of a sick brain! "Rather let me be mad still," I said, "if mad I am; and so dream on that I have been blessed. Were I to wake to such a heaven, I would pray God to let me go and live the life I had but dreamed, with all its sorrows, and all its despair, and all its madness, that when I died again, I might know that such things had been, and could never be awaked from, and left behind with the dream." But I was not mad, any more than Hamlet; though, like him, despair sometimes led me far along the way at the end of which madness lies.

Chapter XVII
The Physician

I was now Captain Campbell, of the Scotch Greys, contriving to live on my half pay, and thinking far more about the past than the present or the future. My father was dead. My only brother was also gone, and the property had passed into other hands. I had no fixed place of abode, but went from one spot to another, as the whim seized me—sometimes remaining months, sometimes removing next day, but generally choosing retired villages about which I knew nothing.

I had spent a week in a small town on the borders of Wales, and intended remaining a fortnight longer, when I was suddenly seized with a violent illness, in which I lay insensible for three weeks. When I recovered consciousness, I found that my head had been shaved, and that the cicatrice of my old wound was occasionally very painful. Of late I have suspected that I had some operation performed upon my skull during my illness; but Dr. Ruthwell never dropped a hint to that effect. This was the friend whom, when first I opened my seeing eyes, I beheld sitting by my bedside, watching the effect of his last prescription. He was one of the few in the profession, whose love of science and love of their fellows combined, would be enough to chain them to the art of healing, irrespective of its emoluments. He was one of the few, also, who see the marvellous in all science, and, therefore, reject nothing merely because the marvellous may seem to predominate in it. Yet neither would he accept anything of the sort as fact, without the strictest use of every experiment within his power, even then remaining often in doubt. This man conferred honour by his friendship; and I am happy to think that before many days of recovery had passed, we were friends indeed. But I lay for months under his care before I was able to leave my bed.

He attributed my illness to the consequences of the sabre-cut, and my recovery to the potency of the drugs he had exhibited. I attributed my illness in great measure to the constant contemplation of my early history, no longer checked by any regular employment; and my recovery in equal measure to the power of his kindness and sympathy, helping from within what could never have been reached from without.

He told me that he had often been greatly perplexed with my symptoms, which would suddenly change in the most unaccountable manner, exhibiting phases which did not, as far as his knowledge went, belong to any variety of the suffering which gave the prevailing character to my ailment; and after I had so far recovered as to render it safe to turn my regard more particularly upon my own case, he said to me one day,

"You would laugh at me, Campbell, were I to confess some of the bother this illness of yours has occasioned me; enough, indeed, to overthrow any conceit I ever had in my own diagnosis."

"Go on," I answered; "I promise not to laugh."

He little knew how far I should be from laughing. "In your case," he continued, "the *pathognomonic,* if you will excuse medical slang, was every now and then broken by the intrusion of altogether foreign symptoms."

I listened with breathless attention.

"Indeed, on several occasions, when, after meditating on your case till I was worn out, I had fallen half asleep by your bedside, I came to myself with the strangest conviction that I was watching by the bedside of a woman."

"Thank Heaven!" I exclaimed, starting up, "She lives still."

I need not describe the doctor's look of amazement, almost consternation; for he thought a fresh access of fever was upon me, and I had already begun to rave. For his reassurance, however, I promised to account fully for my apparently senseless excitement; and that evening I commenced the narrative which forms the preceeding part of this story. Long before I reached its close, my exultation had vanished, and, as I wrote it for him, it ended with the expressed conviction that she must be dead. Ere long, however, the hope once more revived. While, however, the narrative was in progress, I gave him a summary, which amounted to this:—

I had loved a lady—loved her still. I did not know where she was, and had reason to fear that her mind had given way under the suffering of our separation. Between us there existed, as well, the bond of a distant blood relationship; so distant, that but for its probable share in the production of another relationship of a very marvellous nature, it would scarcely have been worth alluding to. This was a kind of psychological attraction, which, when justified and strengthened by the spiritual energies of love, rendered the immediate communication of certain feelings, both mental and bodily, so rapid, that almost the consciousness of the one existed for the time in the mental circumstances of the other. Nay, so complete at times was the communication, that I even doubted her testimony as to some strange correspondence in our past history on this very ground, suspecting that, my memory being open to her retrospection, she saw my story, and took it for her own. It was, therefore, easy for me to account for Dr. Ruthwell's scientific bewilderment at the symptoms I manifested.

As my health revived, my hope and longing increased. But although I loved Lady Alice with more entireness than even during the latest period of our intercourse, a certain calm endurance had supervened, which rendered the relief of fierce action no longer necessary to the continuance of a sane existence. It was as if the concentrated orb of love had diffused itself in a genial warmth through the whole orb of life, imparting fresh vitality to many roots which had remained leafless in my being. For years the field of battle was the only field that had borne the flower of delight; now nature began to live again for me.

One day, the first on which I ventured to walk into the fields alone, I was delighted with the multitude of the daisies peeping from the grass everywhere—the first attempts of the earth, become conscious of blindness, to open eyes, and see what was about and above her. Everything is wonderful after the resurrection from illness. It is a resurrection of all nature. But somehow or other I was not satisfied with the daisies. They did not seem to me so lovely as the daisies I used to see when I was a child. I thought with myself, "This is the cloud that gathers with life, the dimness that passion and suffering cast over the eyes of the mind." That moment my gaze fell upon a single, solitary, red-tipped daisy. My reasoning vanished, and my melancholy with it, slain by the red tips of the lonely beauty. This was the kind of daisy I had loved as a child; and with the sight of it, a whole field of them rushed back into my mind; a field of my father's where, throughout the multitude, you could not have found a white one. My father was dead; the fields had passed into other hands; but perhaps the red-tipped *gowans* were left. I must go and see. At all events, the hill that overlooked the field would still be there, and no change would have passed upon *it*. It would receive me with the same familiar look as of old, still fronting the great mountain from whose sides I had first heard the sound of that clanking horseshoe, which, whatever might be said to account for it, had certainly had a fearful connection with my joys and sorrows both. Did the ghostly rider still haunt the place? or, if he did, should I hear again that sound of coming woe? Whether or not, I defied him. I would not be turned from my desire to see the old place by any fear of a ghostly marauder, whom I should be only too glad to encounter, if there were the smallest chance of coming off with the victory.

As soon as my friend would permit me, I set out for Scotland.

Chapter XVIII
Old Friends

I made the journey by easy stages, chiefly on the back of a favourite black horse, which had carried me well in several fights, and had come out of them scarred, like his master, but sound in wind and limb. It was night when I reached the village lying nearest to my birth place.

When I woke in the morning, I found the whole region filled with a white mist, hiding the mountains around. Now and then a peak looked through, and again retired into the cloudy folds. In the wide, straggling street, below the window at which I had made them place my breakfast-table, a periodical fair was being held; and I sat looking down on the gathering crowd, trying to discover some face known to my childhood, and still to be recognized through the veil which years must have woven across the features. When I had finished my breakfast, I went down and wandered about among the people. Groups of elderly men were talking earnestly; and young men and maidens who had come to be *fee'd*, were joking and laughing. They stared at the Sassenach gentleman, and, little thinking that he understood every word they uttered, made their remarks upon him in no very subdued tones. I approached a stall where a brown old woman was selling gingerbread and apples. She was talking to a man with long, white locks. Near them was a group of young people. One of them must have said something about me; for the old woman, who had been taking stolen glances at me, turned rather sharply towards them, and rebuked them for rudeness.

"The gentleman is no Sassenach," she said. "He understands everything you are saying."

This was spoken in Gaelic, of course. I turned and looked at her with more observance. She made me a courtesy, and said, in the same language:

"Your honour will be a Campbell, I'm thinking."

"I am a Campbell," I answered, and waited.

"Your honour's Christian name wouldn't be Duncan, sir?"

"It is Duncan," I answered; "but there are many Duncan Campbells."

"Only one to me, your honour; and that's yourself. But you will not remember me?"

I did not remember her. Before long, however, urged by her anxiety to associate her Present with my Past, she enabled me to recall in her time-worn features those of a servant in my father's house when I was a child.

"But how could you recollect me?" I said.

"I have often seen you since I left your father's, sir. But it was really, I believe, that I hear more about you than anything else, every day of my life."

"I do not understand you."

"From old Margaret, I mean."

"Dear old Margaret! Is she alive?"

"Alive and hearty, though quite bedridden. Why, sir, she must be within near sight of a hundred."

"Where does she live?"

"In the old cottage, sir. Nothing will make her leave it. The new laird wanted to turn her out; but Margaret muttered something at which he grew as white as his shirt, and he has never ventured across her threshold again."

"How do you see so much of her, though?"

"I never leave her, sir. She can't wait on herself, poor old lady. And she's like a mother to me. Bless her! But your honour will come and see her?"

"Of course I will. Tell her so when you go home."

"Will you honour me by sleeping at my house, sir?" said the old man to whom she had been talking. "My farm is just over the brow of the hill, you know."

I had by this time recognised him, and I accepted his offer at once.

"When may we look for you, sir?" he asked.

"When shall you be home?" I rejoined.

"This afternoon, sir. I have done my business already."

"Then I shall be with you in the evening, for I have nothing to keep me here."

"Will you take a seat in my gig?"

"No, thank you. I have my own horse with me. You can take him in too, I dare say?"

"With pleasure, sir."

We parted for the meantime. I rambled about the neighbourhood till it was time for an early dinner.

Chapter XIX
Old Constancy

The fog cleared off; and, as the hills began to throw long, lazy shadows, their only embraces across the wide valleys, I mounted and set out on the ride of a few miles which should bring me to my old acquaintance's dwelling.

I lingered on the way. All the old places demanded my notice. They seemed to say, "Here we are—waiting for you." Many a tuft of harebells drew me towards the roadside, to look at them and their children, the blue butterflies, hovering over them; and I stopped to gaze at many a wild rosebush, with a sunset of its own roses. The sun had set to me, before I had completed half the distance. But there was a long twilight, and I knew the road well.

My horse was an excellent walker, and I let him walk on, with the reins on his neck; while I, lost in a dream of the past, was singing a song of my own making, with which I often comforted my longing by giving it voice.

The autumn winds are sighing
Over land and sea;
The autumn woods are dying
Over hill and lea;
And my heart is sighing, dying,
Maiden, for thee.

The autumn clouds are flying
Homeless over me;
The homeless birds are crying
In the naked tree;
And my heart is flying, crying,
Maiden, to thee.

My cries may turn to gladness,

And my flying flee;
My sighs may lose the sadness,
Yet sigh on in me;
All my sadness, all my gladness,
Maiden, lost in thee.

I was roused by a heavy drop of rain upon my face. I looked up. A cool wave of wind flowed against me. Clouds had gathered; and over the peak of a hill to the left, the sky was very black. Old Constancy threw his head up, as if he wanted me to take the reins, and let him step out. I remembered that there used to be an awkward piece of road somewhere not far in front, where the path, with a bank on the left side, sloped to a deep descent on the right. If the road was as bad there as it used to be, it would be better to pass it before it grew quite dark. So I took the reins, and away went old Constancy. We had just reached the spot, when a keen flash of lightning broke from the cloud overhead, and my horse instantly stood stock-still, as if paralysed, with his nostrils turned up towards the peak of the mountain. I sat as still as he, to give him time to recover himself. But all at once, his whole frame was convulsed, as if by an agony of terror. He gave a great plunge, and then I felt his muscles swelling and knotting under me, as he rose on his hind legs, and went backwards, with the scaur behind him. I leaned forward on his neck to bring him down, but he reared higher and higher, till he stood bolt upright, and it was time to slip off, lest he should fall upon me. I did so; but my foot alighted upon no support. He had backed to the edge of the shelving ground, and I fell, and went to the bottom. The last thing I was aware of, was the thundering fall of my horse beside me.

When I came to myself, it was dark. I felt stupid and aching all over; but I soon satisfied myself that no bones were broken. A mass of something lay near me. It was poor Constancy. I crawled to him, laid my hand on his neck, and called him by his name. But he made no answer in that gentle, joyful speech—for it was speech in old Constancy—with which he always greeted me, if only after an hour's absence. I felt for his heart. There was just a flutter there. He tried to lift his head, and gave a little kick with one of his hind legs. In doing so, he struck a bit of rock, and the clank of the iron made my flesh creep. I got hold of his leg in the dark, and felt the shoe. *It was loose.* I felt his heart again. The motion had ceased. I needed all my manhood to keep from crying like a child; for my charger was my friend. How long I lay beside him, I do not know; but, at length, I heard the sound of wheels coming along the road. I tried to shout, and, in some measure, succeeded; for a voice, which I recognised as that of my farmer-friend, answered cheerily. He was shocked to discover that his expected guest was in such evil plight. It was still dark, for the rain was falling heavily; but, with his directions, I was soon able to take my seat beside him in the gig. He had been unexpectedly detained, and was now hastening home with the hope of being yet in time to welcome me.

Next morning, after the luxurious rest of a heather-bed, I found myself not much the worse for my adventure, but heart-sore for the loss of my horse.

Chapter XX
Margaret

Early in the forenoon, I came in sight of the cottage of Margaret. It lay unchanged, a grey, stone-fashioned hut, in the hollow of the mountain-basin. I scrambled down the soft green brae, and soon stood within the door of the cottage. There I was met and welcomed by Margaret's attendant. She led me to the bed where my old nurse lay. Her eyes were yet undimmed by years, and little change had passed upon her countenance since I parted with her on that memorable night. The moment she saw me, she broke out into a passionate lamentation such as a mother might utter over the maimed strength and disfigured beauty of her child.

"What ill has he done—my bairn—to be all night the sport of the powers of the air and the wicked of the earth? But the day will dawn for my Duncan yet, and a lovely day it will be!"

Then looking at me anxiously, she said,

"You're not much the worse for last night, my bairn. But woe's me! His grand horse, that carried him so, that I blessed the beast in my prayers!"

I knew that no one could have yet brought her the news of my accident.

"You saw me fall, then, nurse?" I said.

"That I did," she answered. "I see you oftener than you think. But there was a time when I could hardly see you at all, and I thought you were dead, my Duncan."

I stooped to kiss her. She laid the one hand that had still the power of motion upon my head, and dividing the hair, which had begun to be mixed with grey, said: "Eh! The bonny grey hairs! My Duncan's a man in spite of them!"

She searched until she found the scar of the sabre-cut.

"Just where I thought to find it!" she said. "That was a terrible day; worse for me than for you, Duncan."

"You saw me *then!*" I exclaimed.

"Little do folks know," she answered, "who think I'm lying here like a live corpse in its coffin, what liberty my soul—and that's just me—enjoys. Little do they know what I see and hear. And there's no witchcraft or evil-doing in it, my boy; but just what the Almighty made me. Janet, here, declares she heard the cry that I made, when this same cut, that's no so well healed yet, broke out in your bonny head. I saw no sword, only the bursting of the blood from the wound. But sit down, my bairn, and have something to eat after your walk. We'll have time enough for speech."

Janet had laid out the table with fare of the old homely sort, and I was a boy once more as I ate the well-known food. Every now and then I glanced towards the old face. Soon I saw that she was asleep. From her lips broke murmured sounds, so partially connected that I found it impossible to remember them; but the impression they left on my mind was something like this,

"Over the water. Yes; it is a rough sea—green and white. But over the water. There is a path for the pathless. The grass on the hill is long and cool. Never horse came there. If they once sleep in that grass, no harm can hurt them more. Over the water. Up the hill." And then she murmured the words of the psalm: "He that dwelleth in the secret place."

For an hour I sat beside her. It was evidently a sweet, natural sleep, the most wonderful sleep of all, mingled with many a broken dream-rainbow. I rose at last, and, telling Janet that I would return in the evening, went back to my quarters; for my absence from the mid-day meal would have been a disappointment to the household.

When I returned to the cottage, I found Margaret only just awaked, and greatly refreshed. I sat down beside her in the twilight, and the following conversation began:

"You said, nurse, that, some time ago, you could not see me. Did you know nothing about me all that time?"

"I took it to mean that you were ill, my dear. Shortly after you left us, the same thing happened first; but I do not think you were ill then."

"I should like to tell you all my story, dear Margaret," I said, conceiving a sudden hope of assistance from one who hovered so near the unseen that she often flitted across the borders. "But would it tire you?"

"Tire me, my child!" she said, with sudden energy. "Did I not carry you in my bosom, till I loved you more than the darling I had lost? Do I not think about you and your fortunes, till, sitting there, you are no nearer to me than when a thousand miles away? You do not know my love to you, Duncan. I have lived upon it when, I daresay, you did not care whether I was alive or dead. But that was all one to my love. When you leave me now, I shall not care much. My thoughts will only return to their old ways. I think the sight of the eyes is sometimes an intrusion between the heart and its love."

Here was philosophy, or something better, from the lips of an old Highland seeress! For me, I felt it so true, that the joy of hearing her say so turned, by a sudden metamorphosis, into freak. I pretended to rise, and said:

"Then I had better go, nurse. Good-bye."

She put out her one hand, with a smile that revealed her enjoyment of the poor humour, and said, while she held me fast:

"Nay, nay, my Duncan. A little of the scarce is sometimes dearer to us than much of the better. I shall have plenty of time to think about you when I can't see you, my boy." And her philosophy melted away into tears, that filled her two blue eyes.

"I was only joking," I said.

"Do you need to tell me that?" she rejoined, smiling. "I am not so old as to be stupid yet. But I want to hear your story. I am hungering to hear it."

"But," I whispered, "I cannot speak about it before anyone else."

"I will send Janet away. Janet, I want to talk to Mr. Campbell alone."

"Very well, Margaret," answered Janet, and left the room.

"Will she listen?" I asked.

"She dares not," answered Margaret, with a smile; "she has a terrible idea of my powers."

The twilight grew deeper; the glow of the peat-fire became redder; the old woman lay still as death. And I told all the story of Lady Alice. My voice sounded to myself as I spoke, not like my own, but like its echo from the vault of some listening cave, or like the voices one hears beside as sleep is slowly creeping over the sense. Margaret did not once interrupt me. When I had finished she remained still silent, and I began to fear I had talked her asleep.

"Can you help me?" I said.

"I think I can," she answered. "Will you call Janet?" I called her.

"Make me a cup of tea, Janet. Will you have some tea with me, Duncan?"

Janet lighted a little lamp, and the tea was soon set out, with "flour-scons" and butter. But Margaret ate nothing; she only drank her tea, lifting her cup with her one trembling hand. When the remains of our repast had been removed, she said:—

"Now, Janet, you can leave us; and on no account come into the room till Mr. Campbell calls you. Take the lamp with you."

Janet obeyed without a word of reply, and we were left once more alone, lighted only by the dull glow of the fire.

The night had gathered cloudy and dark without, reminding me of that night when she told me the story of the two brothers. But this time no storm disturbed the silence of the night. As soon as Janet was gone, Margaret said:—

"Will you take the pillow from under my head, Duncan, my dear?"

I did so, and she lay in an almost horizontal position. With the living hand she lifted the powerless arm, and drew it across her chest, outside the bed-clothes. Then she laid the other arm over it, and, looking up at me, said:—

"Kiss me, my bairn; I need strength for what I am going to do for your sake."

I kissed her.

"There now!" she said, "I am ready. Good-bye. Whatever happens, do not speak to me; and let no one come near me but yourself. It will be wearisome for you, but it is for your sake, my Duncan. And don't let the fire out. Don't leave me."

I assured her I would attend to all she said. She closed her eyes, and lay still. I went to the fire, and sat down in a high-backed arm-chair, to wait the event.—There was plenty of fuel in the corner. I made up the fire, and then, leaning back, with my eyes fixed on it, let my thoughts roam at will. Where was my old nurse now? What was she seeing or encountering? Would she meet our adversary? Would she be strong enough to foil him? Was she dead for the time, although some bond rendered her return from the regions of the dead inevitable?—But she might never come back, and then I should have no tidings of the kind which I knew she had gone to see, and which I longed to hear!

I sat thus for a long time. I had again replenished the fire—that is all I know about the lapse of the time—when, suddenly, a kind of physical repugnance and terror seized me, and I sat upright in my chair, with every fibre of my flesh protesting against some—shall I call it presence?—in its neighbourhood. But my real self repelled the invading cold, and took courage for any contest that might be at hand. Like Macbeth, I only inhabited trembling; *I* did not tremble. I had withdrawn my gaze from the fire, and fixed it upon the little window, about two feet square, at which the dark night looked in. Why or when I had done so I knew not.

What I next relate, I relate only as what seemed to happen. I do not altogether trust myself in the matter, and think I was subjected to a delusion of some sort or other. My feelings of horror grew as I looked through or rather at the window, till, notwithstanding all my resolution and the continued assurance that nothing could make me turn my back on the cause of the terror, I was yet so far *possessed* by a feeling I could neither account for nor control, that I felt my hair rise upon my head, as if instinct with individual fear of its own—the only instance of the sort in my experience.— In such a condition, the sensuous nerves are so easily operated upon, either from within or from without, that all certainty ceases.

I saw two fiery eyes looking in at the window, huge, and wide apart. Next, I saw the outline of a horse's head, in which the eyes were set; and behind, the dimmer outline of a man's form seated on the horse. The apparition faded and reappeared, just as if it retreated, and again rode up close to the window. Curiously enough, I did not even fancy that I heard any sound. Instinctively I felt for my sword, but there was no sword there. And what would it have availed me? Probably I was in more need of a soothing draught. But the moment I put my hand to the imagined sword-hilt, a dim figure swept between me and the horseman, on my side of the window—a tall, stately female form. She stood facing the window, in an attitude that seemed to dare the further approach of a foe. How long she remained thus, or he confronted her, I have no idea; for when *self*-consciousness returned, I found myself still gazing at the window from which both apparitions had vanished. Whether I had slept, or, from the relaxation of mental tension, had only forgotten, I could not tell; but all fear had vanished, and I proceeded at once to make up the sunken fire. Throughout the time I am certain I never heard the clanking shoe, for that I should have remembered.

The rest of the night passed without any disturbance; and when the first rays of the early morning came into the room, they awoke me from a comforting sleep in the arm-chair. I rose and approached the bed softly.

Margaret lay as still as death. But having been accustomed to similar conditions in my Alice, I believed I saw signs of returning animation, and withdrew to my seat. Nor was I mistaken; for, in a few minutes more, she murmured my name. I hastened to her.

"Call Janet," she said.

I opened the door, and called her. She came in a moment, looking at once frightened and relieved.

"Get me some tea," said Margaret once more.

After she had drunk the tea, she looked at me, and said,

"Go home now, Duncan, and come back about noon. Mind you go to bed."

She closed her eyes once more. I waited till I saw her fast in an altogether different sleep from the former, if sleep that could in any sense be called.

As I went, I looked back on the vision of the night as on one of those illusions to which the mind, busy with its own suggestions, is always liable. The night season, simply because it excludes the external, is prolific in such. The more of the marvellous any one may have experienced in the course of his history, the more sceptical ought he to become, for he is the more exposed to delusion. None have made more blunders in the course of their revelations than genuine seers. Was it any wonder that, as I sat at midnight beside the woman of a hundred years, who had voluntarily died for a time that she might discover what most of all things it concerned me to know, the ancient tale, on which, to her mind, my whole history turned, and which she had herself told me in this very cottage, should take visible shape to my excited brain and watching eyes?

I have one thing more to tell, which strengthens still further this view of the matter. As I walked home, before I had gone many hundred yards from the cottage, I suddenly came upon my own old Constancy. He was limping about, picking the best grass he could find from among the roots of the heather and cranberry bushes. He gave a start when I came upon him, and then a jubilant neigh.

But he could not be so glad as I was. When I had taken sufficient pains to let him know this fact, I walked on, and he followed me like a dog, with his head at my heel; but as he limped much, I turned to examine him; and found one cause of his lameness to be, that the loose shoe, which was a hind one, was broken at the toe; and that one half, held only at the toe, had turned round and was sticking right out, striking his forefoot every time he moved. I soon remedied this, and he walked much better.

But the phenomena of the night, and the share my old horse might have borne in them, were not the subjects, as may well be supposed, that occupied my mind most, on my walk to the farm. Was it possible that Margaret might have found out something about *her*? That was the one question.

After removing the anxiety of my hostess, and partaking of their Highland breakfast, a ceremony not to be completed without a glass of peaty whisky, I wandered to my ancient haunt on the hill. Thence I could look down on my old home, where it lay unchanged, though not one human form, which had made it home to me, moved about its precincts. I went no nearer. I no more felt that that was home, than one feels that the form in the coffin is the departed dead. I sat down in my old study-chamber among the rocks, and thought that if I could but find Alice she would be my home—of the past as well as of the future;—for in her mind my necromantic words would recall the departed, and we should love them together.

Towards noon I was again at the cottage.

Margaret was sitting up in bed, waiting for me. She looked weary, but cheerful; and a clean white *mutch* gave her a certain *company*-air. Janet left the room directly, and Margaret motioned me to a chair by her side. I sat down. She took my hand, and said,

"Duncan, my boy, I fear I can give you but little help; but I will tell you all I know. If I were to try to put into words the things I had to encounter before I could come near her, you would not understand what I meant. Nor do I understand the things myself. They seem quite plain to me at the time, but very cloudy when I come back. But I did succeed in getting one glimpse of her. She was fast asleep. She seemed to have suffered much, for her face was very thin, and as patient as it was pale."

"But where was she?"

"I must leave you to find out that, if you can, from my description. But, alas! it is only the places immediately about the persons that I can see. Where they are, or how far I have gone to get there, I cannot tell."

She then gave me a rather minute description of the chamber in which the lady was lying. Though most of the particulars were unknown to me, the conviction, or hope at least, gradually dawned upon me, that I knew the room. Once or twice I had peeped into the sanctuary of Lady Alice's chamber, when I knew she was not there; and some points in the description Margaret gave set my heart in a tremor with the bare suggestion that she might now be at Hilton Hall.

"Tell me, Margaret," I said, almost panting for utterance, "was there a mirror over the fireplace, with a broad gilt frame, carved into huge representations of crabs and lobsters, and all crawling sea-creatures with shells on them—very ugly, and very strange?"

She would have interrupted me before, but I would not be stopped.

"I must tell you, my dear Duncan," she answered, "that in none of these trances, or whatever you please to call them, did I ever see a mirror. It has struck me before as a curious thing, that a mirror is then an absolute blank to me—I see nothing on which I could put a name. It does not even seem a vacant space to me. A mirror must have nothing in common with the state I am then in, for I feel a kind of repulsion from it; and indeed it would be rather an awful thing to look at, for of course I should see no reflection of myself in it."

(Here I beg once more to remind the reader, that Margaret spoke in Gaelic, and that my translation into ordinary English does not in the least represent the extreme simplicity of the forms of her speculations, any more than of the language which conveyed them.)

"But," she continued, "I have a vague recollection of seeing some broad, big, gilded thing with figures on it. It might be something else, though, altogether."

"I will go in hope," I answered, rising at once.

"Not already, Duncan?"

"Why should I stay longer?"

"Stay over to-night."

"What is the use? I cannot."

"For my sake, Duncan!"

"Yes, dear Margaret; for your sake. Yes, surely."

"Thank you," she answered. "I will not keep you longer now. But if I send Janet to you, come at once. And, Duncan, wear this for my sake."

She put into my hand an ancient gold cross, much worn. To my amazement I recognised the counterpart of one Lady Alice had always worn. I pressed it to my heart.

"I am a Catholic; you are a Protestant, Duncan; but never mind: that's the same sign to both of us. You won't part with it. It has been in our family for many long years."

"Not while I live," I answered, and went out, half wild with hope, into the keen mountain air. How deliciously it breathed upon me!

I passed the afternoon in attempting to form some plan of action at Hilton Hall, whither I intended to proceed as soon as Margaret set me at liberty. That liberty came sooner than I expected; and yet I did not go at once. Janet came for me towards sundown. I thought she looked troubled. I rose at once and followed her, but asked no questions. As I entered the cottage, the sun was casting the shadow of the edge of the hollow in which the cottage stood just at my feet; that is, the sun was more than half set to one who stood at the cottage door. I entered.

Margaret sat, propped with pillows. I saw some change had passed upon her. She held out her hand to me. I took it. She smiled feebly, closed her eyes, and went with the sun, down the hill of night. But down the hill of night is up the hill of morning in other lands, and no doubt Margaret soon found that she was more at home there than here.

I sat holding the dead hand, as if therein lay some communion still with the departed. Perhaps she who saw more than others while yet alive, could see when dead that I held her cold hand in my warm grasp. Had I not good cause to love her? She had exhausted the last remnants of her life in that effort to find for me my lost Alice. Whether she had succeeded I had yet to discover. Perhaps she knew now.

I hastened the funeral a little, that I might follow my quest. I had her grave dug amidst her own people and mine; for they lay side by side. The whole neighbourhood for twenty miles round followed Margaret to the grave. Such was her character and reputation, that the belief in her supernatural powers had only heightened the notion of her venerableness.

When I had seen the last sod placed on her grave, I turned and went, with a desolate but hopeful heart. I had a kind of feeling that her death had sealed the truth of her last vision. I mounted old Constancy at the churchyard gate, and set out for Hilton Hall.

Chapter XXI
Hilton

It was a dark, drizzling night when I arrived at the little village of Hilton, within a mile of the Hall. I knew a respectable second-rate inn on the side next the Hall, to which the gardener and other servants had been in the habit of repairing of an evening; and I thought I might there stumble upon some information, especially as the old-fashioned place had a large kitchen in which all sorts of guests met. When I reflected on the utter change which time, weather, and a great scar must have made upon me, I feared no recognition. But what was my surprise when, by one of those coincidences which have so often happened to me, I found in the ostler one of my own troop at Waterloo! His countenance and salute convinced me that he recognised me. I said to him:

"I know you perfectly, Wood; but you must not know me. I will go with you to the stable."

He led the way instantly.

"Wood," I said, when we had reached the shelter of the stable, "I don't want to be known here, for reasons which I will explain to you another time."

"Very well, sir. You may depend on me, sir."

"I know I may, and I shall. Do you know anybody about the Hall?"

"Yes, sir. The gardener comes here sometimes, sir. I believe he's in the house now. Shall I ask him to step this way, sir?"

"No. All I want is to learn who is at the Hall now. Will you get him talking? I shall be by, having something to drink."

"Yes, sir. As soon as I have rubbed down the old horse, sir—bless him!"

"You'll find me there."

I went in, and, with my condition for an excuse, ordered something hot by the kitchen-fire. Several country people were sitting about it. They made room for me, and I took my place at a table on one side. I soon discovered the gardener, although time had done what he could to disguise him. Wood came in presently, and, loitering about, began to talk to him.

"What's the last news at the Hall, William?" he said.

"News!" answered the old man, somewhat querulously. "There's never nothing but news up there, and very new-fangled news, too. What do you think, now, John? They do talk of turning all them greenhouses into hothouses; for, to be sure, there's nothing the new missus cares about but just the finest grapes in the country; and the flowers, purty creatures, may go to the devil for her. There's a lady for ye!"

"But you'll be glad to have her home, and see what she's like, won't you? It's rather dull up there now, isn't it?"

"I don't know what you call dull," replied the old man, as if half offended at the suggestion. "I don't believe a soul missed his lordship when he died; and there's always Mrs. Blakesley and me, as is the best friends in the world, besides the three maids and the stableman, who helps me in the garden, now there's no horses. And then there's Jacob and—"

"But you don't mean," said Wood, interrupting him, "that there's *none* o' the family at home now?"

"No. Who should there be? Least ways, only the poor lady. And she hardly counts now—bless her sweet face!"

"Do you ever see her?" interposed one of the by-sitters.

"Sometimes."

"Is she quite crazy?"

"Al-to-gether; but that quiet *and* gentle, you would think she was an angel instead of a mad woman. But not a notion has she in *her* head, no more than the babe unborn."

It was a dreadful shock to me. Was this to be the end of all? Were it not better she had died? For me, life was worthless now. And there were no wars, with the chance of losing it honestly.

I rose, and went to my own room. As I sat in dull misery by the fire, it struck me that it might not have been Lady Alice after all that the old man spoke about. That moment a tap came to my door, and Wood entered. After a few words, I asked him who was the lady the gardener had said was crazy.

"Lady Alice," he answered, and added: "A love story, that came to a bad end up at the Hall years ago. A tutor was in it, they say. But I don't know the rights of it."

When he left me, I sat in a cold stupor, in which the thoughts—if thoughts they could be called—came and went of themselves. Overcome by the appearances of things—as what man the strongest may not sometimes be?—I felt as if I had lost her utterly, as if there was no Lady Alice anywhere, and as if, to add to the vacant horror of the world without her, a shadow of her, a goblin *simulacrum*, soul-less, unreal, yet awfully like her, went wandering about the place which had once been glorified by her presence— as to the eyes of seers the phantoms of events which have happened years before are still visible, clinging to the room in which they have indeed *taken place*. But, in a little while, something warm began to throb and flow in my being; and I thought that if she were dead, I should love her still; that now she was not worse than dead; it was only that her soul was out of sight. Who could tell but it might be wandering in worlds of too noble shapes and too high a speech, to permit of representation in the language of the world in which her bodily presentation remained, and therefore her speech and behaviour seemed to men to be mad? Nay, was it not in some sense better for me that it should be so? To see once the pictured likeness of her of whom I had no such memorial, would I not give years of my poverty-stricken life? And here was such a statue of her, as that of his wife which the widowed king was bending before, when he said:—

"*What fine chisel*

Could ever yet cut breath?"

This statue I might see, "looking like an angel," as the gardener had said. And, while the bond of visibility remained, must not the soul be, somehow, nearer to the earth, than if the form lay decaying beneath it? Was there not some possibility that the love for whose sake the reason had departed, might be able to recall that reason once more to the windows of sense,—make it look forth at those eyes, and lie listening in the recesses of those ears? In her somnambulic sleeps, the present body was the sign that the soul was within reach: so it might be still.

Mrs. Blakesley was still at the lodge, then: I would call upon her to-morrow. I went to bed, and dreamed all night that Alice was sitting somewhere in a land "full of dark mountains," and that I was wandering about in the darkness, alternately calling and listening; sometimes fancying I heard a faint reply, which might be her voice or an echo of my own; but never finding her. I woke in an outburst of despairing tears, and my despair was not comforted by my waking.

Chapter XXII
The Sleeper

It was a lovely morning in autumn. I walked to the Hall. I entered at the same gate by which I had entered first, so many years before. But it was not Mrs. Blakesley that opened it. I inquired after her, and the woman told me that she lived at the Hall now, and took care of Lady Alice. So far, this was hopeful news.

I went up the same avenue, through the same wide grassy places, saw the same statue from whose base had arisen the lovely form which soon became a part of my existence. Then everything looked rich, because I had come from a poor, grand country. In all my wanderings I had seen nothing so rich; yet now it seemed poverty-stricken. That it was autumn could not account for this; for I had always found that the sadness of autumn vivified the poetic sense; and that the colours of decay had a pathetic glory more beautiful than the glory of the most gorgeous summer with all its flowers. It was winter within me—that was the reason; and I could feel no autumn around me, because I saw no spring beyond me. It had fared with my mind as with the garden in the *Sensitive Plant,* when the lady was dead. I was amazed and troubled at the stolidity with which I walked up to the door, and, having rung the bell, waited. No sweet memories of the past arose in my mind; not one of the well-known objects around looked at me as claiming a recognition. Yet, when the door was opened, my heart beat so violently at the thought that I might see her, that I could hardly stammer out my inquiry after Mrs. Blakesley.

I was shown to a room. None of the sensations I had had on first crossing the threshold were revived. I remembered them all; I felt none of them. Mrs. Blakesley came. She did not recognise me. I told her who I was. She stared at me for a moment, seemed to see the same face she had known still glimmering through all the changes that had crowded upon it, held out both her hands, and burst into tears.

"Mr. Campbell," she said, "you *are* changed! But not like her. She's the same to look at; but, oh dear!"

We were both silent for some time. At length she resumed:—

"Come to my room; I have been mistress here for some time now."

I followed her to the room Mrs. Wilson used to occupy. She put wine on the table. I told her my story. My labours, and my wounds, and my illness, slightly touched as I trust they were in the course of the tale, yet moved all her womanly sympathies.

"What can I do for you, Mr. Campbell?" she said.

"Let me see her," I replied.

She hesitated for a moment.

"I dare not, sir. I don't know what it might do to her. It might send her raving; and she is so quiet."

"Has she ever raved?"

"Not often since the first week or two. Now and then occasionally, for an hour or so, she would be wild, wanting to get out. But she gave that over altogether; and she has had her liberty now for a long time. But, Heaven bless her! at the worst she was always a lady."

"And am I to go away without even seeing her?"

"I am very sorry for you, Mr. Campbell."

I felt hurt—foolishly, I confess—and rose. She put her hand on my arm.

"I'll tell you what I'll do, sir. She always falls asleep in the afternoon; you may see her asleep, if you like."

"Thank you; thank you," I answered. "That will be much better. When shall I come?"

"About three o'clock."

I went wandering about the woods, and at three I was again in the housekeeper's room. She came to me presently, looking rather troubled.

"It is very odd," she began, the moment she entered, "but for the first time, I think, for years, she's not for her afternoon sleep."

"Does she sleep at night?" I asked.

"Like a bairn. But she sleeps a great deal; and the doctor says that's what keeps her so quiet. She would go raving again, he says, if the sleep did not soothe her poor brain."

"Could you not let me see her when she is asleep to-night?"

Again she hesitated, but presently replied:—

"I will, sir; but I trust to you never to mention it."

"Of course I will not."

"Come at ten o'clock, then. You will find the outer door on this side open. Go straight to my room."

With renewed thanks I left her and, once again betaking myself to the woods, wandered about till night, notwithstanding signs of an approaching storm. I thus kept within the boundaries of the demesne, and had no occasion to request re-admittance at any of the gates.

As ten struck on the tower-clock, I entered Mrs. Blakesley's room. She was not there. I sat down. In a few minutes she came.

"She is fast asleep," she said. "Come this way."

I followed, trembling. She led me to the same room Lady Alice used to occupy. The door was a little open. She pushed it gently, and I followed her in. The curtains towards the door were drawn. Mrs. Blakesley took me round to the other side.—There lay the lovely head, so phantom-like for years, coming only in my dreams; filling now, with a real presence, the eyes that had longed for it, as if in them dwelt an appetite of sight. It calmed my heart at once, which had been almost choking me with the violence of its palpitation. "That is not the face of insanity," I said to myself. "It is clear as the morning light." As I stood gazing, I made no comparisons between the past and the present, although I was aware of some difference—of some measure of the unknown fronting me; I was filled with the delight of beholding the face I loved—full, as it seemed to me, of mind and womanhood; sleeping— nothing more. I murmured a fervent "Thank God!" and was turning away with a feeling of satisfaction for all the future, and a strange great hope beginning to throb in my heart, when, after a little restless motion of her head on the pillow, her patient lips began to tremble. My soul rushed into my ears.

"Mr. Campbell," she murmured, "I cannot spell; what am I to do to learn?"

The unexpected voice, naming my name, sounded in my ears like a voice from the far-off regions where sighing is over. Then a smile gleamed up from the depths unseen, and broke and melted away all over her face. But her nurse had heard her speak, and now approached in alarm. She laid hold of my arm, and drew me towards the door. I yielded at once, but heard a moan from the bed as I went. I looked back—the curtains hid her from my view. Outside the door, Mrs. Blakesley stood listening for a moment, and then led the way downstairs.

"You made her restless. You see, sir, she never was like other people, poor dear!"

"Her face is not like one insane," I rejoined.

"I often think she looks more like herself when she's asleep," answered she. "And then I have often seen her smile. She never smiles when she's awake. But, gracious me, Mr. Campbell! what *shall* I do?"

This exclamation was caused by my suddenly falling back in my chair and closing my eyes. I had almost fainted. I had eaten nothing since breakfast; and had been wandering about in a state of excitement all day. I greedily swallowed the glass of wine she brought me, and then first became aware that the storm which I had seen gathering while I was in the woods had now broken loose. "What a night in the old hall!" thought I. The wind was dashing itself like a thousand eagles against the house, and the rain was trampling the roofs and the court like troops of galloping steeds. I rose to go.

But Mrs. Blakesley interfered.

"You don't leave this house to-night, Mr. Campbell," she said. "I won't have your death laid at my door."

I laughed.

"Dear Mrs. Blakesley,—" I said, seeing her determined.

"I won't hear a word," she interrupted. "I wouldn't let a horse out in such a tempest. No, no; you shall just sleep in your old quarters, across the passage there."

I did not care for any storm. It hardly even interested me. That beautiful face filled my whole being. But I yielded to Mrs. Blakesley, and not unwillingly.

Chapter XXIII
My Old Room

Once more I was left alone in that room of dark oak, looking out on the little ivy-mantled court, of which I was now reminded by the howling of the storm within its high walls. Mrs. Blakesley had extemporised a bed for me on the old sofa; and the fire was already blazing away splendidly. I sat down beside it, and the sombre-hued Past rolled back upon me.

After I had floated, as it were, upon the waves of memory for some time, I suddenly glanced behind me and around the room, and a new and strange experience dawned upon me. Time became to my consciousness what some metaphysicians say it is in itself—only a *form* of human thought. For the Past had returned and had become the Present. I could not be sure that the Past had passed, that I had not been dreaming through the whole series of years and adventures, upon which I was able to look back. For here was the room, all as before; and here was I, the same man, with the same love glowing in my heart. I went on thinking. The storm went on howling. The logs went on cheerily burning. I rose and walked about the room, looking at everything as I had looked at it on the night of my first arrival. I said to myself, "How strange that I should feel as if all this had happened to me before!" And then I said, "Perhaps it *has* happened to me before." Again I said, "And when it did happen before, I felt as if it had happened before that; and perhaps it has been happening to me at intervals for ages." I opened the door of the closet, and looked at the door behind it, which led into the hall of the old house. It was bolted. But the bolt slipped back at my touch; twelve years were nothing in the history of its rust; or was it only yesterday I had forced the iron free from the adhesion of the rust-welded surfaces? I stood for a moment hesitating whether to open the door, and have one peep into the wide hall, full of intent echoes, listening breathless for one air of sound, that they might catch it up jubilant and dash it into the ears of—Silence—their ancient enemy—their Death. But I drew back, leaving the door unopened; and, sitting down again by my fire, sank into a kind of unconscious weariness. Perhaps I slept—I do not know; but as I became once more aware of myself, I awoke, as it were, in the midst of an old long-buried night. I was sitting in my own room, waiting for Lady

Alice. And, as I sat waiting, and wishing she would come, by slow degrees my wishes intensified themselves, till I found myself, with all my gathered might, willing that she should come. The minutes passed, but the will remained.

How shall I tell what followed? The door of the closet opened—slowly, gently—and in walked Lady Alice, pale as death, her eyes closed, her whole person asleep. With a gliding motion as in a dream, where the volition that produces motion is unfelt, she seemed to me to dream herself across the floor to my couch, on which she laid herself down as gracefully, as simply, as in the old beautiful time. Her appearance did not startle me, for my whole condition was in harmony with the phenomenon. I rose noiselessly, covered her lightly from head to foot, and sat down, as of old to watch. How beautiful she was! I thought she had grown taller; but, perhaps, it was only that she had gained in form without losing anything in grace. Her face was, as it had always been, colourless; but neither it nor her figure showed any signs of suffering. The holy sleep had fed her physical as well as shielded her mental nature. But what would the waking be? Not all the power of the revived past could shut out the anticipation of the dreadful difference to be disclosed, the moment she should open those sleeping eyes. To what a frightfully farther distance was that soul now removed, whose return I had been wont to watch, as from the depths of the unknown world! That was strange; this was terrible. Instead of the dawn of rosy intelligence I had now to look for the fading of the loveliness as she woke, till her face withered into the bewildered and indigent expression of the insane.

She was waking. My love with the unknown face was at hand. The reviving flush came, grew, deepened. She opened her eyes. God be praised! They were lovelier than ever. And the smile that broke over her face was the very sunlight of the soul.

"Come again, you see!" she said gently, as she stretched her beautiful arms towards me.

I could not speak. I could only submit to her embrace, and hold myself with all my might, lest I should burst into helpless weeping. But a sob or two broke their prison, and she felt the emotion she had not seen. Relaxing her hold, she pushed me gently from her, and looked at me with concern that grew as she looked.

"You are dreadfully changed, my Duncan! What is the matter? Has Lord Hilton been rude to you? You look so much older, somehow. What can it be?"

I understood at once how it was. The whole of those dreary twelve years was gone. The thread of her consciousness had been cut, those years dropped out, and the ends reunited. She thought this was one of her old visits to me, when, as now, she had walked in her sleep. I answered,

"I will tell you all another time. I don't want to waste the moments with you, my Alice, in speaking about it. Lord Hilton *has* behaved very badly to me; but never mind."

She half rose in anger; and her eyes looked insane for the first time.

"How dares he?" she said, and then checked herself with a sigh at her own helplessness.

"But it will all come right, Alice," I went on in terror lest I should disturb her present conception of her circumstances. I felt as if the very face I wore, with the changes of those twelve forgotten years, which had passed over her like the breath of a spring wind, were a mask of which I had to be ashamed before her. Her consciousness was my involuntary standard of fact. Hope of my life as she was, there was thus mingled with my delight in her presence a restless fear that made me wish fervently that she would go. I wanted time to quiet my thoughts and resolve how I should behave to her.

"Alice," I said, "it is nearly morning. You were late to-night. Don't you think you had better go—for fear, you know?"

"Ah!" she said, with a smile, in which there was no doubt of fear, "you are tired of me already! But I will go at once to dream about you."

She rose.

"Go, my darling," I said; "and mind you get some right sleep. Shall I go with you?"

Much to my relief, she answered,

"No, no; please not. I can go alone as usual. When a ghost meets me, I just walk through him, and then he's nowhere; and I laugh."

One kiss, one backward lingering look, and the door closed behind her. I heard the echo of the great hall. I was alone. But what a loneliness—a loneliness crowded with presence! I paced up and down the room, threw myself on the couch she had left, started up, and paced again. It was long before I could think. But the conviction grew upon me that she would be mine yet. Mine yet? Mine she *was*, beyond all the power of madness or demons; and mine I trusted she would be beyond the dispute of the world. About me, at least, she was not insane. But what should I do? The only chance of her recovery lay in seeing me still; but I could resolve on nothing till I knew whether Mrs. Blakesley had discovered her absence from her room; because, if I drew her, and she were watched and prevented from coming, it would kill her, or worse. I must take to-morrow to think.

Yet at the moment, by a sudden impulse, I opened the window gently, stepped into the little grassy court, where the last of the storm was still moaning, and withdrew the bolts of a door which led into an alley of trees running along one side of the kitchen-garden. I felt like a housebreaker; but I said, "It is *her* right." I pushed the bolts forward again, so as just to touch the sockets and look as if they went in, and then retreated into my own room, where I paced about till the household was astir.

Chapter XXIV
Prison-Breaking

It was with considerable anxiety that I repaired to Mrs. Blakesley's room. There I found the old lady at the breakfast-table, so thoroughly composed, that I was at once reassured as to her ignorance of what had occurred while she slept. But she seemed uneasy till I should take my departure, which I attributed to the fear that I might happen to meet Lady Alice.

Arrived at my inn, I kept my room, my dim-seen plans rendering it desirable that I should attract as little attention in the neighbourhood as might be. I had now to concentrate these plans, and make them definite to myself. It was clear that there was no chance of spending another night at Hilton Hall by invitation: would it be honourable to go there without one, as I, knowing all the *outs and ins* of the place, could, if I pleased? I went over the whole question of Alice's position in that house, and of the crime committed against her. I saw that, if I could win my wife by restoring to her the exercise of reason, that very success would justify the right I already possessed in her. And could she not demand of me to climb over any walls, or break open whatsoever doors, to free her from her prison—from the darkness of a clouded brain? Let them say what they would of the meanness and wickedness of gaining such access to, and using such power over, the insane—she was mine, and as safe with me as with her mother. There is a love that tears and destroys; and there is a love that enfolds and saves. I hated mesmerism and its vulgar impertinences; but here was a power I possessed, as far as I knew, only over one, and that one allied to me by a reciprocal influence, as well as long-tried affection. Did not love give me the right to employ this power?

My cognitions concluded in the resolve to use the means in my hands for the rescue of Lady Alice. Midnight found me in the alley of the kitchen-garden. The door of the little court opened easily. Nor had I withdrawn its bolts without knowing that I could manage to open the window of my old room from the outside. I stood in the dark, a stranger and housebreaker, where so often I had sat waiting the visits of my angel. I secured the door of the room, struck a light, lighted a remnant of taper which I found on the table, threw myself on the couch, and said to my Alice—"Come."

And she came. I rose. She laid herself down. I pulled off my coat—it was all I could find—and laid it over her. The night was chilly. She revived with the same sweet smile, but, giving a little shiver, said:

"Why have you no fire, Duncan? I must give orders about it. That's some trick of old Clankshoe."

"Dear Alice, do not breath a word about me to any one. I have quarrelled with Lord Hilton. He has turned me away, and I have no business to be in the house."

"Oh!" she replied, with a kind of faint recollecting hesitation. "That must be why you never come to the haunted chamber now. I go there every night, as soon as the sun is down."

"Yes, that is it, Alice."

"Ah! that must be what makes the day so strange to me too."

She looked very bewildered for a moment, and then resumed:

"Do you know, Duncan, I feel very strange all day—as if I was walking about in a dull dream that would never come to an end? But it is very different at night—is it not, dear?"

She had not yet discovered any distinction between my presence to her dreams and my presence to her waking sight. I hardly knew what reply to make; but she went on:

"They won't let me come to you now, I suppose. I shall forget my Euclid and everything. I feel as if I had forgotten it all already. But you won't be vexed with your poor Alice, will you? She's only a beggar-girl, you know."

I could answer only by a caress.

"I had a strange dream the other night. I thought I was sitting on a stone in the dark. And I heard your voice calling me. And it went all round about me, and came nearer, and went farther off, but I could not move to go to you. I tried to answer you, but I could only make a queer sound, not like my own voice at all."

"I dreamed it too, Alice."

"The same dream?"

"Yes, the very same."

"I am so glad. But I didn't like the dream. Duncan, my head feels so strange sometimes. And I am so sleepy. Duncan, dearest—am I dreaming now? Oh! tell me that I am awake and that I hold you; for to-morrow, when I wake, I shall fancy that I have lost you. They've spoiled my poor brain, somehow. I am all right, I know, but I cannot get at it. The red is withered, somehow."

"You are wide awake, my Alice. I know all about it. I will help you to understand it all, only you must do exactly as I tell you."

"Yes, yes."

"Then go to bed now, and sleep as much as you can; else I will not let you come to me at night."

"That would be too cruel, when it is all I have."

"Then go, dearest, and sleep."

"I will."

She rose and went. I, too, went, making all close behind me. The moon was going down. Her light looked to me strange, and almost malignant. I feared that when she came to the full she would hurt my darling's brain, and I longed to climb the sky, and cut her in pieces. Was I too going mad? I needed rest, that was all.

Next morning, I called again upon Mrs. Blakesley, to inquire after Lady Alice, anxious to know how yesterday had passed.

"Just the same," answered the old lady. "You need not look for any change. Yesterday I did see her smile once, though."

And was that nothing?

In her case there was a reversal of the usual facts of nature—(*I say facts, not laws*): the dreams of most people are more or less insane; those of Lady Alice were sound; thus, with her, restoring the balance of sane life. That smile was the sign of the dream-life beginning to leaven the waking and false life.

"Have you heard of young Lord Hilton's marriage?" asked Mrs. Blakesley.

"I have only heard some rumours about it," I answered. "Who is the new countess?"

"The daughter of a rich merchant somewhere. They say she isn't the best of tempers. They're coming here in about a month. I am just terrified to think how it may fare with my lamb now. They won't let her go wandering about wherever she pleases, I doubt. And if they shut her up, she will die."

I vowed inwardly that she should be free, if I carried her off, madness and all.

Chapter XXV
New Entrenchments

But this way of breaking into the house every night did not afford me the facility I wished. For I wanted to see Lady Alice during the day, or at least in the evening before she went to sleep; as otherwise I could not thoroughly judge of her condition. So I got Wood to pack up a small stock of provisions for me in his haversack, which I took with me; and when I entered the house that night, I bolted the door of the court behind me, and made all fast.

I waited till the usual time for her appearance had passed; and, always apprehensive now, as was very natural, I had begun to grow uneasy, when I heard her voice, as I had heard it once before, singing. Fearful of disturbing her, I listened for a moment. Whether the song was her own or not, I cannot be certain. When I questioned her afterwards, she knew nothing about it. It was this,—

> *Days of old,*
>
> *Ye are not dead, though gone from me;*
>
> *Ye are not cold,*
>
> *But like the summer-birds gone o'er the sea.*
>
> *The sun brings back the swallows fast,*
>
> *O'er the sea:*
>
> *When thou comest at the last,*
>
> *The days of old come back to me.*

She ceased singing. Still she did not enter. I went into the closet, and found that the door was bolted. When I opened it, she entered, as usual; and, when she came to herself, seemed still better than before.

"Duncan," she said, "I don't know how it is, but I believe I must have forgotten everything I ever knew. I feel as if I had. I don't think I can even read. Will you teach me my letters?"

She had a book in her hand. I hailed this as another sign that her waking and sleeping thoughts bordered on each other; for she must have taken the book during her somnambulic condition. I did as she desired. She seemed to know nothing till I told her. But the moment I told her anything, she knew it perfectly. Before she left me that night she was reading tolerably, with many pauses of laughter that she should ever have forgotten how. The moment she shared the light of my mind, all was plain; where that had not shone, all was dark. The fact was, she was living still in the shadow of that shock which her nervous constitution had received from our discovery and my ejection.

As she was leaving me, I said,

"Shall you be in the haunted room at sunset tomorrow, Alice?"

"Of course I shall," she answered.

"You will find me there then," I rejoined—"that is, if you think there is no danger of being seen."

"Not the least," she answered. "No one follows me there; not even Mrs. Blakesley, good soul! They are all afraid, as usual."

"And you won't be frightened to see me there?"

"Frightened? No. Why? Oh! you think me queer too, do you?"

She looked vexed, but tried to smile.

"I? I would trust you with my life," I said. "That's not much, though— with my soul, whatever that means, Alice."

"Then don't talk nonsense," she rejoined coaxingly, "about my being frightened to see you."

When she had gone, I followed into the old hall, taking my sack with me; for, after having found the door in the closet bolted, I was determined not to spend one night more in my old quarters, and never to allow Lady Alice to go there again, if I could prevent her. And I had good hopes that, if we met in the day, the same consequences would follow as had followed long ago—namely, that she would sleep at night.

It was just such a night as that on which I had first peeped into the hall. The moon shone through one of the high windows, scarcely more dim than before, and showed all the dreariness of the place. I went up the great old staircase, hoping I trod in the very footsteps of Lady Alice, and reached the old gallery in which I had found her on that night when our strangely-knit intimacy began. My object was to choose one of the deserted rooms in which I might establish myself without chance of discovery. I had not turned many corners, or gone through many passages, before I found one exactly to my mind. I will not trouble my reader with a description of its odd position and shape. All I wanted was concealment, and that it provided plentifully. I lay down on the floor, and was soon fast asleep.

Next morning, having breakfasted from the contents of my bag, I proceeded to make myself thoroughly acquainted with the bearings, etc., of this portion of the house. Before evening, I knew it all thoroughly.

But I found it very difficult to wait for the evening. By the windows of one of the rooms looking westward, I sat watching the down-going of the sun. When he set, my moon would rise. As he touched the horizon, I went the old, well-known way to the haunted chamber. What a night had passed for me since I left Alice in that charmed room! I had a vague feeling, however, notwithstanding the misfortune that had befallen us there, that the old phantoms that haunted it were friendly to Alice and me. But I waited her arrival in fear. Would she come? Would she be as in the night? Or should I find her but half awake to life, and perhaps asleep to me?

One moment longer, and a light hand was laid on the door. It opened gently, and Alice, entering, flitted across the room straight to my arms. How beautiful she was! her old-fashioned dress bringing her into harmony with the room and its old consecrated twilight! For this room looked eastward, and there was only twilight here. She brought me some water, at my request; and then we read, and laughed over our reading. Every moment she not only knew something fresh, but knew that she had known it before. The dust of the years had to be swept away; but it was only dust, and flew at a breath. The light soon failed us in that dusky chamber; and we sat and whispered, till only when we kissed could we see each other's eyes. At length Lady Alice said:

"They are looking for me; I had better go. Shall I come at night?"

"No," I answered. "Sleep, and do not move."

"Very well, I will."

She went, and I returned to my den. There I lay and thought. Had she ever been insane at all? I doubted it. A kind of mental sleep or stupor had come upon her—nothing more. True it might be allied to madness; but is there a strong emotion that man or woman experiences that is not *allied* to madness? Still her mind was not clear enough to reflect the past. But if she never recalled that entirely, not the less were her love and tenderness—all womanliness—entire in her.

Next evening we met again, and the next, and many evenings. Every time I was more convinced than before that she was thoroughly sane in every practical sense, and that she would recall everything as soon as I reminded her. But this I forbore to do, fearing a reaction.

Meantime, after a marvellous fashion, I was living over again the old lovely time that had gone by twelve years ago; living it over again, partly in virtue of the oblivion that had invaded the companion and source of the blessedness of the time. She had never ceased to live it; but had renewed it in dreams, unknown as such, from which she awoke to forgetfulness and quiet, while I awoke from my troubled fancies to tears and battles.

It was strange, indeed, to live the past over again thus.

Chapter XXVI
Escape

It was time, however, to lay some plan, and make some preparations, for our departure. The first thing to be secured was a convenient exit from the house. I searched in all directions, but could discover none better than that by which I had entered. Leaving the house one evening, as soon as Lady Alice had retired, I communicated my situation to Wood, who entered with all his heart into my projects. Most fortunately, through all her so-called madness, Lady Alice had retained and cherished the feeling that there was something sacred about the diamond-ring and the little money which had been intended for our flight before; and she had kept them carefully concealed, where she could find them in a moment. I had sent the ring to a friend in London, to sell it for me; and it produced more than I expected. I had then commissioned Wood to go to the county town and buy a light gig for me; and in this he had been very fortunate. My dear old Constancy had the accomplishment, not at all common to chargers, of going admirably in harness; and I had from the first enjoined upon Wood to get him into as good condition as possible. I now fixed a certain hour at which Wood was to be at a certain spot on one of the roads skirting the park, where I had found a crazy door in the plank-fence—with Constancy in the dogcart, and plenty of wraps for Alice.

"And for Heaven's sake, Wood," I concluded, "look to his shoes."

It may seem strange that I should have been able to go and come thus without detection; but it must be remembered that I had made myself more familiar with the place than any of its inhabitants, and that there were only a very few domestics in the establishment. The gardener and stableman slept in the house, for its protection; but I knew their windows perfectly, and most of their movements. I could watch them all day long, if I liked, from some loophole or other of my quarter; where, indeed, I sometimes found that the only occupation I could think of.

The next evening I said, "Alice, I must leave the house: will you go with me?"

"Of course I will, Duncan. When?"

"The night after to-morrow, as soon as every one is in bed and the house quiet. If you have anything you value very much, take it; but the lighter we go the better."

"I have nothing, Duncan. I will take a little bag—that will do for me."

"But dress as warmly as you can. It will be cold."

"Oh, yes; I won't forget that. Good night."

She took it as quietly as going to church.

I had not seen Mrs. Blakesley since she had told me that the young earl and countess were expected in about a month; else I might have learned one fact which it was very important I should have known, namely, that their arrival had been hastened by eight or ten days. The very morning of our intended departure, I was looking into the court through a little round hole I had cleared for observation in the dust of one of the windows, believing I had observed signs of unusual preparation on the part of the household, when a carriage drove up, followed by two others, and Lord and Lady Hilton descended and entered, with an attendance of some eight or ten.

There was a great bustle in the house all day. Of course I felt uneasy, for if anything should interfere with our flight, the presence of so many would increase whatever difficulty might occur. I was also uneasy about the treatment my Alice might receive from the new-comers. Indeed, it might be put out of her power to meet me at all. It had been arranged between us that she should not come to the haunted chamber at the usual hour, but towards midnight.

I was there waiting for her. The hour arrived; the house seemed quiet; but she did not come. I began to grow very uneasy. I waited half an hour more, and then, unable to endure it longer, crept to her door. I tried to open it, but found it fast. At the same moment I heard a light sob inside. I put my lips to the keyhole, and called "*Alice.*" She answered in a moment:—

"They have locked me in."

The key was gone. There was no time to be lost. Who could tell what they might do to-morrow, if already they were taking precautions against her madness? I would try the key of a neighbouring door, and if that would not fit, I would burst the door open, and take the chance. As it was, the key fitted the lock, and the door opened. We locked it again on the outside, restored the key, and in another moment were in the haunted chamber. Alice was dressed, ready for flight. To me, it was very pathetic to see her in the shapes of years gone by. She looked faded and ancient, notwithstanding that this was the dress in which I had seen her so often of old. Her stream had been standing still, while mine had flowed on. She was a portrait of my own young Alice, a picture of her own former self.

One or two lights glancing about below detained us for a little while. We were standing near the window, feeling now very anxious to be clear of the house; Alice was holding me and leaning on me with the essence of trust; when, all at once, she dropped my arm, covered her face with her hands, and called out: "The horse with the clanking shoe!" At the same moment, the heavy door which communicated with this part of the house flew open with a crash, and footsteps came hurrying along the passage. A light gleamed into the room, and by it I saw that Lady Alice, who was standing close to me still, was gazing, with flashing eyes, at the door. She whispered hurriedly:

"I remember it all now, Duncan. My brain is all right. It is come again. But they shall not part us this time. You follow me for once."

As she spoke, I saw something glitter in her hand. She had caught up an old Malay creese that lay in a corner, and was now making for the door, at which half a dozen domestics were by this time gathered. They, too, saw the glitter, and made way. I followed close, ready to fell the first who offered to lay hands on her. But she walked through them unmenaced, and, once clear, sped like a bird into the recesses of the old house. One fellow started to follow. I tripped him up. I was collared by another. The same instant he lay by his companion, and I followed Alice. She knew the route well enough, and I overtook her in the great hall. We heard pursuing feet rattling down the echoing stair. To enter my room and bolt the door behind us was a moment's work; and a few moments more took us into the alley of the kitchen-garden. With speedy, noiseless steps, we made our way to the park, and across it to the door in the fence, where Wood was waiting for us, old Constancy pawing the ground with impatience for a good run.

He had had enough of it before twelve hours were over.

Was I not well recompensed for my long years of despair? The cold stars were sparkling overhead; a wind blew keen against us—the wind of our own flight; Constancy stepped out with a will; and I urged him on, for he bore my beloved and me into the future life. Close beside me she sat, wrapped warm from the cold, rejoicing in her deliverance, and now and then looking up with tear-bright eyes into my face. Once and again I felt her sob, but I knew it was a sob of joy, and not of grief. The spell was broken at last, and she was mine. I felt that not all the spectres of the universe could tear her from me, though now and then a slight shudder would creep through me, when the clank of Constancy's bit would echo sharply back from the trees we swept past.

We rested no more than was absolutely necessary; and in as short a space as ever horse could perform the journey, we reached the Scotch border, and before many more hours had gone over us, Alice was my wife.

Chapter XXVII
Freedom

Honest Wood joined us in the course of a week or two, and has continued in my service ever since. Nor was it long before Mrs. Blakesley was likewise added to our household, for she had been instantly dismissed from the countess's service on the charge of complicity in Lady Alice's abduction.

We lived for some months in a cottage on a hill-side, overlooking one of the loveliest of the Scotch lakes. Here I was once more tutor to my Alice. And a quick scholar she was, as ever. Nor, I trust, was I slow in my part. Her character became yet clearer to me, every day. I understood her better and better.

She could endure marvellously; but without love and its joy she could not *live*, in any real sense. In uncongenial society, her whole mental faculty had frozen; when love came, her mental world, like a garden in the spring sunshine, blossomed and budded. When she lost me, the Present vanished, or went by her like an ocean that has no milestones; she caring only for the Past, living only in the Past, and that reflection of it in the dim glass of her hope, which prefigured the Future.

We have never again heard the clanking shoe. Indeed, after we had passed a few months in the absorption of each other's society, we began to find that we doubted a great deal of what seemed to have happened to us. It was as if the gates of the unseen world were closing against us, because we had shut ourselves up in the world of the present. But we let it go gladly. We felt that love was the gate to an unseen world infinitely beyond that region of the psychological in which we had hitherto moved; for this love was teaching us to love all men, and live for all men. In fact, we are now, I am glad to say, very much like other people; and wonder, sometimes, how much of the story of our lives might be accounted for on the supposition that unusual coincidences had fallen in with psychological peculiarities. Dr. Ruthwell, who is sometimes our most welcome guest, has occasionally hinted at the sabre-cut as the key to all the mysteries of the story, seeing nothing of it was at least recorded before I came under his charge. But I have only to remind him of one or two circumstances, to elicit from his honesty and immediate confession of bewilderment, followed by silence; although he evidently still clings to the notion that in that sabre-cut lies the solution of much of the marvel. At all events, he considers me sane enough now, else he would hardly honour me with so much of his confidence as he does. Having examined into Lady Alice's affairs, I claimed the fortune which she had inherited. Lord Hilton, my former pupil, at once acknowledged the justice of the claim, and was considerably astonished to find how much more might have been demanded of him, which had been spent over the allowance made from her income for her maintenance. But we had enough without claiming that.

My wife purchased for me the possession of my forefathers, and there we live in peace and hope. To her I owe the delight which I feel every day of my life in looking upon the haunts of my childhood as still mine. They help me to keep young. And so does my Alice's hair; for although much grey now mingles with mine, hers is as dark as ever. For her heart, I know that cannot grow old; and while the heart is young, man may laugh old Time in the face, and dare him to do his worst.

THE CRUEL PAINTER

Among the young men assembled at the University of Prague, in the year 159—, was one called Karl von Wolkenlicht. A somewhat careless student, he yet held a fair position in the estimation of both professors and men, because he could hardly look at a proposition without understanding it. Where such proposition, however, had to do with anything relating to the deeper insights of the nature, he was quite content that, for him, it should remain a proposition; which, however, he laid up in one of his mental cabinets, and was ready to reproduce at a moment's notice. This mental agility was more than matched by the corresponding corporeal excellence, and both aided in producing results in which his remarkable strength was equally apparent. In all games depending upon the combination of muscle and skill, he had scarce rivalry enough to keep him in practice. His strength, however, was embodied in such a softness of muscular outline, such a rare Greek-like style of beauty, and associated with such a gentleness of manner and behaviour, that, partly from the truth of the resemblance, partly from the absurdity of the contrast, he was known throughout the university by the diminutive of the feminine form of his name, and was always called Lottchen.

"I say, Lottchen," said one of his fellow-students, called Richter, across the table in a wine-cellar they were in the habit of frequenting, "do you know, Heinrich Höllenrachen here says that he saw this morning, with mortal eyes, whom do you think?—Lilith."

"Adam's first wife?" asked Lottchen, with an attempt at carelessness, while his face flushed like a maiden's.

"None of your chaff!" said Richter. "Your face is honester than your tongue, and confesses what you cannot deny, that you would give your chance of salvation—a small one to be sure, but all you've got—for one peep at Lilith. Wouldn't you now, Lottchen?"

"Go to the devil!" was all Lottchen's answer to his tormentor; but he turned to Heinrich, to whom the students had given the surname above mentioned, because of the enormous width of his jaws, and said with eagerness and envy, disguising them as well as he could, under the appearance of curiosity—

"You don't mean it, Heinrich? You've been taking the beggar in! Confess now."

"Not I. I saw her with my two eyes."

"Notwithstanding the different planes of their orbits," suggested Richter.

"Yes, notwithstanding the fact that I can get a parallax to any of the fixed stars in a moment, with only the breadth of my nose for the base," answered Heinrich, responding at once to the fun, and careless of the personal defect insinuated. "She was near enough for even me to see her perfectly."

"When? Where? How?" asked Lottchen.

"Two hours ago. In the churchyard of St. Stephen's. By a lucky chance. Any more little questions, my child?" answered Höllenrachen.

"What could have taken her there, who is seen nowhere?" said Richter.

"She was seated on a grave. After she left, I went to the place; but it was a new-made grave. There was no stone up. I asked the sexton about her. He said he supposed she was the daughter of the woman buried there last Thursday week. I knew it was Lilith."

"Her mother dead!" said Lottchen, musingly. Then he thought with himself—"She will be going there again, then!" But he took care that this ghost-thought should wander unembodied. "But how did you know her, Heinrich? You never saw her before."

"How do you come to be over head and ears in love with her, Lottchen, and you haven't seen her at all?" interposed Richter.

"Will you or will you not go to the devil?" rejoined Lottchen, with a comic crescendo; to which the other replied with a laugh.

"No one could miss knowing her," said Heinrich.

"Is she so very like, then?"

"It is always herself, her very self."

A fresh flask of wine, turning out to be not up to the mark, brought the current of conversation against itself; not much to the dissatisfaction of Lottchen, who had already resolved to be in the churchyard of St. Stephen's at sun-down the following day, in the hope that he too might be favoured with a vision of Lilith.

This resolution he carried out. Seated in a porch of the church, not knowing in what direction to look for the apparition he hoped to see, and desirous as well of not seeming to be on the watch for one, he was gazing at the fallen rose-leaves of the sunset, withering away upon the sky; when, glancing aside by an involuntary movement, he saw a woman seated upon a new-made grave, not many yards from where he sat, with her face buried in her hands, and apparently weeping bitterly. Karl was in the shadow of the porch, and could see her perfectly, without much danger of being discovered by her; so he sat and watched her. She raised her head for a moment, and the rose-flush of the west fell over it, shining on the tears with which it was wet, and giving the whole a bloom which did not belong to it, for it was always pale, and now pale as death. It was indeed the face of Lilith, the most celebrated beauty of Prague.

Again she buried her face in her hands; and Karl sat with a strange feeling of helplessness, which grew as he sat; and the longing to help her whom he could not help, drew his heart towards her with a trembling reverence which was quite new to him. She wept on. The western roses withered slowly away, and the clouds blended with the sky, and the stars gathered like drops of glory sinking through the vault of night, and the trees about the churchyard grew black, and Lilith almost vanished in the wide darkness. At length she lifted her head, and seeing the night around her, gave a little broken cry of dismay. The minutes had swept over her head, not through her mind, and she did not know that the dark had come.

Hearing her cry, Karl rose and approached her. She heard his footsteps, and started to her feet. Karl spoke—

"Do not be frightened," he said. "Let me see you home. I will walk behind you."

"Who are you?" she rejoined.

"Karl Wolkenlicht."

"I have heard of you. Thank you. I can go home alone."

Yet, as if in a half-dreamy, half-unconscious mood, she accepted his offered hand to lead her through the graves, and allowed him to walk beside her, till, reaching the corner of a narrow street, she suddenly bade him good-night and vanished. He thought it better not to follow her, so he returned her good-night and went home.

How to see her again was his first thought the next day; as, in fact, how to see her at all had been his first thought for many days. She went nowhere that ever he heard of; she knew nobody that he knew; she was never seen at church, or at market; never seen in the street. Her home had a dreary, desolate aspect. It looked as if no one ever went out or in. It was like a place on which decay had fallen because there was no indwelling spirit. The mud of years was baked upon its door, and no faces looked out of its dusty windows.

How then could she be the most celebrated beauty of Prague? How then was it that Heinrich Höllenrachen knew her the moment he saw her? Above all, how was it that Karl Wolkenlicht had, in fact, fallen in love with her before ever he saw her? It was thus—

Her father was a painter. Belonging thus to the public, it had taken the liberty of re-naming him. Every one called him Teufelsbürst, or Devilsbrush. It was a name with which, to judge from the nature of his representations, he could hardly fail to be pleased. For, not as a nightmare dream, which may alternate with the loveliest visions, but as his ordinary everyday work, he delighted to represent human suffering.

Not an aspect of human woe or torture, as expressed in countenance or limb, came before his willing imagination, but he bore it straightway to his easel. In the moments that precede sleep, when the black space before the eyes of the poet teems with lovely faces, or dawns into a spirit-landscape, face after face of suffering, in all varieties of expression, would crowd, as if compelled by the accompanying fiends, to present themselves, in awful levee, before the inner eye of the expectant master. Then he would rise, light his lamp, and, with rapid hand, make notes of his visions; recording, with swift successive sweeps of his pencil, every individual face which had rejoiced his evil fancy. Then he would return to his couch, and, well satisfied, fall asleep to dream yet further embodiments of human ill.

What wrong could man or mankind have done him, to be thus fearfully pursued by the vengeance of the artist's hate?

Another characteristic of the faces and form which he drew was, that they were all beautiful in the original idea. The lines of each face, however distorted by pain, would have been, in rest, absolutely beautiful; and the whole of the execution bore witness to the fact that upon this original beauty the painter had directed the artillery of anguish to bring down the sky-soaring heights of its divinity to the level of a hated existence. To do this, he worked in perfect accordance with artistic law, falsifying no line of the original forms. It was the suffering, rather than his pencil, that wrought the change. The latter was the willing instrument to record what the imagination conceived with a cruelty composed enough to be correct.

To enhance the beauty he had thus distorted, and so to enhance yet further the suffering that produced the distortion, he would often represent attendant demons, whom he made as ugly as his imagination could compass; avoiding, however, all grotesqueness beyond what was sufficient to indicate that they were demons, and not men. Their ugliness rose from hate, envy, and all evil passions; amongst which he especially delighted to represent a gloating exultation over human distress. And often in the midst of his clouds of demon faces, would some one who knew him recognise the painter's own likeness, such as the mirror might have presented it to him when he was busiest over the incarnation of some exquisite torture.

But apparently with the wish to avoid being supposed to choose such representations for their own sakes, he always found a story, often in the histories of the church, whose name he gave to the painting, and which he pretended to have inspired the pictorial conception. No one, however, who looked upon his suffering martyrs, could suppose for a moment that he honoured their martyrdom. They were but the vehicles for his hate of humanity. He was the torturer, and not Diocletian or Nero.

But, stranger yet to tell, there was no picture, whatever its subject, into which he did not introduce one form of placid and harmonious loveliness. In this, however, his fierceness was only more fully displayed. For in no case did this form manifest any relation either to the actors or the endurers in the picture. Hence its very loveliness became almost hateful to those who beheld it. Not a shade crossed the still sky of that brow, not a ripple disturbed the still sea of that cheek. She did not hate, she did not love the sufferers: the painter would not have her hate, for that would be to the injury of her loveliness: would not have her love, for he hated. Sometimes she floated above, as a still, unobservant angel, her gaze turned upward, dreaming along, careless as a white summer cloud, across the blue. If she looked down on the scene below, it was only that the beholder might see that she saw and did not care—that not a feather of her outspread pinions would quiver at the sight. Sometimes she would stand in the crowd, as if she had been copied there from another picture, and had nothing to do with this one, nor any right to be in it at all. Or when the red blood was trickling drop by drop from the crushed limb, she might be seen standing nearest, smiling over a primrose or the bloom on a peach. Some had said that she was the painter's wife; that she had been false to him; that he had killed her; and, finding that that was no sufficing revenge, thus half in love, and half in deepest hate, immortalised his vengeance. But it was now universally understood that it was his daughter, of whose loveliness extravagant reports went abroad; though all said, doubtless reading this from her father's pictures, that she was a beauty without a heart. Strange theories of something else supplying its place were rife among the anatomical students. With the girl in the pictures, the wild imagination of Lottchen, probably in part from her apparently absolute unattainableness and her undisputed heartlessness, had fallen in love, as far as the mere imagination can fall in love.

But again, how was he to see her? He haunted the house night after night. Those blue eyes never met his. No step responsive to his came from that door. It seemed to have been so long unopened that it had grown as fixed and hard as the stones that held its bolts in their passive clasp. He dared not watch in the daytime, and with all his watching at night, he never saw father or daughter or domestic cross the threshold. Little he thought that, from a shot-window near the door, a pair of blue eyes, like Lilith's, but paler and colder, were watching him just as a spider watches the fly that is likely ere long to fall into his toils. And into those toils Karl soon fell. For her form darkened the page; her form stood on the threshold of sleep; and when, overcome with watching, he did enter its precincts, her form entered with him, and walked by his side. He must find her; or the world might go to the bottomless pit for him. But how?

Yes. He would be a painter. Teufelsbürst would receive him as a humble apprentice. He would grind his colours, and Teufelsbürst would teach him the mysteries of the science which is the handmaiden of art. Then he might see her, and that was all his ambition.

In the clear morning light of a day in autumn, when the leaves were beginning to fall seared from the hand of that Death which has his dance in the chapels of nature as well as in the cathedral aisles of men—he walked up and knocked at the dingy door. The spider painter opened it himself. He was a little man, meagre and pallid, with those faded blue eyes, a low nose in three distinct divisions, and thin, curveless, cruel lips. He wore no hair on his face; but long grey locks, long as a woman's, were scattered over his shoulders, and hung down on his breast. When Wolkenlicht had explained his errand, he smiled a smile in which hypocrisy could not hide the cunning, and, after many difficulties, consented to receive him as a pupil, on condition that he would become an inmate of his house. Wolkenlicht's heart bounded with delight, which he tried to hide: the second smile of Teufelsbürst might have shown him that he had ill succeeded. The fact that he was not a native of Prague, but coming from a distant part of the country, was entirely his own master in the city, rendered this condition perfectly easy to fulfil; and that very afternoon he entered the studio of Teufelsbürst as his scholar and servant.

It was a great room, filled with the appliances and results of art. Many pictures, festooned with cobwebs, were hung carelessly on the dirty walls. Others, half finished, leaned against them, on the floor. Several, in different stages of progress, stood upon easels. But all spoke the cruel bent of the artist's genius. In one corner a lay figure was extended on a couch, covered with a pall of black velvet. Through its folds, the form beneath was easily discernible; and one hand and forearm protruded from beneath it, at right angles to the rest of the frame. Lottchen could not help shuddering when he saw it. Although he overcame the feeling in a moment, he felt a great repugnance to seating himself with his back towards it, as the arrangement of an easel, at which Teufelsbürst wished him to draw, rendered necessary. He contrived to edge himself round, so that when he lifted his eyes he should see the figure, and be sure that it could not rise without his being aware of it. But his master saw and understood his altered position; and under some pretence about the light, compelled him to resume the position in which he had placed him at first; after which he sat watching, over the top of his picture, the expression of his countenance as he tried to draw; reading in it the horrid fancy that the figure under the pall had risen, and was stealthily approaching to look over his shoulder. But Lottchen resisted the feeling, and, being already no contemptible draughtsman, was soon interested enough to forget it. And then, any moment *she* might enter.

Now began a system of slow torture, for the chance of which the painter had been long on the watch—especially since he had first seen Karl lingering about the house. His opportunities of seeing physical suffering were nearly enough even for the diseased necessities of his art; but now he had one in his power, on whom, his own will fettering him, he could try any experiments he pleased for the production of a kind of suffering, in the observation of which he did not consider that he had yet sufficient experience. He would hold the very heart of the youth in his hand, and wring it and torture it to his own content. And lest Karl should be strong enough to prevent those expressions of pain for which he lay on the watch, he would make use of further means, known to himself, and known to few besides.

All that day Karl saw nothing of Lilith; but he heard her voice once— and that was enough for one day. The next, she was sitting to her father the greater part of the day, and he could see her as often as he dared glance up from his drawing. She had looked at him when she entered, but had shown no sign of recognition; and all day long she took no further notice of him. He hoped, at first, that this came of the intelligence of love; but he soon began to doubt it. For he saw that, with the holy shadow of sorrow, all that distinguished the expression of her countenance from that which the painter so constantly reproduced, had vanished likewise. It was the very face of the unheeding angel whom, as often as he lifted his eyes higher than hers, he saw on the wall above her, playing on a psaltery in the smoke of the torment ascending for ever from burning Babylon.—The power of the painter had not merely wrought for the representation of the woman of his imagination; it had had scope as well in realising her.

Karl soon began to see that communication, other than of the eyes, was all but hopeless; and to any attempt in that way she seemed altogether indisposed to respond. Nor if she had wished it, would it have been safe; for as often as he glanced towards her, instead of hers, he met the blue eyes of the painter gleaming upon him like winter lightning. His tones, his gestures, his words, seemed kind: his glance and his smile refused to be disguised.

The first day he dined alone in the studio, waited upon by an old woman; the next he was admitted to the family table, with Teufelsbürst and Lilith. The room offered a strange contrast to the study. As far as handicraft, directed by a sumptuous taste, could construct a house-paradise, this was one. But it seemed rather a paradise of demons; for the walls were covered with Teufelsbürst's paintings. During the dinner, Lilith's gaze scarcely met that of Wolkenlicht; and once or twice, when their eyes did meet, her glance was so perfectly unconcerned, that Karl wished he might look at her for ever without the fear of her looking at him again. She seemed like one whose love had rushed out glowing with seraphic fire, to be frozen to death in a more than wintry cold: she now walked lonely without her love. In the evenings, he was expected to continue his drawing by lamplight; and at night he was conducted by Teufelsbürst to his chamber. Not once did he allow him to proceed thither alone, and not once did he leave him there without locking and bolting the door on the outside. But he felt nothing except the coldness of Lilith.

Day after day she sat to her father, in every variety of costume that could best show the variety of her beauty. How much greater that beauty might be, if it ever blossomed into a beauty of soul, Wolkenlicht never imagined; for he soon loved her enough to attribute to her all the possibilities of her face as actual possessions of her being. To account for everything that seemed to contradict this perfection, his brain was prolific in inventions; till he was compelled at last to see that she was in the condition of a rose-bud, which, on the point of blossoming, had been chilled into a changeless bud by the cold of an untimely frost. For one day, after the father and daughter had become a little more accustomed to his silent presence, a conversation began between them, which went on until he saw that Teufelsbürst believed in nothing except his art. How much of his feeling for that could be dignified by the name of belief, seeing its objects were such as they were, might have been questioned. It seemed to Wolkenlicht to amount only to this: that, amidst a thousand distastes, it was a pleasant thing to reproduce on the canvas the forms he beheld around him, modifying them to express the prevailing feelings of his own mind.

A more desolate communication between souls than that which then passed between father and daughter could hardly be imagined. The father spoke of humanity and all its experiences in a tone of the bitterest scorn. He despised men, and himself amongst them; and rejoiced to think that the generations rose and vanished, brood after brood, as the crops of corn grew and disappeared. Lilith, who listened to it all unmoved, taking only an intellectual interest in the question, remarked that even the corn had more life than that; for, after its death, it rose again in the new crop. Whether she meant that the corn was therefore superior to man, forgetting that the superior can produce being without losing its own, or only advanced an objection to her father's argument, Wolkenlicht could not tell. But Teufelsbürst laughed like the sound of a saw, and said: "Follow out the analogy, my Lilith, and you will see that man is like the corn that springs again after it is buried; but unfortunately the only result we know of is a vampire."

Wolkenlicht looked up, and saw a shudder pass through the frame, and over the pale thin face of the painter. This he could not account for. But Teufelsbürst could have explained it, for there were strange whispers abroad, and they had reached his ear; and his philosophy was not quite enough for them. But the laugh with which Lilith met this frightful attempt at wit, grated dreadfully on Wolkenlicht's feeling. With her, too, however, a reaction seemed to follow. For, turning round a moment after, and looking at the picture on which her father was working, the tears rose in her eyes, and she said: "Oh! father, how like my mother you have made me this time!" "Child!" retorted the painter with a cold fierceness, "you have no mother. That which is gone out is gone out. Put no name in my hearing on that which is not. Where no substance is, how can there be a name?"

Lilith rose and left the room. Wolkenlicht now understood that Lilith was a frozen bud, and could not blossom into a rose. But pure love lives by faith. It loves the vaguely beheld and unrealised ideal. It dares believe that the loved is not all that she ever seemed. It is in virtue of this that love loves on. And it was in virtue of this, that Wolkenlicht loved Lilith yet more after he discovered what a grave of misery her unbelief was digging for her within her own soul. For her sake he would bear anything—bear even with calmness the torments of his own love; he would stay on, hoping and hoping.—The text, that we know not what a day may bring forth, is just as true of good things as of evil things; and out of Time's womb the facts must come.

But with the birth of this resolution to endure, his suffering abated; his face grew more calm; his love, no less earnest, was less imperious; and he did not look up so often from his work when Lilith was present. The master could see that his pupil was more at ease, and that he was making rapid progress in his art. This did not suit his designs, and he would betake himself to his further schemes.

For this purpose he proceeded first to simulate a friendship for Wolkenlicht, the manifestations of which he gradually increased, until, after a day or two, he asked him to drink wine with him in the evening. Karl readily agreed. The painter produced some of his best; but took care not to allow Lilith to taste it; for he had cunningly prepared and mingled with it a decoction of certain herbs and other ingredients, exercising specific actions upon the brain, and tending to the inordinate excitement of those portions of it which are principally under the rule of the imagination. By the reaction of the brain during the operation of these stimulants, the imagination is filled with suggestions and images. The nature of these is determined by the prevailing mood of the time. They are such as the imagination would produce of itself, but increased in number and intensity. Teufelsbürst, without philosophising about it, called his preparation simply a love-philtre, a concoction well known by name, but the composition of which was the secret of only a few. Wolkenlicht had, of course, not the least suspicion of the treatment to which he was subjected.

Teufelsbürst was, however, doomed to fresh disappointment. Not that his potion failed in the anticipated effect, for now Karl's real sufferings began; but that such was the strength of Karl's will, and his fear of doing anything that might give a pretext for banishing him from the presence of Lilith, that he was able to conceal his feelings far too successfully for the satisfaction of Teufelsbürst's art. Yet he had to fetter himself with all the restraints that self-exhortation could load him with, to refrain from falling at the feet of Lilith and kissing the hem of her garment. For that, as the lowliest part of all that surrounded her, itself kissing the earth, seemed to come nearest within the reach of his ambition, and therefore to draw him the most.

No doubt the painter had experience and penetration enough to perceive that he was suffering intensely; but he wanted to see the suffering embodied in outward signs, bringing it within the region over which his pencil held sway. He kept on, therefore, trying one thing after another, and rousing the poor youth to agony; till to his other sufferings were added, at length, those of failing health; a fact which notified itself evidently enough even for Teufelsbürst, though its signs were not of the sort he chiefly desired. But Karl endured all bravely.

Meantime, for various reasons, he scarcely ever left the house.

I must now interrupt the course of my story to introduce another element.

A few years before the period of my tale, a certain shoemaker of the city had died under circumstances more than suggestive of suicide. He was buried, however, with such precautions, that six weeks elapsed before the rumour of the facts broke out; upon which rumour, not before, the most fearful reports began to be circulated, supported by what seemed to the people of Prague incontestable evidence.—A *spectrum* of the deceased appeared to multitudes of persons, playing horrible pranks, and occasioning indescribable consternation throughout the whole town. This went on till at last, about eight months after his burial, the magistrates caused his body to be dug up; when it was found in just the condition of the bodies of those who in the eastern countries of Europe are called *vampires*. They buried the corpse under the gallows; but neither the digging up nor the reburying were of avail to banish the spectre. Again the spade and pick-axe were set to work, and the dead man being found considerably improved in *condition* since his last interment, was, with various horrible indignities, burnt to ashes, "after which the *spectrum* was never seen more."

And a second epidemic of the same nature had broken out a little before the period to which I have brought my story.

About midnight, after a calm frosty day, for it was now winter, a terrible storm of wind and snow came on. The tempest howled frightfully about the house of the painter, and Wolkenlicht found some solace in listening to the uproar, for his troubled thoughts would not allow him to sleep. It raged on all the next three days, till about noon on the fourth day, when it suddenly fell, and all was calm. The following night, Wolkenlicht, lying awake, heard unaccountable noises in the next house, as of things thrown about, of kicking and fighting horses, and of opening and shutting gates. Flinging wide his lattice and looking out, the noise of howling dogs came to him from every quarter of the town. The moon was bright and the air was still. In a little while he heard the sounds of a horse going at full gallop round the house, so that it shook as if it would fall; and flashes of light shone into his room. How much of this may have been owing to the effect of the drugs on poor Lottchen's brain, I leave my readers to determine. But when the family met at breakfast in the morning, Teufelsbürst, who had been already out of doors, reported that he had found the marks of strange feet in the snow, all about the house and through the garden at the back; stating, as his belief, that the tracks must be continued over the roofs, for there was no passage otherwise. There was a wicked gleam in his eye as he spoke; and Lilith believed that he was only trying an experiment on Karl's nerves. He persisted that he had never seen any footprints of the sort before. Karl informed him of his experiences during the night; upon which Teufelsbürst looked a little graver still, and proceeded to tell them that the storm, whose snow was still covering the ground, had arisen the very moment that their next door neighbour died, and had ceased as suddenly the moment he was buried, though it had raved furiously all the time of the funeral, so that "it made men's bodies quake and their teeth chatter in their heads." Karl had heard that the man, whose name was John Kuntz, was dead and buried. He knew that he had been a very wealthy, and therefore most respectable, alderman of the town; that he had been very fond of horses; and that he had died in consequence of a kick received from one of his own, as he was looking at his hoof. But he had not heard that, just before he died, a black cat "opened the casement with her nails, ran to his bed, and violently scratched his face and the bolster, as if she endeavoured by force to remove him out of the place where he lay. But the cat afterwards was suddenly gone, and she was no sooner gone, but he breathed his last."

So said Teufelsbürst, as the reporter of the town talk. Lilith looked very pale and terrified; and it was perhaps owing to this that the painter brought no more tales home with him. There were plenty to bring, but he heard them all and said nothing. The fact was that the philosopher himself could not resist the infection of the fear that was literally raging in the city; and perhaps the reports that he himself had sold himself to the devil had sufficient response from his own evil conscience to add to the influence of the epidemic upon him. The whole place was infested with the presence of the dead Kuntz, till scarce a man or woman would dare to be alone. He strangled old men; insulted women; squeezed children to death; knocked out the brains of dogs against the ground; pulled up posts; turned milk into blood; nearly killed a worthy clergyman by breathing upon him the intolerable airs of the grave, cold and malignant and noisome; and, in short, filled the city with a perfect madness of fear, so that every report was believed without the smallest doubt or investigation.

Though Teufelsbürst brought home no more of the town talk, the old servant was a faithful purveyor, and frequented the news-mart assiduously. Indeed she had some nightmare experiences of her own that she was proud to add to the stock of horrors which the city enjoyed with such a hearty community of goods. For those regions were not far removed from the birthplace and home of the vampire. The belief in vampires is the quintessential concentration and embodiment of all the passion of fear in Hungary and the adjacent regions. Nor, of all the other inventions of the human imagination, has there ever been one so perfect in crawling terror as this. Lilith and Karl were quite familiar with the popular ideas on the subject. It did not require to be explained to them, that a vampire was a body retaining a kind of animal life after the soul had departed. If any relation existed between it and the vanished ghost, it was only sufficient to make it restless in its grave. Possessed of vitality enough to keep it uncorrupted and pliant, its only instinct was a blind hunger for the sole food which could keep its awful life persistent—living human blood. Hence it, or, if not it, a sort of semi-material exhalation or essence of it, retaining its form and material relations, crept from its tomb, and went roaming about till it found some one asleep, towards whom it had an attraction, founded on old affection. It sucked the blood of this unhappy being, transferring so much of its life to itself as a vampire could assimilate. Death was the certain consequence. If suspicion conjectured aright, and they opened the proper grave, the body of the vampire would be found perfectly fresh and plump, sometimes indeed of rather florid complexion;—with grown hair, eyes half open, and the stains of recent blood about its greedy, leech-like lips. Nothing remained but to consume the corpse to ashes, upon which the vampire would show itself no more. But what added infinitely to the horror was the certainty that whoever died from the mouth of the vampire, wrinkled grandsire or delicate maiden, must in turn rise from the grave, and go forth a vampire, to suck the blood of the dearest left behind. This was the generation of the vampire brood. Lilith trembled at the very name of the creature. Karl was too much in love to be afraid of anything. Yet the evident fear of the unbelieving painter took a hold of his imagination; and, under the influence of the potions of which he still partook unwittingly, when he was not thinking about Lilith, he was thinking about the vampire.

Meantime, the condition of things in the painter's household continued much the same for Wolkenlicht—work all day; no communication between the young people; the dinner and the wine; silent reading when work was done, with stolen glances many over the top of the book, glances that were never returned; the cold good-night; the locking of the door; the wakeful night and the drowsy morning. But at length a change came, and sooner than any of the party had expected. For, whether it was that the impatience of Teufelsbürst had urged him to yet more dangerous experiments, or that the continuance of those he had been so long employing had overcome at length the vitality of Wolkenlicht—one afternoon, as he was sitting at his work, he suddenly dropped from his chair, and his master hurrying to him in some alarm, found him rigid and apparently lifeless. Lilith was not in the study when this took place. In justice to Teufelsbürst, it must be confessed that he employed all the skill he was master of, which for beneficent purposes was not very great, to restore the youth; but without avail. At last, hearing the footsteps of Lilith, he desisted in some consternation; and that she might escape being shocked by the sight of a dead body where she had been accustomed to see a living one, he removed the lay figure from the couch, and laid Karl in its place, covering him with a black velvet pall. He was just in time. She started at seeing no one in Karl's place and said—

"Where is your pupil, father?"

"Gone home," he answered, with a kind of convulsive grin.

She glanced round the room, caught sight of the lay figure where it had not been before, looked at the couch, and saw the pall yet heaved up from beneath, opened her eyes till the entire white sweep around the iris suggested a new expression of consternation to Teufelsbürst, though from a quarter whence he did not desire or look for it; and then, without a word, sat down to a drawing she had been busy upon the day before. But her father, glancing at her now, as Wolkenlicht had used to do, could not help seeing that she was frightfully pale. She showed no other sign of uneasiness. As soon as he released her, she withdrew, with one more glance, as she passed, at the couch and the figure blocked out in black upon it. She hastened to her chamber, shut and locked the door, sat down on the side of the couch, and fell, not a-weeping, but a-thinking. Was he dead? What did it matter? They would all be dead soon. Her mother was dead already. It was only that the earth could not bear more children, except she devoured those to whom she had already given birth. But what if they had to come back in another form, and live another sad, hopeless, love-less life over again?—And so she went on questioning, and receiving no replies; while through all her thoughts passed and repassed the eyes of Wolkenlicht, which she had often felt to be upon her when she did not see them, wild with repressed longing, the light of their love shining through the veil of diffused tears, ever gathering and never overflowing. Then came the pale face, so worshipping, so distant in its self-withdrawn devotion, slowly dawning out of the vapours of her reverie. When it vanished, she tried to see it again. It would not come when she called it; but when her thoughts left knocking at the door of the lost, and wandered away, out came the pale, troubled, silent face again, gathering itself up from some unknown nook in her world of phantasy, and once more, when she tried to steady it by the fixedness of her own regard, fading back into the mist. So the phantasm of the dead drew near and wooed, as the living had never dared.—What if there were any good in loving? What if men and women did not die all out, but some dim shade of each, like that pale, mind-ghost of Wolkenlicht, floated through the eternal vapours of chaos? And what if they might sometimes cross each other's path, meet, know that they met, love on? Would not that revive the withered memory, fix the fleeting ghost, give a new habitation, a body even, to the poor, unhoused wanderers, frozen by the eternal frosts, no longer thinking beings, but thoughts wandering through the brain of the "Melancholy Mass?" Back with the thought came the face of the dead Karl, and the maiden threw herself on her bed in a flood of bitter tears. She could have loved him if he had only lived: she did love him, for he was dead. But even in the midst of the remorse that followed—for had she not killed him?—life seemed a less hard and hopeless thing than before. For it is love itself and not its responses or results that is the soul of life and its pleasures.

Two hours passed ere she could again show herself to her father, from whom she seemed in some new way divided by the new feeling in which he did not, and could not share. But at last, lest he should seek her, and finding her, should suspect her thoughts, she descended and sought him.—For there is a maidenliness in sorrow, that wraps her garments close around her.—But he was not to be seen; the door of the study was locked. A shudder passed through her as she thought of what her father, who lost no opportunity of furthering his all but perfect acquaintance with the human form and structure, might be about with the figure which she knew lay dead beneath that velvet pall, but which had arisen to haunt the hollow caves and cells of her living brain. She rushed away, and up once more to her silent room, through the darkness which had now settled down in the house; threw herself again on her bed, and lay almost paralysed with horror and distress.

But Teufelsbürst was not about anything so frightful as she supposed, though something frightful enough. I have already implied that Wolkenlicht was, in form, as fine an embodiment of youthful manhood as any old Greek republic could have provided one of its sculptors with as model for an Apollo. It is true, that to the eye of a Greek artist he would not have been more acceptable in consequence of the regimen he had been going through for the last few weeks; but the emaciation of Wolkenlicht's frame, and the consequent prominence of the muscles, indicating the pain he had gone through, were peculiarly attractive to Teufelsbürst.—He was busy preparing to take a cast of the body of his dead pupil, that it might aid to the perfection of his future labours.

He was deep in the artistic enjoyment of a form, at the same time so beautiful and strong, yet with the lines of suffering in every limb and feature, when his daughter's hand was laid on the latch. He started, flung the velvet drapery over the body, and went to the door. But Lilith had vanished. He returned to his labours. The operation took a long time, for he performed it very carefully. Towards midnight, he had finished encasing the body in a close-clinging shell of plaster, which, when broken off, and fitted together, would be the matrix to the form of the dead Wolkenlicht. Before leaving it to harden till the morning, he was just proceeding to strengthen it with an additional layer all over, when a flash of lightning, reflected in all its dazzle from the snow without, almost blinded him. A peal of long-drawn thunder followed; the wind rose; and just such a storm came on as had risen some time before at the death of Kuntz, whose spectre was still tormenting the city. The gnomes of terror, deep hidden in the caverns of Teufelsbürst's nature, broke out jubilant. With trembling hands he tried to cast the pall over the awful white chrysalis,—failed, and fled to his chamber. And there lay the studio naked to the eyes of the lightning, with its tortured forms throbbing out of the dark, and quivering, as with life, in the almost continuous palpitations of the light; while on the couch lay the motionless mass of whiteness, gleaming blue in the lightning, almost more terrible in its crude indications of the human form, than that which it enclosed. It lay there as if dropped from some tree of chaos, haggard with the snows of eternity—a huge mis-shapen nut, with a corpse for its kernel.

But the lightning would soon have revealed a more terrible sight still, had there been any eyes to behold it. At midnight, while a peal of thunder was just dying away in the distance, the crust of death flew asunder, rending in all directions; and, pale as his investiture, staring with ghastly eyes, the form of Karl started up sitting on the couch. Had he not been far beyond ordinary men in strength, he could not thus have rent his sepulchre. Indeed, had Teufelsbürst been able to finish his task by the additional layer of gypsum which he contemplated, he must have died the moment life revived; although, so long as the trance lasted, neither the exclusion from the air, nor the practical solidification of the walls of his chest, could do him any injury. He had lain unconscious throughout the operations of Teufelsbürst, but now the catalepsy had passed away, possibly under the influence of the electric condition of the atmosphere. Very likely the strength he now put forth was intensified by a convulsive reaction of all the powers of life, as is not infrequently the case in sudden awakenings from similar interruptions of vital activity. The coming to himself and the bursting of his case were simultaneous. He sat staring about him, with, of all his mental faculties, only his imagination awake, from which the thoughts that occupied it when he fell senseless had not yet faded. These thoughts had been compounded of feelings about Lilith, and speculations about the vampire that haunted the neighbourhood; and the fumes of the last drug of which he had partaken, still hovering in his brain, combined with these thoughts and fancies to generate the delusion that he had just broken from the embrace of his coffin, and risen, the last-born of the vampire race. The sense of unavoidable obligation to fulfil his doom, was yet mingled with a faint flutter of joy, for he knew that he must go to Lilith. With a deep sigh, he rose, gathered up the pall of black velvet, flung it around him, stepped from the couch, and left the study to find her.

Meantime, Teufelsbürst had sufficiently recovered to remember that he had left the door of the studio unfastened, and that any one entering would discover in what he had been engaged, which, in the case of his getting into any difficulty about the death of Karl, would tell powerfully against him. He was at the farther end of a long passage, leading from the house to the studio, on his way to make all secure, when Karl appeared at the door, and advanced towards him. The painter, seized with invincible terror, turned and fled. He reached his room, and fell senseless on the floor. The phantom held on its way, heedless.

Lilith, on gaining her room the second time, had thrown herself on her bed as before, and had wept herself into a troubled slumber. She lay dreaming—and dreadful dreams. Suddenly she awoke in one of those peals of thunder which tormented the high regions of the air, as a storm billows the surface of the ocean. She lay awake and listened. As it died away, she thought she heard, mingling with its last muffled murmurs, the sound of moaning. She turned her face towards the room in keen terror. But she saw nothing. Another light, long-drawn sigh reached her ear, and at the same moment a flash of lightning illuminated the room. In the corner farthest from her bed, she spied a white face, nothing more. She was dumb and motionless with fear. Utter darkness followed, a darkness that seemed to enter into her very brain. Yet she felt that the face was slowly crossing the black gulf of the room, and drawing near to where she lay. The next flash revealed, as it bended over her, the ghastly face of Karl, down which flowed fresh tears. The rest of his form was lost in blackness. Lilith did not faint, but it was the very force of her fear that seemed to keep her alive. It became for the moment the atmosphere of her life. She lay trembling and staring at the spot in the darkness where she supposed the face of Karl still to be. But the next flash showed her the face far off, looking at her through the panes of her lattice-window.

For Lottchen, as soon as he saw Lilith, seemed to himself to go through a second stage of awaking. Her face made him doubt whether he could be a vampire after all; for instead of wanting to bite her arm and suck the blood, he all but fell down at her feet in a passion of speechless love. The next moment he became aware that his presence must be at least very undesirable to her; and in an instant he had reached her window, which he knew looked upon a lower roof that extended between two different parts of the house, and before the next flash came, he had stepped through the lattice and closed it behind him.

Believing his own room to be attainable from this quarter, he proceeded along the roof in the direction he judged best. The cold winter air by degrees restored him entirely to his right mind, and he soon comprehended the whole of the circumstances in which he found himself. Peeping through a window he was passing, to see whether it belonged to his room, he spied Teufelsbürst, who, at the very moment, was lifting his head from the faint into which he had fallen at the first sight of Lottchen. The moon was shining clear, and in its light the painter saw, to his horror, the pale face staring in at his window. He thought it had been there ever since he had fainted, and dropped again in a deeper swoon than before. Karl saw him fall, and the truth flashed upon him that the wicked artist took him for what he had believed himself to be when first he recovered from his trance—namely, the vampire of the former Karl Wolkenlicht. The moment he comprehended it, he resolved to keep up the delusion if possible. Meantime he was innocently preparing a new ingredient for the popular dish of horrors to be served at the ordinary of the city the next day. For the old servant's were not the only eyes that had seen him besides those of Teufelsbürst. What could be more like a vampire, dragging his pall after him, than this apparition of poor, half-frozen Lottchen, crawling across the roof? Karl remembered afterwards that he had heard the dogs howling awfully in every direction, as he crept along; but this was hardly necessary to make those who saw him conclude that it was the same phantasm of John Kuntz, which had been infesting the whole city, and especially the house next door to the painter's, which had been the dwelling of the respectable alderman who had degenerated into this most disreputable of moneyless vagabonds. What added to the consternation of all who heard of it, was the sickening conviction that the extreme measures which they had resorted to in order to free the city from the ghoul, beyond which nothing could be done, had been utterly unavailing, successful as they had proved in every other known case of the kind. For, urged as well by various horrid signs about his grave, which not even its close proximity to the altar could render a place of repose, they had opened it, had found in the body every peculiarity belonging to a vampire, had pulled it out with the greatest difficulty on account of a quite supernatural ponderosity; which rendered the horse which had killed him—a strong animal—all but unable to drag it along, and had at last, after cutting it in pieces, and expending on the fire two hundred and sixteen great billets, succeeded in conquering its incombustibleness, and reducing it to ashes. Such, at least, was the story which had reached the painter's household, and was believed by many; and if all this did not compel the perturbed corpse to rest, what more could be done?

When Karl had reached his room, and was dressing himself, the thought struck him that something might be made of the report of the extreme weight of the body of old Kuntz, to favour the continuance of the delusion of Teufelsbürst, although he hardly knew yet to what use he could turn this delusion. He was convinced that he would have made no progress however long he might have remained in his house; and that he would have more chance of favour with Lilith if he were to meet her in any other circumstances whatever than those in which he invariably saw her—namely, surrounded by her father's influences, and watched by her father's cold blue eyes.

As soon as he was dressed, he crept down to the studio, which was now quiet enough, the storm being over, and the moon filling it with her steady shine. In the corner lay in all directions the fragments of the mould which his own body had formed and filled. The bag of plaster and the bucket of water which the painter had been using stood beside. Lottchen gathered all the pieces together, and then making his way to an outhouse where he had seen various odds and ends of rubbish lying, chose from the heap as many pieces of old iron and other metal as he could find. To these he added a few large stones from the garden. When he had got all into the studio, he locked the door, and proceeded to fit together the parts of the mould, filling up the hollow as he went on with the heaviest things he could get into it, and solidifying the whole by pouring in plaster; till, having at length completed it, and obliterated, as much as possible, the marks of joining, he left it to harden, with the conviction that now it would make a considerable impression on Teufelsbürst's imagination, as well as on his muscular sense. He then left everything else as nearly undisturbed as he could; and, knowing all the ways of the house, was soon in the street, without leaving any signs of his exit.

Karl soon found himself before the house in which his friend Höllenrachen resided. Knowing his studious habits, he had hoped to see his light still burning, nor was he disappointed. He contrived to bring him to his window, and a moment after, the door was cautiously opened.

"Why, Lottchen, where do you come from?"

"From the grave, Heinrich, or next door to it."

"Come in, and tell me all about it. We thought the old painter had made a model of you, and tortured you to death."

"Perhaps you were not far wrong. But get me a horn of ale, for even a vampire is thirsty, you know."

"A vampire!" exclaimed Heinrich, retreating a pace, and involuntarily putting himself upon his guard.

Karl laughed.

"My hand was warm, was it not, old fellow?" he said. "Vampires are cold, all but the blood."

"What a fool I am!" rejoined Heinrich. "But you know we have been hearing such horrors lately that a fellow may be excused for shuddering a little when a pale-faced apparition tells him at two o'clock in the morning that he is a vampire, and thirsty, too."

Karl told him the whole story; and the mental process of regarding it for the sake of telling it, revealed to him pretty clearly some of the treatment of which he had been unconscious at the time. Heinrich was quite sure that his suspicions were correct. And now the question was, what was to be done next?

"At all events," said Heinrich, "we must keep you out of the way for some time. I will represent to my landlady that you are in hiding from enemies, and her heart will rule her tongue. She can let you have a garret-room, I know; and I will do as well as I can to bear you company. We shall have time then to invent some plan of operation."

To this proposal Karl agreed with hearty thanks, and soon all was arranged. The only conclusion they could yet arrive at was, that somehow or other the old demon-painter must be tamed.

Meantime, how fared it with Lilith? She too had no doubt that she had seen the body-ghost of poor Karl, and that the vampire had, according to rule, paid her the first visit because he loved her best. This was horrible enough if the vampire were not really the person he represented; but if in any sense it were Karl himself, at least it gave some expectation of a more prolonged existence than her father had taught her to look for; and if love anything like her mother's still lasted, even along with the habits of a vampire, there was something to hope for in the future. And then, though he had visited her, he had not, as far as she was aware, deprived her of a drop of blood. She could not be certain that he had not bitten her, for she had been in such a strange condition of mind that she might not have felt it, but she believed that he had restrained the impulses of his vampire nature, and had left her, lest he should yet yield to them. She fell fast asleep; and, when morning came, there was not, as far as she could judge, one of those triangular leech-like perforations to be found upon her whole body. Will it be believed that the moment she was satisfied of this, she was seized by a terrible jealousy, lest Karl should have gone and bitten some one else? Most people will wonder that she should not have gone out of her senses at once; but there was all the difference between a visit from a real vampire and a visit from a man she had begun to love, even although she took him for a vampire. All the difference does *not* lie in a name. They were very different causes, and the effects must be very different.

When Teufelsbürst came down in the morning, he crept into the studio like a murderer. There lay the awful white block, seeming to his eyes just the same as he had left it. What was to be done with it? He dared not open it. Mould and model must go together. But whither? If inquiry should be made after Wolkenlicht, and this were discovered anywhere on his premises, would it not be enough to bring him at once to the gallows? Therefore it would be dangerous to bury it in the garden, or in the cellar.

"Besides," thought he, with a shudder, "that would be to fix the vampire as a guest for ever." — And the horrors of the past night rushed back upon his imagination with renewed intensity. What would it be to have the dead Karl crawling about his house for ever, now inside, now out, now sitting on the stairs, now staring in at the windows?

He would have dragged it to the bottom of his garden, past which the Moldau flowed, and plunged it into the stream; but then, should the spectre continue to prove troublesome, it would be almost impossible to reach the body so as to destroy it by fire; besides which, he could not do it without assistance, and the probability of discovery. If, however, the apparition should turn out to be no vampire, but only a respectable ghost, they might manage to endure its presence, till it should be weary of haunting them.

He resolved at last to convey the body for the meantime into a concealed cellar in the house, seeing something must be done before his daughter came down. Proceeding to remove it, his consternation as greatly increased when he discovered how the body had grown in weight since he had thus disposed of it, leaving on his mind scarcely a hope that it could turn out not to be a vampire after all. He could scarcely stir it, and there was but one whom he could call to his assistance — the old woman who acted as his housekeeper and servant.

He went to her room, roused her, and told her the whole story. Devoted to her master for many years, and not quite so sensitive to fearful influences as when less experienced in horrors, she showed immediate readiness to render him assistance. Utterly unable, however, to lift the mass between them, they could only drag and push it along; and such a slow toil was it that there was no time to remove the traces of its track, before Lilith came down and saw a broad white line leading from the door of the studio down the cellarstairs. She knew in a moment what it meant; but not a word was uttered about the matter, and the name of Karl Wolkenlicht seemed to be entirely forgotten.

But how could the affairs of a house go on all the same when every one of the household knew that a dead body lay in the cellar? — nay more, that, although it lay still and dead enough all day, it would come half alive at nightfall, and, turning the whole house into a sepulchre by its presence, go creeping about like a cat all over it in the dark—perhaps with phosphorescent eyes? So it was not surprising that the painter abandoned his studio early, and that the three found themselves together in the gorgeous room formerly described, as soon as twilight began to fall.

Already Teufelsbürst had begun to experience a kind of shrinking from the horrid faces in his own pictures, and to feel disgusted at the abortions of his own mind. But all that he and the old woman now felt was an increasing fear as the night drew on, a kind of sickening and paralysing terror. The thing down there would not lie quiet—at least its phantom in the cellars of their imagination would not. As much as possible, however, they avoided alarming Lilith, who, knowing all they knew, was as silent as they. But her mind was in a strange state of excitement, partly from the presence of a new sense of love, the pleasure of which all the atmosphere of grief into which it grew could not totally quench. It comforted her somehow, as a child may comfort when his father is away.

Bedtime came, and no one made a move to go. Without a word spoken on the subject, the three remained together all night; the elders nodding and slumbering occasionally, and Lilith getting some share of repose on a couch. All night the shape of death might be somewhere about the house; but it did not disturb them. They heard no sound, saw no sight; and when the morning dawned, they separated, chilled and stupid, and for the time beyond fear, to seek repose in their private chambers. There they remained equally undisturbed.

But when the painter approached his easel a few hours after, looking more pale and haggard still than he was wont, from the fears of the night, a new bewilderment took possession of him. He had been busy with a fresh embodiment of his favourite subject, into which he had sketched the form of the student as the sufferer. He had represented poor Wolkenlicht as just beginning to recover from a trance, while a group of surgeons, unaware of the signs of returning life, were absorbed in a minute dissection of one of the limbs. At an open door he had painted Lilith passing, with her face buried in a bunch of sweet peas. But when he came to the picture, he found, to his astonishment and terror, that the face of one of the group was now turned towards that of the victim, regarding his revival with demoniac satisfaction, and taking pains to prevent the others from discovering it. The face of this prince of torturers was that of Teufelsbürst himself. Lilith had altogether vanished, and in her place stood the dim vampire reiteration of the body that lay extended on the table, staring greedily at the assembled company. With trembling hands the painter removed the picture from the easel, and turned its face to the wall.

Of course this was the work of Lottchen. When he left the house, he took with him the key of a small private door, which was so seldom used that, while it remained closed, the key would not be missed, perhaps for many months. Watching the windows, he had chosen a safe time to enter, and had been hard at work all night on these alterations. Teufelsbürst attributed them to the vampire, and left the picture as he found it, not daring to put brush to it again.

The next night was passed much after the same fashion. But the fear had begun to die away a little in the hearts of the women, who did not know what had taken place in the studio on the previous night. It burrowed, however, with gathered force in the vitals of Teufelsbürst. But this night likewise passed in peace; and before it was over, the old woman had taken to speculating in her own mind as to the best way of disposing of the body, seeing it was not at all likely to be troublesome. But when the painter entered his studio in trepidation the next morning, he found that the form of the lovely Lilith was painted out of every picture in the room. This could not be concealed; and Lilith and the servant became aware that the studio was the portion of the house in haunting which the vampire left the rest in peace.

Karl recounted all the tricks he had played to his friend Heinrich, who begged to be allowed to bear him company the following night. To this Karl consented, thinking it would be considerably more agreeable to have a companion. So they took a couple of bottles of wine and some provisions with them, and before midnight found themselves snug in the studio. They sat very quiet for some time, for they knew that if they were seen, two vampires would not be so terrible as one, and might occasion discovery. But at length Heinrich could bear it no longer.

"I say, Lottchen, let's go and look; for your dead body. What has the old beggar done with it?"

"I think I know. Stop; let me peep out. All right! Come along."

With a lamp in his hand, he led the way to the cellars, and after searching about a little they discovered it.

"It looks horrid enough," said Heinrich, "but think a drop or two of wine would brighten it up a little."

So he took a bottle from his pocket, and after they had had a glass apiece, he dropped a third in blots all over the plaster. Being red wine, it had the effect Höllenrachen desired.

"When they visit it next, they will know that the vampire can find the food he prefers," said he.

In a corner close by the plaster, they found the clothes Karl had worn.

"Hillo!" said Heinrich, "we'll make something of this find."

So he carried them with him to the studio. There he got hold of the lay-figure.

"What are you about, Heinrich?"

"Going to make a scarecrow to keep the ravens off old Teufel's pictures," answered Heinrich, as he went on dressing the lay-figure in Karl's clothes. He next seated the creature at an easel with its back to the door, so that it should be the first thing the painter should see when he entered. Karl meant to remove this before he went, for it was too comical to fall in with the rest of his proceedings. But the two sat down to their supper, and by the time they had finished the wine, they thought they should like to go to bed. So they got up and went home, and Karl forgot the lay-figure, leaving it in busy motionlessness all night before the easel. When Teufelsbürst saw it, he turned and fled with a cry that brought his daughter to his help. He rushed past her, able only to articulate:

"The vampire! The vampire! Painting!"

Far more courageous than he, because her conscience was more peaceful, Lilith passéd on to the studio. She too recoiled a step or two when she saw the figure; but with the sight of the back of Karl, as she supposed it to be, came the longing to see the face that was on the other side. So she crept round and round by the wall, as far off as she could. The figure remained motionless. It was a strange kind of shock that she experienced when she saw the face, disgusting from its inanity. The absurdity next struck her; and with the absurdity flashed into her mind the conviction that this was not the doing of a vampire; for of all creatures under the moon, he could not be expected to be a humorist. A wild hope sprang up in her mind that Karl was not dead. Of this she soon resolved to make herself sure.

She closed the door of the studio; in the strength of her new hope undressed the figure, put it in its place, concealed the garments—all the work of a few minutes; and then, finding her father just recovering from the worst of his fear, told him there was nothing in the studio but what ought to be there, and persuaded him to go and see. He not only saw no one, but found that no further liberties had been taken with his pictures. Reassured, he soon persuaded himself that the spectre in this case had been the offspring of his own terror-haunted brain. But he had no spirit for painting now. He wandered about the house, himself haunting it like a restless ghost.

When night came, Lilith retired to her own room. The waters of fear had begun to subside in the house; but the painter and his old attendant did not yet follow her example.

As soon, however, as the house was quite still, Lilith glided noiselessly down the stairs, went into the studio, where as yet there assuredly was no vampire, and concealed herself in a corner.

As it would not do for an earnest student like Heinrich to be away from his work very often, he had not asked to accompany Lottchen this time. And indeed Karl himself, a little anxious about the result of the scarecrow, greatly preferred going alone.

While she was waiting for what might happen, the conviction grew upon Lilith, as she reviewed all the past of the story, that these phenomena were the work of the real Karl, and of no vampire. In a few moments she was still more sure of this. Behind the screen where she had taken refuge, hung one of the pictures out of which her portrait had been painted the night before last. She had taken a lamp with her into the studio, with the intention of extinguishing it the moment she heard any sign of approach; but as the vampire lingered, she began to occupy herself with examining the picture beside her. She had not looked at it long, before she wetted the tip of her forefinger, and began to rub away at the obliteration. Her suspicions were instantly confirmed: the substance employed was only a gummy wash over the paint. The delight she experienced at the discovery threw her into a mischievous humour.

"I will see," she said to herself, "whether I cannot match Karl Wolkenlicht at this game."

In a closet in the room hung a number of costumes, which Lilith had at different times worn for her father. Among them was a large white drapery, which she easily disposed as a shroud. With the help of some chalk, she soon made herself ghastly enough, and then placing her lamp on the floor behind the screen, and setting a chair over it, so that it should throw no light in any direction, she waited once more for the vampire. Nor had she much longer to wait. She soon heard a door move, the sound of which she hardly knew, and then the studio door opened. Her heart beat dreadfully, not with fear lest it should be a vampire after all, but with hope that it was Karl. To see him once more was too great joy. Would she not make up to him for all her coldness! But would he care for her now? Perhaps he had been quite cured of his longing for a hard heart like hers. She peeped. It was he sure enough, looking as handsome as ever. He was holding his light to look at her last work, and the expression of his face, even in regarding her handiwork, was enough to let her know that he loved her still. If she had not seen this, she dared not have shown herself from her hiding-place. Taking the lamp in her hand, she got upon the chair, and looked over the screen, letting the light shine from below upon her face. She then made a slight noise to attract Karl's attention. He looked up, evidently rather startled, and saw the face of Lilith in the air: He gave a stifled cry threw himself on his knees with his arms stretched towards her, and moaned—

"I have killed her! I have killed her!"

Lilith descended, and approached him noiselessly. He did not move. She came close to him and said—

"Are you Karl Wolkenlicht?"

His lips moved, but no sound came.

"If you are a vampire, and I am a ghost," she said—but a low happy laugh alone concluded the sentence.

Karl sprang to his feet. Lilith's laugh changed into a burst of sobbing and weeping, and in another moment the ghost was in the arms of the vampire.

Lilith had no idea how far her father had wronged Karl, and though, from thinking over the past, he had no doubt that the painter had drugged him, he did not wish to pain her by imparting this conviction. But Lilith was afraid of a reaction of rage and hatred in her father after the terror was removed; and Karl saw that he might thus be deprived of all further intercourse with Lilith, and all chance of softening the old man's heart towards him; while Lilith would not hear of forsaking him who had banished all the human race but herself. They managed at length to agree upon a plan of operation.

The first thing they did was to go to the cellar where the plaster mass lay, Karl carrying with him a great axe used for cleaving wood. Lilith shuddered when she saw it, stained as it was with the wine Heinrich had spilt over it, and almost believed herself the midnight companion of a vampire after all, visiting with him the terrible corpse in which he lived all day. But Karl soon reassured her; and a few good blows of the axe revealed a very different core to that which Teufelsbürst supposed to be in it. Karl broke it into pieces, and with Lilith's help, who insisted on carrying her share, the whole was soon at the bottom of the Moldau and every trace of its ever having existed removed. Before morning, too, the form of Lilith had dawned anew in every picture. There was no time to restore to its former condition the one Karl had first altered; for in it the changes were all that they seemed; nor indeed was he capable of restoring it in the master's style; but they put it quite out of the way, and hoped that sufficient time might elapse before the painter thought of it again.

When they had done, and Lilith, for all his entreaties, would remain with him no longer, Karl took his former clothes with him, and having spent the rest of the night in his old room, dressed in them in the morning. When Teufelsbürst entered his studio next day, there sat Karl, as if nothing had happened, finishing the drawing on which he had been at work when the fit of insensibility came upon him. The painter started, stared, rubbed his eyes, thought it was another spectral illusion, and was on the point of yielding to his terror, when Karl rose, and approached him with a smile. The healthy, sunshiny countenance of Karl, let him be ghost or goblin, could not fail to produce somewhat of a tranquillising effect on Teufelsbürst. He took his offered hand mechanically, his countenance utterly vacant with idiotic bewilderment. Karl said—

"I was not well, and thought it better to pay a visit to a friend for a few days; but I shall soon make up for lost time, for I am all right now."

He sat down at once, taking no notice of his master's behaviour, and went on with his drawing. Teufelsbürst stood staring at him for some minutes without moving, then suddenly turned and left the room. Karl heard him hurrying down the cellar stairs. In a few moments he came up again. Karl stole a glance at him. There he stood in the same spot, no doubt more full of bewilderment than ever, but it was not possible that his face should express more. At last he went to his easel, and sat down with a long-drawn sigh as if of relief. But though he sat at his easel, he painted none that day; and as often as Karl ventured a glance, he saw him still staring at him. The discovery that his pictures were restored to their former condition aided, no doubt, in leading him to the same conclusion as the other facts, whatever that conclusion might be—probably that he had been the sport of some evil power, and had been for the greater part of a week utterly bewitched. Lilith had taken care to instruct the old woman, with whom she was all-powerful; and as neither of them showed the smallest traces of the astonishment which seemed to be slowly vitrifying his own brain, he was at last perfectly satisfied that things had been going on all right everywhere but in his inner man; and in this conclusion he certainly was not far wrong, in more senses than one. But when all was restored again to the old routine, it became evident that the peculiar direction of his art in which he had hitherto indulged had ceased to interest him. The shock had acted chiefly upon that part of his mental being which had been so absorbed. He would sit for hours without doing anything, apparently plunged in meditation.— Several weeks elapsed without any change, and both Lilith and Karl were getting dreadfully anxious about him. Karl paid him every attention; and the old man, for he now looked much older than before, submitted to receive his services as well as those of Lilith. At length, one morning, he said in a slow thoughtful tone—

"Karl Wolkenlicht, I should like to paint you."

"Certainly, sir," answered Karl, jumping up, "where would you like me to sit?"

So the ice of silence and inactivity was broken, and the painter drew and painted; and the spring of his art flowed once more; and he made a beautiful portrait of Karl—a portrait without evil or suffering. And as soon as he had finished Karl, he began once more to paint Lilith; and when he had painted her, he composed a picture for the very purpose of introducing them together; and in this picture there was neither ugliness nor torture, but human feeling and human hope instead. Then Karl knew that he might speak to him of Lilith; and he spoke, and was heard with a smile. But he did not dare to tell him the truth of the vampire story till one day that Teufelsbürst was lying on the floor of a room in Karl's ancestral castle, half smothered in grandchildren; when the only answer it drew from the old man was a kind of shuddering laugh and the words "Don't speak of it, Karl, my boy!"

THE CASTLE

On the top of a high cliff, forming part of the base of a great mountain, stood a lofty castle. When or how it was built, no man knew; nor could any one pretend to understand its architecture. Every one who looked upon it felt that it was lordly and noble; and where one part seemed not to agree with another, the wise and modest dared not to call them incongruous, but presumed that the whole might be constructed on some higher principle of architecture than they yet understood. What helped them to this conclusion was, that no one had ever seen the whole of the edifice; that, even of the portion best known, some part or other was always wrapped in thick folds of mist from the mountain; and that, when the sun shone upon this mist, the parts of the building that appeared through the vaporous veil were strangely glorified in their indistinctness, so that they seemed to belong to some aerial abode in the land of the sunset; and the beholders could hardly tell whether they had ever seen them before, or whether they were now for the first time partially revealed.

Nor, although it was inhabited, could certain information be procured as to its internal construction. Those who dwelt in it often discovered rooms they had never entered before—yea, once or twice,—whole suites of apartments, of which only dim legends had been handed down from former times. Some of them expected to find, one day, secret places, filled with treasures of wondrous jewels; amongst which they hoped to light upon Solomon's ring, which had for ages disappeared from the earth, but which had controlled the spirits, and the possession of which made a man simply what a man should be, the king of the world. Now and then, a narrow, winding stair, hitherto untrodden, would bring them forth on a new turret, whence new prospects of the circumjacent country were spread out before them. How many more of these there might be, or how much loftier, no one could tell. Nor could the foundations of the castle in the rock on which it was built be determined with the smallest approach to precision. Those of the family who had given themselves to exploring in that direction, found such a labyrinth of vaults and passages, and endless successions of down-going stairs, out of one underground space into a yet lower, that they came to the conclusion that at least the whole mountain was perforated and honeycombed in this fashion. They had a dim consciousness, too, of the presence, in those awful regions, of beings whom they could not comprehend. Once they came upon the brink of a great black gulf, in which the eye could see nothing but darkness: they recoiled with horror; for the conviction flashed upon them that that gulf went down into the very central spaces of the earth, of which they had hitherto been wandering only in the upper crust; nay, that the seething blackness before them had relations mysterious, and beyond human comprehension, with the far-off voids of space, into which the stars dare not enter.

At the foot of the cliff whereon the castle stood, lay a deep lake, inaccessible save by a few avenues, being surrounded on all sides with precipices which made the water look very black, although it was pure as the nightsky. From a door in the castle, which was not to be otherwise entered, a broad flight of steps, cut in the rock, went down to the lake, and disappeared below its surface. Some thought the steps went to the very bottom of the water.

Now in this castle there dwelt a large family of brothers and sisters. They had never seen their father or mother. The younger had been educated by the elder, and these by an unseen care and ministration, about the sources of which they had, somehow or other, troubled themselves very little—for what people are accustomed to, they regard as coming from nobody; as if help and progress and joy and love were the natural crops of Chaos or old Night. But Tradition said that one day—it was utterly uncertain *when*—their father would come, and leave them no more; for he was still alive, though where he lived nobody knew. In the meantime all the rest had to obey their eldest brother, and listen to his counsels.

But almost all the family was very fond of liberty, as they called it; and liked to run up and down, hither and thither, roving about, with neither law nor order, just as they pleased. So they could not endure their brother's tyranny, as they called it. At one time they said that he was only one of themselves, and therefore they would not obey him; at another, that he was not like them, and could not understand them, and *therefore* they would not obey him. Yet, sometimes, when he came and looked them full in the face, they were terrified, and dared not disobey, for he was stately and stern and strong. Not one of them loved him heartily, except the eldest sister, who was very beautiful and silent, and whose eyes shone as if light lay somewhere deep behind them. Even she, although she loved him, thought him very hard sometimes; for when he had once said a thing plainly, he could not be persuaded to think it over again. So even she forgot him sometimes, and went her own ways, and enjoyed herself without him. Most of them regarded him as a sort of watchman, whose business it was to keep them in order; and so they were indignant and disliked him. Yet they all had a secret feeling that they ought to be subject to him; and after any particular act of disregard, none of them could think, with any peace, of the old story about the return of their father to his house. But indeed they never thought much about it, or about their father at all; for how could those who cared so little for their brother, whom they saw every day, care for their father whom they had never seen?—One chief cause of complaint against him was that he interfered with their favourite studies and pursuits; whereas he only sought to make them give up trifling with earnest things, and seek for truth, and not for amusement, from the many wonders around them. He did not want them to turn to other studies, or to eschew pleasures; but, in those studies, to seek the highest things most, and other things in proportion to their true worth and nobleness. This could not fail to be distasteful to those who did not care for what was higher than they. And so matters went on for a time. They thought they could do better without their brother; and their brother knew they could not do at all without him, and tried to fulfil the charge committed into his hands.

At length, one day, for the thought seemed to strike them simultaneously, they conferred together about giving a great entertainment in their grandest rooms to any of their neighbours who chose to come, or indeed to any inhabitants of the earth or air who would visit them. They were too proud to reflect that some company might defile even the dwellers in what was undoubtedly the finest palace on the face of the earth. But what made the thing worse, was, that the old tradition said that these rooms were to be kept entirely for the use of the owner of the castle. And, indeed, whenever they entered them, such was the effect of their loftiness and grandeur upon their minds, that they always thought of the old story, and could not help believing it. Nor would the brother permit them to forget it now; but, appearing suddenly amongst them, when they had no expectation of being interrupted by him, he rebuked them, both for the indiscriminate nature of their invitation, and for the intention of introducing any one, not to speak of some who would doubtless make their appearance on the evening in question, into the rooms kept sacred for the use of the unknown father. But by this time their talk with each other had so excited their expectations of enjoyment, which had previously been strong enough, that anger sprung up within them at the thought of being deprived of their hopes, and they looked each other in the eyes; and the look said: "We are many and he is one—let us get rid of him, for he is always finding fault, and thwarting us in the most innocent pleasures;—as if we would wish to do anything wrong!" So without a word spoken, they rushed upon him; and although he was stronger than any of them, and struggled hard at first, yet they overcame him at last. Indeed some of them thought he yielded to their violence long before they had the mastery of him; and this very submission terrified the more tender-hearted amongst them. However, they bound him; carried him down many stairs, and, having remembered an iron staple in the wall of a certain vault, with a thick rusty chain attached to it, they bore him thither, and made the chain fast around him. There they left him, shutting the great gnarring brazen door of the vault, as they departed for the upper regions of the castle.

Now all was in a tumult of preparation. Every one was talking of the coming festivity; but no one spoke of the deed they had done. A sudden paleness overspread the face, now of one, and now of another; but it passed away, and no one took any notice of it; they only plied the task of the moment the more energetically. Messengers were sent far and near, not to individuals or families, but publishing in all places of concourse a general invitation to any who chose to come on a certain day, and partake for certain succeeding days of the hospitality of the dwellers in the castle. Many were the preparations immediately begun for complying with the invitation. But the noblest of their neighbours refused to appear; not from pride, but because of the unsuitableness and carelessness of such a mode. With some of them it was an old condition in the tenure of their estates, that they should go to no one's dwelling except visited in person, and expressly solicited. Others, knowing what sort of persons would be there, and that, from a certain physical antipathy, they could scarcely breathe in their company, made up their minds at once not to go. Yet multitudes, many of them beautiful and innocent as well as gay, resolved to appear.

Meanwhile the great rooms of the castle were got in readiness—that is, they proceeded to deface them with decorations; for there was a solemnity and stateliness about them in their ordinary condition, which was at once felt to be unsuitable for the light-hearted company so soon to move about in them with the self-same carelessness with which men walk abroad within the great heavens and hills and clouds. One day, while the workmen were busy, the eldest sister, of whom I have already spoken, happened to enter, she knew not why. Suddenly the great idea of the mighty halls dawned upon her, and filled her soul. The so-called decorations vanished from her view, and she felt as if she stood in her father's presence. She was at one elevated and humbled. As suddenly the idea faded and fled, and she beheld but the gaudy festoons and draperies and paintings which disfigured the grandeur. She wept and sped away. Now it was too late to interfere, and things must take their course. She would have been but a Cassandra-prophetess to those who saw but the pleasure before them. She had not been present when her brother was imprisoned; and indeed for some days had been so wrapt in her own business, that she had taken but little heed of anything that was going on. But they all expected her to show herself when the company was gathered; and they had applied to her for advice at various times during their operations.

At length the expected hour arrived, and the company began to assemble. It was a warm summer evening. The dark lake reflected the rose-coloured clouds in the west, and through the flush rowed many gaily painted boats, with various coloured flags, towards the massy rock on which the castle stood. The trees and flowers seemed already asleep, and breathing forth their sweet dream-breath. Laughter and low voices rose from the breast of the lake to the ears of the youths and maidens looking forth expectant from the lofty windows. They went down to the broad platform at the top of the stairs in front of the door to receive their visitors. By degrees the festivities of the evening commenced. The same smiles flew forth both at eyes and lips, darting like beams through the gathering crowd. Music, from unseen sources, now rolled in billows, now crept in ripples through the sea of air that filled the lofty rooms. And in the dancing halls, when hand took hand, and form and motion were moulded and swayed by the indwelling music, it governed not these alone, but, as the ruling spirit of the place, every new burst of music for a new dance swept before it a new and accordant odour, and dyed the flames that glowed in the lofty lamps with a new and accordant stain. The floors bent beneath the feet of the time-keeping dancers. But twice in the evening some of the inmates started, and the pallor occasionally common to the household overspread their faces, for they felt underneath them a counter-motion to the dance, as if the floor rose slightly to answer their feet. And all the time their brother lay below in the dungeon, like John the Baptist in the castle of Herod, when the lords and captains sat around, and the daughter of Herodias danced before them. Outside, all around the castle, brooded the dark night unheeded; for the clouds had come up from all sides, and were crowding together overhead. In the unfrequent pauses of the music, they might have heard, now and then, the gusty rush of a lonely wind, coming and going no one could know whence or whither, born and dying unexpected and unregarded.

But when the festivities were at their height, when the external and passing confidence which is produced between superficial natures by a common pleasure was at the full, a sudden crash of thunder quelled the music, as the thunder quells the noise of the uplifted sea. The windows were driven in, and torrents of rain, carried in the folds of a rushing wind, poured into the halls. The lights were swept away; and the great rooms, now dark within, were darkened yet more by the dazzling shoots of flame from the vault of blackness overhead. Those that ventured to look out of the windows saw, in the blue brilliancy of the quick-following jets of lightning, the lake at the foot of the rock, ordinarily so still and so dark, lighted up, not on the surface only, but down to half its depth; so that, as it tossed in the wind, like a tortured sea of writhing flames, or incandescent half-molten serpents of brass, they could not tell whether a strong phosphorescence did not issue from the transparent body of the waters, as if earth and sky lightened together, one consenting source of flaming utterance.

Sad was the condition of the late plastic mass of living form that had flowed into shape at the will and law of the music. Broken into individuals, the common transfusing spirit withdrawn, they stood drenched, cold, and benumbed, with clinging garments; light, order, harmony, purpose departed, and chaos restored; the issuings of life turned back on their sources, chilly and dead. And in every heart reigned the falsest of despairing convictions, that this was the only reality, and that was but a dream. The eldest sister stood with clasped hands and down-bent head, shivering and speechless, as if waiting for something to follow. Nor did she wait long. A terrible flash and thunder-peal made the castle rock; and in the pausing silence that followed, her quick sense heard the rattling of a chain far off, deep down; and soon the sound of heavy footsteps, accompanied with the clanking of iron, reached her ear. She felt that her brother was at hand. Even in the darkness, and amidst the bellowing of another deep-bosomed cloud-monster, she knew that he had entered the room. A moment after, a continuous pulsation of angry blue light began, which, lasting for some moments, revealed him standing amidst them, gaunt, haggard, and motionless; his hair and beard untrimmed, his face ghastly, his eyes large and hollow. The light seemed to gather around him as a centre. Indeed some believed that it throbbed and radiated from his person, and not from the stormy heavens above them. The lightning had rent the wall of his prison, and released the iron staple of his chain, which he had wound about him like a girdle. In his hand he carried an iron fetter-bar, which he had found on the floor of the vault. More terrified at his aspect than at all the violence of the storm, the visitors, with many a shriek and cry, rushed out into the tempestuous night. By degrees, the storm died away. Its last flash revealed the forms of the brothers and sisters lying prostrate, with their faces on the floor, and that fearful shape standing motionless amidst them still.

Morning dawned, and there they lay, and there he stood. But at a word from him, they arose and went about their various duties, though listlessly enough. The eldest sister was the last to rise; and when she did, it was only by a terrible effort that she was able to reach her room, where she fell again on the floor. There she remained lying for days. The brother caused the doors of the great suite of rooms to be closed, leaving them just as they were, with all the childish adornment scattered about, and the rain still falling in through the shattered windows. "Thus let them lie," said he, "till the rain and frost have cleansed them of paint and drapery: no storm can hurt the pillars and arches of these halls."

The hours of this day went heavily. The storm was gone, but the rain was left; the passion had departed, but the tears remained behind. Dull and dark the low misty clouds brooded over the castle and the lake, and shut out all the neighbourhood. Even if they had climbed to the loftiest known turret, they would have found it swathed in a garment of clinging vapour, affording no refreshment to the eye, and no hope to the heart. There was one lofty tower that rose sheer a hundred feet above the rest, and from which the fog could have been seen lying in a grey mass beneath; but that tower they had not yet discovered, nor another close beside it, the top of which was never seen, nor could be, for the highest clouds of heaven clustered continually around it. The rain fell continuously, though not heavily, without; and within, too, there were clouds from which dropped the tears which are the rain of the spirit. All the good of life seemed for the time departed, and their souls lived but as leafless trees that had forgotten the joy of the summer, and whom no wind prophetic of spring had yet visited. They moved about mechanically, and had not strength enough left to wish to die.

The next day the clouds were higher, and a little wind blew through such loopholes in the turrets as the false improvements of the inmates had not yet filled with glass, shutting out, as the storm, so the serene visitings of the heavens. Throughout the day, the brother took various opportunities of addressing a gentle command, now to one and now to another of his family. It was obeyed in silence. The wind blew fresher through the loopholes and the shattered windows of the great rooms, and found its way, by unknown passages, to faces and eyes hot with weeping. It cooled and blessed them.— When the sun arose the next day, it was in a clear sky.

By degrees, everything fell into the regularity of subordination. With the subordination came increase of freedom. The steps of the more youthful of the family were heard on the stairs and in the corridors more light and quick than ever before. Their brother had lost the terrors of aspect produced by his confinement, and his commands were issued more gently, and oftener with a smile, than in all their previous history. By degrees his presence was universally felt through the house. It was no surprise to any one at his studies, to see him by his side when he lifted up his eyes, though he had not before known that he was in the room. And although some dread still remained, it was rapidly vanishing before the advances of a firm friendship. Without immediately ordering their labours, he always influenced them, and often altered their direction and objects. The change soon evident in the household was remarkable. A simpler, nobler expression was visible on all the countenances. The voices of the men were deeper, and yet seemed by their very depth more feminine than before; while the voices of the women were softer and sweeter, and at the same time more full and decided. Now the eyes had often an expression as if their sight was absorbed in the gaze of the inward eyes; and when the eyes of two met, there passed between those eyes the utterance of a conviction that both meant the same thing. But the change was, of course, to be seen more clearly, though not more evidently, in individuals.

One of the brothers, for instance, was very fond of astronomy. He had his observatory on a lofty tower, which stood pretty clear of the others, towards the north and east. But hitherto, his astronomy, as he had called it, had been more of the character of astrology. Often, too, he might have been seen directing a heaven-searching telescope to catch the rapid transit of a fiery shooting-star, belonging altogether to the earthly atmosphere, and not to the serene heavens. He had to learn that the signs of the air are not the signs of the skies. Nay, once, his brother surprised him in the act of examining through his longest tube a patch of burning heath upon a distant hill. But now he was diligent from morning till night in the study of the laws of the truth that has to do with stars; and when the curtain of the sunlight was about to rise from before the heavenly worlds which it had hidden all day long, he might be seen preparing his instruments with that solemn countenance with which it becometh one to look into the mysterious harmonies of Nature. Now he learned what law and order and truth are, what consent and harmony mean; how the individual may find his own end in a higher end, where law and freedom mean the same thing, and the purest certainty exists without the slightest constraint. Thus he stood on the earth, and looked to the heavens.

Another, who had been much given to searching out the hollow places and recesses in the foundations of the castle, and who was often to be found with compass and ruler working away at a chart of the same which he had been in process of constructing, now came to the conclusion, that only by ascending the upper regions of his abode could he become capable of understanding what lay beneath; and that, in all probability, one clear prospect, from the top of the highest attainable turret, over the castle as it lay below, would reveal more of the idea of its internal construction, than a year spent in wandering through its subterranean vaults. But the fact was, that the desire to ascend wakening within him had made him forget what was beneath; and having laid aside his chart for a time at least, he was now to be met in every quarter of the upper parts, searching and striving upward, now in one direction, now in another; and seeking, as he went, the best outlooks into the clear air of outer realities.

And they began to discover that they were all meditating different aspects of the same thing; and they brought together their various discoveries, and recognised the likeness between them; and the one thing often explained the other, and combining with it helped to a third. They grew in consequence more and more friendly and loving; so that every now and then one turned to another and said, as in surprise, "Why, you are my brother!"—"Why, you are my sister!" And yet they had always known it.

The change reached to all. One, who lived on the air of sweet sounds, and who was almost always to be found seated by her harp or some other instrument, had, till the late storm, been generally merry and playful, though sometimes sad. But for a long time after that, she was often found weeping, and playing little simple airs which she had heard in childhood—backward longings, followed by fresh tears. Before long, however, a new element manifested itself in her music. It became yet more wild, and sometimes retained all its sadness, but it was mingled with anticipation and hope. The past and the future merged in one; and while memory yet brought the rain-cloud, expectation threw the rainbow across its bosom—and all was uttered in her music, which rose and swelled, now to defiance, now to victory; then died in a torrent of weeping.

As to the eldest sister, it was many days before she recovered from the shock. At length, one day, her brother came to her, took her by the hand, led her to an open window, and told her to seat herself by it, and look out. She did so; but at first saw nothing more than an unsympathising blaze of sunlight. But as she looked, the horizon widened out, and the dome of the sky ascended, till the grandeur seized upon her soul, and she fell on her knees and wept. Now the heavens seemed to bend lovingly over her, and to stretch out wide cloud-arms to embrace her; the earth lay like the bosom of an infinite love beneath her, and the wind kissed her cheek with an odour of roses. She sprang to her feet, and turned, in an agony of hope, expecting to behold the face of the father, but there stood only her brother, looking calmly though lovingly on her emotion. She turned again to the window. On the hilltops rested the sky: Heaven and Earth were one; and the prophecy awoke in her soul, that from betwixt them would the steps of the father approach.

Hitherto she had seen but Beauty; now she beheld Truth. Often had she looked on such clouds as these, and loved the strange ethereal curves into which the winds moulded them; and had smiled as her little pet sister told her what curious animals she saw in them, and tried to point them out to her. Now they were as troops of angels, jubilant over her new birth, for they sang, in her soul, of beauty, and truth, and love. She looked down, and her little sister knelt beside her.

She was a curious child, with black, glittering eyes, and dark hair; at the mercy of every wandering wind; a frolicsome, daring girl, who laughed more than she smiled. She was generally in attendance on her sister, and was always finding and bringing her strange things. She never pulled a primrose, but she knew the haunts of all the orchis tribe, and brought from them bees and butterflies innumerable, as offerings to her sister. Curious moths and glow-worms were her greatest delight; and she loved the stars, because they were like the glow-worms. But the change had affected her too; for her sister saw that her eyes had lost their glittering look, and had become more liquid and transparent. And from that time she often observed that her gaiety was more gentle, her smile more frequent, her laugh less bell-like; and although she was as wild as ever, there was more elegance in her motions, and more music in her voice. And she clung to her sister with far greater fondness than before.

The land reposed in the embrace of the warm summer days. The clouds of heaven nestled around the towers of the castle; and the hearts of its inmates became conscious of a warm atmosphere—of a presence of love. They began to feel like the children of a household, when the mother is at home. Their faces and forms grew daily more and more beautiful, till they wondered as they gazed on each other. As they walked in the gardens of the castle, or in the country around, they were often visited, especially the eldest sister, by sounds that no one heard but themselves, issuing from woods and waters; and by forms of love that lightened out of flowers, and grass, and great rocks. Now and then the young children would come in with a slow, stately step, and, with great eyes that looked as if they would devour all the creation, say that they had met the father amongst the trees, and that he had kissed them; "And," added one of them once, "I grew so big!" But when the others went out to look, they could see no one. And some said it must have been the brother, who grew more and more beautiful, and loving, and reverend, and who had lost all traces of hardness, so that they wondered they could ever have thought him stern and harsh. But the eldest sister held her peace, and looked up, and her eyes filled with tears. "Who can tell," thought she, "but the little children know more about it than we?"

Often, at sunrise, might be heard their hymn of praise to their unseen father, whom they felt to be near, though they saw him not. Some words thereof once reached my ear through the folds of the music in which they floated, as in an upward snowstorm of sweet sounds. And these are some of the words I heard—but there was much I seemed to hear which I could not understand, and some things which I understood but cannot utter again.

"We thank thee that we have a father, and not a maker; that thou hast begotten us, and not moulded us as images of clay; that we have come forth of thy heart, and have not been fashioned by thy hands. It *must* be so. Only the heart of a father is able to create. We rejoice in it, and bless thee that we know it. We thank thee for thyself. Be what thou art—our root and life, our beginning and end, our all in all. Come home to us. Thou livest; therefore we live. In thy light we see. Thou art—that is all our song."

Thus they worship, and love, and wait. Their hope and expectation grow ever stronger and brighter, that one day, ere long, the Father will show Himself amongst them, and thenceforth dwell in His own house for evermore. What was once but an old legend has become the one desire of their hearts.

And the loftiest hope is the surest of being fulfilled.

THE WOW O'RIVEN

Elsie Scott had let her work fall on her knees, and her hands on her work, and was looking out of the wide, low window of her room, which was on one of the ground floors of the village street. Through a gap in the household shrubbery of fuchsias and myrtles filling the window-sill, one passing on the foot pavement might get a momentary glimpse of her pale face, lighted up with two blue eyes, over which some inward trouble had spread a faint, gauze-like haziness. But almost before her thoughts had had time to wander back to this trouble, a shout of children's voices, at the other end of the street, reached her ear. She listened a moment. A shadow of displeasure and pain crossed her countenance; and rising hastily, she betook herself to an inner apartment, and closed the door behind her.

Meantime the sounds drew nearer; and by and by an old man, whose strange appearance and dress showed that he had little capacity either for good or evil, passed the window. His clothes were comfortable enough in quality and condition, for they were the annual gift of a benevolent lady in the neighbourhood; but, being made to accommodate his taste, both known and traditional, they were somewhat peculiar in cut and adornment. Both coat and trousers were of a dark grey cloth; but the former, which, in its shape, partook of the military, had a straight collar of yellow, and narrow cuffs of the same; while upon both sleeves, about the place where a corporal wears his stripes, was expressed, in the same yellow cloth, a somewhat singular device. It was as close an imitation of a bell, with its tongue hanging out of its mouth, as the tailor's skill could produce from a single piece of cloth. The origin of the military cut of his coat was well known. IIis preference for it arose in the time of the wars of the first Napoleon, when the threatened invasion of the country caused the organisation of many volunteer regiments. The martial show and exercises captivated the poor man's fancy; and from that time forward nothing pleased his vanity, and consequently conciliated his goodwill more, than to style him by his favourite title—the *Colonel*. But the badge on his arm had a deeper origin, which will be partially manifest in the course of the story—if story it can be called. It was, indeed, the baptism of the fool, the outward and visible sign of his relation to the infinite and unseen. His countenance, however, although the features were not of any peculiarly low or animal type, showed no corresponding sign of the consciousness of such a relation, being as vacant as human countenance could well be.

The cause of Elsie's annoyance was that the fool was annoyed; he was followed by a troop of boys, who turned his rank into scorn, and assailed him with epithets hateful to him. Although the most harmless of creatures when left alone, he was dangerous when roused; and now he stooped repeatedly to pick up stones and hurl them at his tormentors, who took care, while abusing him, to keep at a considerable distance, lest he should get hold of them. Amidst the sounds of derision that followed him, might be heard the words frequently repeated—"*Come hame, come hame.*" But in a few minutes the noise ceased, either from the interference of some friendly inhabitant, or that the boys grew weary, and departed in search of other amusement. By and by, Elsie might be seen again at her work in the window; but the cloud over her eyes was deeper, and her whole face more sad.

Indeed, so much did the persecution of this poor man affect her, that an onlooker would have been compelled to seek the cause in some yet deeper sympathy than that commonly felt for the oppressed, even by women. And such a sympathy existed, strange as it may seem, between the beautiful girl (for many called her *a bonnie lassie*) and this "tatter of humanity". Nothing would have been farther from the thoughts of those that knew them, than the supposition of any correspondence or connection between them; yet this sympathy sprang in part from a real similarity in their history and present condition.

All the facts that were known about *Feel Jock's* origin were these: that seventy years ago, a man who had gone with his horse and cart some miles from the village, to fetch home a load of peat from a desolate *moss*, had heard, while toiling along as rough a road on as lonely a hillside as any in Scotland, the cry of a child; and, searching about, had found the infant, hardly wrapt in rags, and untended, as if the earth herself had just given birth—that desert moor, wide and dismal, broken and watery, the only bosom for him to lie upon, and the cold, clear night-heaven his only covering. The man had brought him home, and the parish had taken parish-care of him. He had grown up, and proved what he now was—almost an idiot. Many of the townspeople were kind to him, and employed him in fetching water for them from the river or wells in the neighbourhood, paying him for his trouble in victuals, or whisky, of which he was very fond. He seldom spoke; and the sentences he could utter were few; yet the tone, and even the words of his limited vocabulary, were sufficient to express gratitude and some measure of love towards those who were kind to him, and hatred of those who teased and insulted him. He lived a life without aim, and apparently to no purpose; in this resembling most of his more gifted fellow-men, who, with all the tools and materials necessary for building a noble mansion, are yet content with a clay hut.

Elsie, on the contrary, had been born in a comfortable farmhouse, amidst homeliness and abundance. But at a very early age she had lost both father and mother; not so early, however, but that she had faint memories of warm soft times on her mother's bosom, and of refuge in her mother's arms from the attacks of geese, and the pursuit of pigs. Therefore, in after-times, when she looked forward to heaven, it was as much a reverting to the old heavenly times of childhood and mother's love, as an anticipation of something yet to be revealed. Indeed, without some such memory, how should we ever picture to ourselves a perfect rest? But sometimes it would seem as if the more a heart was made capable of loving, the less it had to love; and poor Elsie, in passing from a mother's to a brother's guardianship, felt a change of spiritual temperature too keen. He was not a bad man, or incapable of benevolence when touched by the sight of want in anything of which he would himself have felt the privation; but he was so coarsely made that only the purest animal necessities affected him, and a hard word, or unfeeling speech, could never have reached the quick of his nature through the hide that enclosed it. Elsie, on the contrary, was excessively and painfully sensitive, as if her nature constantly portended an invisible multitude of half-spiritual, half-nervous antenna, which shrank and trembled in every current of air at all below their own temperature. The effect of this upon her behaviour was such that she was called odd; and the poor girl felt she was not like other people, yet could not help it. Her brother, too, laughed at her without the slightest idea of the pain he occasioned, or the remotest feeling of curiosity as to what the inward and consistent causes of the outward abnormal condition might be. Tenderness was the divine comforting she needed; and it was altogether absent from her brother's character and behaviour.

Her neighbours looked on her with some interest, but they rather shunned than courted her acquaintance; especially after the return of certain nervous attacks, to which she had been subject in childhood, and which were again brought on by the events I must relate. It is curious how certain diseases repel, by a kind of awe, the sympathies of the neighbours: as if, by the fact of being subject to them, the patient were removed into another realm of existence, from which, like the dead with the living, she can hold communion with those around her only partially, and with a mixture of dread pervading the intercourse. Thus some of the deepest, purest wells of spiritual life, are, like those in old castles, choked up by the decay of the outer walls. But what tended more than anything, perhaps, to keep up the painful unrest of her soul (for the beauty of her character was evident in the fact that the irritation seldom reached her *mind*), was a circumstance at which, in its present connection, some of my readers will smile, and others feel a shudder corresponding in kind to that of Elsie.

Her brother was very fond of a rather small, but ferocious-looking bull-dog, which followed close at his heels, wherever he went, with hanging head and slouching gait, never leaping or racing about like other dogs. When in the house, he always lay under his master's chair. He seemed to dislike Elsie, and she felt an unspeakable repugnance to him. Though she never mentioned her aversion, her brother easily saw it by the way in which she avoided the animal; and attributing it entirely to fear—which indeed had a great share in the matter—he would cruelly aggravate it, by telling her stories of the fierce hardihood and relentless persistency of this kind of animal. He dared not yet further increase her terror by offering to set the creature upon her, because it was doubtful whether he might be able to restrain him; but the mental suffering which he occasioned by this heartless conduct, and for which he had no sympathy, was as severe as many bodily sufferings to which he would have been sorry to subject her. Whenever the poor girl happened inadvertently to pass near the dog, which was seldom, a low growl made her aware of his proximity, and drove her to a quick retreat. He was, in fact, the animal impersonation of the animal opposition which she had continually to endure. Like chooses like; and the bulldog *in* her brother made choice of the bull-dog *out of* him for his companion. So her day was one of shrinking fear and multiform discomfort.

But a nature capable of so much distress, must of necessity be *capable* of a corresponding amount of pleasure; and in her case this was manifest in the fact that sleep and the quiet of her own room restored her wonderfully. If she were only let alone, a calm mood, filled with images of pleasure, soon took possession of her mind.

Her acquaintance with the fool had commenced some ten years previous to the time I write of, when she was quite a little girl, and had come from the country with her brother, who, having taken a small farm close to the town, preferred residing in the town to occupying the farmhouse, which was not comfortable. She looked at first with some terror on his uncouth appearance, and with much wonderment on his strange dress. This wonder was heightened by a conversation she overheard one day in the street, between the fool and a little pale-faced boy, who, approaching him respectfully, said, "Weel, cornel!" "Weel, laddie!" was the reply. "Fat dis the wow say, cornel?" "Come hame, come hame!" answered the *colonel*, with both accent and quantity heaped on the word *hame*. What the wow could be, she had no idea; only, as the years passed on, the strange word became in her mind indescribably associated with the strange shape in yellow cloth on his sleeves. Had she been a native of the town, she could not have failed to know its import, so familiar was every one with it, although it did not belong to the local vocabulary; but, as it was, years passed away before she discovered its meaning. And when, again and again, the fool, attempting to convey his gratitude for some kindness she had shown him mumbled over the words—"*The wow o' Rivven—the wow o' Rivven,*" the wonder would return as to what could be the idea associated with them in his mind, but she made no advance towards their explanation.

That, however, which most attracted her to the old man, was his persecution by the children. They were to him what the bull-dog was to her—the constant source of irritation and annoyance. They could hardly hurt him, nor did he appear to dread other injury from them than insult, to which, fool though he was, he was keenly alive. Human gadflies that they were! they sometimes stung him beyond endurance, and he would curse them in the impotence of his anger. Once or twice Elsie had been so far carried beyond her constitutional timidity, by sympathy for the distress of her friend, that she had gone out and talked to the boys—even scolded them, so that they slunk away ashamed, and began to stand as much in dread of her as of the clutches of their prey. So she, gentle and timid to excess, acquired among them the reputation of a termagant. Popular opinion among children, as among men, is of ten just, but as often very unjust; for the same manifestations may proceed from opposite principles; and, therefore, as indices to character, may mislead as often as enlighten.

Next door to the house in which Elsie resided, dwelt a tradesman and his wife, who kept an indefinite sort of shop, in which various kinds of goods were exposed for sale. Their youngest son was about the same age as Elsie; and while they were rather more than children, and less than young people, he spent many of his evenings with her, somewhat to the loss of position in his classes at the parish school. They were, indeed, much attached to each other; and, peculiarly constituted as Elsie was, one may imagine what kind of heavenly messenger a companion stronger than herself must have been to her. In fact, if she could have framed the undefinable need of her childlike nature into an articulate prayer, it would have been—"Give me some one to love me stronger than I." Any love was helpful, yes, in its degree, saving to her poor troubled soul; but the hope, as they grew older together, that the powerful, yet tender-hearted youth, really loved her, and would one day make her his wife, was like the opening of heavenly eyes of life and love in the hitherto blank and deathlike face of her existence. But nothing had been said of love, although they met and parted like lovers.

Doubtless, if the circles of their thought and feeling had continued as now to intersect each other, there would have been no interruption to their affection; but the time at length arrived when the old couple, seeing the rest of their family comfortably settled in life, resolved to make a gentleman of the youngest; and so sent him from school to college. The facilities existing in Scotland for providing a professional training enabled them to educate him as a surgeon. He parted from Elsie with some regret; but, far less dependent on her than she was on him, and full of the prospects of the future, he felt none of that sinking at the heart which seemed to lay her whole nature open to a fresh inroad of all the terrors and sorrows of her peculiar existence. No correspondence took place between them. New pursuits and relations, and the development of his tastes and judgments, entirely altered the position of poor Elsie in his memory. Having been, during their intercourse, far less of a man than she of a woman, he had no definite idea of the place he had occupied in her regard; and in his mind she receded into the background of the past, without his having any idea that she would suffer thereby, or that he was unjust towards her; while, in her thoughts, his image stood in the highest and clearest relief. It was the centre-point from which and towards which all lines radiated and converged; and although she could not but be doubtful about the future, yet there was much hope mingled with her doubts.

But when, at the close of two years, he visited his native village, and she saw before her, instead of the homely youth who had left her that winter evening, one who, to her inexperienced eyes, appeared a finished gentleman, her heart sank within her, as if she had found Nature herself false in her ripening processes, destroying the beautiful promise of a former year by changing instead of developing her creations. He spoke kindly to her, but not cordially. To her ear the voice seemed to come from a great distance out of the past; and while she looked upon him, that optical change passed over her vision, which all have experienced after gazing abstractedly on any object for a time: his form grew very small, and receded to an immeasurable distance; till, her imagination mingling with the twilight haze of her senses, she seemed to see him standing far off on a hill, with the bright horizon of sunset for a background to his clearly defined figure.

She knew no more till she found herself in bed in the dark; and the first message that reached her from the outer world was the infernal growl of the bull-dog from the room below. Next day she saw her lover walking with two ladies, who would have thought it some degree of condescension to speak to her; and he passed the house without once looking towards it.

One who is sufficiently possessed by the demon of nervousness to be glad of the magnetic influences of a friend's company in a public promenade, or of a horse beneath him in passing through a churchyard, will have some faint idea of how utterly exposed and defenceless poor Elsie now felt on the crowded thoroughfare of life. And so the insensibility which had overtaken her, was not the ordinary swoon with which Nature relieves the overstrained nerves, but the return of the epileptic fits of her early childhood; and if the condition of the poor girl had been pitiable before, it was tenfold more so now. Yet she did not complain, but bore all in silence, though it was evident that her health was giving way. But now, help came to her from a strange quarter; though many might not be willing to accord the name of help to that which rather hastened than retarded the progress of her decline.

She had gone to spend a few of the summer days with a relative in the country, some miles from her home, if home it could be called. One evening, towards sunset, she went out for a solitary walk. Passing from the little garden gate, she went along a bare country road for some distance, and then, turning aside by a footpath through a thicket of low trees, she came out in a lonely little churchyard on the hillside. Hardly knowing whether or not she had intended to go there, she seated herself on a mound covered with long grass, one of many. Before her stood the ruins of an old church which was taking centuries to crumble. Little remained but the gable wall, immensely thick, and covered with ancient ivy. The rays of the setting sun fell on a mound at its foot, not green like the rest, but of a rich red-brown in the rosy sunset, and evidently but newly heaped up. Her eyes, too, rested upon it. Slowly the sun sank below the near horizon.

As the last brilliant point disappeared, the ivy darkened, and a wind arose and shook all its leaves, making them look cold and troubled; and to Elsie's ear came a low faint sound, as from a far-off bell. But close beside her—and she started and shivered at the sound—rose a deep, monotonous, almost sepulchral voice, "*Come hame, come hame! The wow, the wow!*"

At once she understood the whole. She sat in the churchyard of the ancient parish church of Ruthven; and when she lifted up her eyes, there she saw, in the half-ruined belfry, the old bell, all but hidden with ivy, which the passing wind had roused to utter one sleepy tone; and there beside her, stood the fool with the bell on his arm; and to him and to her the *wow o' Rivven* said, "*Come hame, come hame!*" Ah, what did she want in the whole universe of God but a home? And though the ground beneath was hard, and the sky overhead far and boundless, and the hillside lonely and companionless, yet somewhere within the visible and beyond these the outer surface of creation, there might be a home for her; as round the wintry house the snows lie heaped up cold and white and dreary all the long *forenight*, while within, beyond the closed shutters, and giving no glimmer through the thick stone wall, the fires are blazing joyously, and the voice and laughter of young unfrozen children are heard, and nothing belongs to winter but the grey hairs on the heads of the parents, within whose warm hearts childlike voices are heard, and childlike thoughts move to and fro. The kernel of winter itself is spring, or a sleeping summer.

It was no wonder that the fool, cast out of the earth on a far more desolate spot than this, should seek to return within her bosom at this place of open doors, and should call it *home*. For surely the surface of the earth had no home for him. The mound at the foot of the gable contained the body of one who had shown him kindness. He had followed the funeral that afternoon from the town, and had remained behind with the bell. Indeed it was his custom, though Elsie had not known it, to follow every funeral going to this, his favourite churchyard of Ruthven; and, possibly in imitation of its booming, for it was still tolled at the funerals, he had given the old bell the name of *the wow*, and had translated its monotonous clangour into the articulate sounds—*come hame, come hame*. What precise meaning he attached to the words, it is impossible to say; but it was evident that the place possessed a strange attraction for him, drawing him towards it by the cords of some spiritual magnetism. It is possible that in the mind of the idiot there may have been some feeling about this churchyard and bell, which, in the mind of another, would have become a grand poetic thought; a feeling as if the ghostly old bell hung at the church door of the invisible world, and ever and anon rung out joyous notes (though they sounded sad in the ears of the living), calling to the children of the unseen to *come home, come home*. She sat for some time in silence; for the bell did not ring again, and the fool spoke no more; till the dews began to fall, when she rose and went home, followed by her companion, who passed the night in the barn. From that hour Elsie was furnished with a visual image of the rest she sought; an image which, mingling with deeper and holier thoughts, became, like the bow set in the cloud, the earthly pledge and sign of the fulfilment of heavenly hopes. Often when the wintry fog of cold discomfort and homelessness filled her soul, all at once the picture of the little churchyard—with the old gable and belfry, and the slanting sunlight steeping down to the very roots of the long grass on the graves—arose in the darkened chamber (*camera obscura,*) of her soul; and again she heard the faint Aeolian sound of the bell, and the voice of the prophet-fool who interpreted the oracle; and the inward weariness was soothed by the promise of a long sleep. Who can tell how many have been counted fools simply because they were prophets; or how much of the madness in the world may be the utterance of thoughts true and just, but belonging to a region differing from ours in its nature and scenery!

But to Elsie looking out of her window came the mocking tones of the idle boys who had chosen as the vehicle of their scorn the very words which showed the relation of the fool to the eternal, and revealed in him an element higher far than any yet developed in them. They turned his glory into shame, like the enemies of David when they mocked the would-be king. And the best in a man is often that which is most condemned by those who have not attained to his goodness. The words, however, even as repeated by the boys, had not solely awakened indignation at the persecution of the old man: they had likewise comforted her with the thought of the refuge that awaited both him and her.

But the same evening a worse trial was in store for her. Again she sat near the window, oppressed by the consciousness that her brother had come in. He had gone upstairs, and his dog had remained at the door, exchanging surly compliments with some of his own kind, when the fool came strolling past, and, I do not know from what cause, the dog flew at him. Elsie heard his cry and looked up. Her fear of the brute vanished in a moment before her sympathy for her friend. She darted from the house, and rushed towards the dog to drag him off the defenceless idiot, calling him by his name in a tone of anger and dislike. He left the fool, and, springing at Elsie, seized her by the arm above the elbow with such a grip that, in the midst of her agony, she fancied she heard the bone crack. But she uttered no cry, for the most apprehensive are sometimes the most courageous. Just then, however, her former lover was coming along the street, and, catching a glimpse of what had happened, was on the spot in an instant, took the dog by the throat with a gripe not inferior to his own, and having thus compelled him to relax his hold, dashed him on the ground with a force that almost stunned him, and then with a superadded kick sent him away limping and howling; whereupon the fool, attacking him furiously with a stick, would certainly have finished him, had not his master descried his plight and come to his rescue.

Meantime the young surgeon had carried Elsie into the house; for, as soon as she was rescued from the dog, she had fallen down in one of her fits, which were becoming more and more frequent of themselves, and little needed such a shock as this to increase their violence. He was dressing her arm when she began to recover; and when she opened her eyes, in a state of half-consciousness, he first object she beheld was his face bending over her. Recalling nothing of what had occurred, it seemed to her, in the dreamy condition in which the fit had left her, the same face, unchanged, which had once shone in upon her tardy springtime, and promised to ripen it into summer. She forgot it had departed and left her in the wintry cold. And so she uttered wild words of love and trust; and the youth, while stung with remorse at his own neglect, was astonished to perceive the poetic forms of beauty in which the soul of the uneducated maiden burst into flower. But as her senses recovered themselves, the face gradually changed to her, as if the slow alteration of two years had been phantasmagorically compressed into a few moments; and the glow departed from the maiden's thoughts and words, and her soul found itself at the narrow window of the present, from which she could behold but a dreary country.—From the street came the iambic cry of the fool, *"Come hame, come hame."*

Tycho Brahe, I think, is said to have kept a fool, who frequently sat at his feet in his study, and to whose mutterings he used to listen in the pauses of his own thought. The shining soul of the astronomer drew forth the rainbow of harmony from the misty spray of words ascending ever from the dark gulf into which the thoughts of the idiot were ever falling. He beheld curious concurrences of words therein; and could read strange meanings from them—sometimes even received wondrous hints for the direction of celestial inquiry, from what, to any other, and it may be to the fool himself, was but a ceaseless and aimless babble. Such power lieth in words. It is not then to be wondered at, that the sounds I have mentioned should fall on the ears of Elsie, at such a moment, as a message from God Himself. This then—all this dreariness—was but a passing show like the rest, and there lay somewhere for her a reality—a home. The tears burst up from her oppressed heart. She received the message, and prepared to go home. From that time her strength gradually sank, but her spirits as steadily rose.

The strength of the fool, too, began to fail, for he was old. He bore all the signs of age, even to the grey hairs, which betokened no wisdom. But one cannot say what wisdom might be in him, or how far he had fought his own battle, and been victorious. Whether any notion of a continuance of life and thought dwelt in his brain, it is impossible to tell; but he seemed to have the idea that this was not his home; and those who saw him gradually approaching his end, might well anticipate for him a higher life in the world to come. He had passed through this world without ever awaking to such a consciousness of being as is common to mankind. He had spent his years like a weary dream through a long night—a strange, dismal, unkindly dream; and now the morning was at hand. Often in his dream had he listened with sleepy senses to the ringing of the bell, but that bell would awake him at last. He was like a seed buried too deep in the soil, to which the light has never penetrated, and which, therefore, has never forced its way upwards to the open air, ever experienced the resurrection of the dead. But seeds will grow ages after they have fallen into the earth; and, indeed, with many kinds, and within some limits, the older the seed before it germinates, the more plentiful the fruit. And may it not be believed of many human beings, that, the Great Husbandman having sown them like seeds in the soil of human affairs, there they lie buried a life long; and only after the upturning of the soil by death reach a position in which the awakening of their aspiration and the consequent growth become possible. Surely He has made nothing in vain.

A violent cold and cough brought him at last near to his end, and hearing that he was ill, Elsie ventured one bright spring day to go to see him. When she entered the miserable room where he lay, he held out his hand to her with something like a smile, and muttered feebly and painfully, "I'm gaein' to the wow, nae to come back again." Elsie could not restrain her tears; while the old man, looking fixedly at her, though with meaningless eyes, muttered, for the last time, "*Come hame! come hame!*" and sank into a lethargy, from which nothing could rouse him, till, next morning, he was waked by friendly death from the long sleep of this world's night. They bore him to his favourite churchyard, and buried him within the site of the old church, below his loved bell, which had ever been to him as the cuckoo-note of a coming spring. Thus he at length obeyed its summons, and went home.

Elsie lingered till the first summer days lay warm on the land. Several kind hearts in the village, hearing of her illness, visited her and ministered to her. Wondering at her sweetness and patience, they regretted they had not known her before. How much consolation might not their kindness have imparted, and how much might not their sympathy have strengthened her on her painful road! But they could not long have delayed her going home. Nor, mentally constituted as she was, would this have been at all to be desired. Indeed it was chiefly the expectation of departure that quieted and soothed her tremulous nature. It is true that a deep spring of hope and faith kept singing on in her heart, but this alone, without the anticipation of speedy release, could only have kept her mind at peace. It could not have reached, at least for a long time, the border land between body and mind, in which her disease lay.

One still night of summer, the nurse who watched by her bedside heard her murmur through her sleep, "I hear it: *come hame—come hame.* I'm comin', I'm comin'—I'm gaein' hame to the wow, nae to come back." She awoke at the sound of her own words, and begged the nurse to convey to her brother her last request, that she might be buried by the side of the fool, within the old church of Ruthven. Then she turned her face to the wall, and in the morning was found quiet and cold. She must have died within a few minutes after her last words. She was buried according to her request; and thus she too went home.

Side by side rest the aged fool and the young maiden; for the bell called them, and they obeyed; and surely they found the fire burning bright, and heard friendly voices, and felt sweet lips on theirs, in the home to which they went. Surely both intellect and love were waiting them there.

Still the old bell hangs in the old gable; and whenever another is borne to the old churchyard, it keeps calling to those who are left behind, with the same sad, but friendly and unchanging voice— *"Come hame! come hame! come hame!"*

"Thy sun shall no more go down; neither shall thy moon withdraw itself: for the Lord shall be thine everlasting light, and the days of thy mourning shall be ended."—ISA. LX 20.

THE BROKEN SWORDS

The eyes of three, two sisters and a brother, gazed for the last time on a great pale-golden star, that followed the sun down the steep west. It went down to arise again; and the brother about to depart might return, but more than the usual doubt hung upon his future. For between the white dresses of the sisters, shone his scarlet coat and golden sword-knot, which he had put on for the first time, more to gratify their pride than his own vanity. The brightening moon, as if prophetic of a future memory, had already begun to dim the scarlet and the gold, and to give them a pale, ghostly hue. In her thoughtful light the whole group seemed more like a meeting in the land of shadows, than a parting in the substantial earth. But which should be called the land of realities?—the region where appearance, and space, and time drive between, and stop the flowing currents of the soul's speech? or that region where heart meets heart, and appearance has become the slave to utterance, and space and time are forgotten?

Through the quiet air came the far-off rush of water, and the near cry of the land-rail. Now and then a chilly wind blew unheeded through the startled and jostling leaves that shaded the ivy-seat. Else, there was calm everywhere, rendered yet deeper and more intense by the dusky sorrow that filled their hearts. For, far away, hundreds of miles beyond the hearing of their ears, roared the great war-guns; next week their brother must sail with his regiment to join the army; and tomorrow he must leave his home.

The sisters looked on him tenderly, with vague fears about his fate. Yet little they divined it. That the face they loved might lie pale and bloody, in a heap of slain, was the worst image of it that arose before them; but this, had they seen the future, they would, in ignorance of the further future, have infinitely preferred to that which awaited him. And even while they looked on him, a dim feeling of the unsuitableness of his lot filled their minds. For, indeed, to all judgments it must have seemed unsuitable that the home-boy, the loved of his mother, the pet of his sisters, who was happy womanlike (as Coleridge says), if he possessed the signs of love, having never yet sought for its proofs—that he should be sent amongst soldiers, to command and be commanded; to kill, or perhaps to be himself crushed out of the fair earth in the uproar that brings back for the moment the reign of

Night and Chaos. No wonder that to his sisters it seemed strange and sad. Yet such was their own position in the battle of life, in which their father had died with doubtful conquest, that when their old military uncle sent the boy an ensign's commission, they did not dream of refusing the only path open, as they thought, to an honourable profession, even though it might lead to the trench-grave. They heard it as the voice of destiny, wept, and yielded.

If they had possessed a deeper insight into his character, they would have discovered yet further reason to doubt the fitness of the profession chosen for him; and if they had ever seen him at school, it is possible the doubt of fitness might have strengthened into a certainty of incongruity. His comparative inactivity amongst his schoolfellows, though occasioned by no dulness of intellect, might have suggested the necessity of a quiet life, if inclination and liking had been the arbiters in the choice. Nor was this inactivity the result of defective animal spirits either, for sometimes his mirth and boyish frolic were unbounded; but it seemed to proceed from an over-activity of the inward life, absorbing, and in some measure checking, the outward manifestation. He had so much to do in his own hidden kingdom, that he had not time to take his place in the polity and strife of the commonwealth around him. Hence, while other boys were acting, he was thinking. In this point of difference, he felt keenly the superiority of many of his companions; for another boy would have the obstacle overcome, or the adversary subdued, while he was meditating on the propriety, or on the means, of effecting the desired end. He envied their promptitude, while they never saw reason to envy his wisdom; for his conscience, tender and not strong, frequently transformed slowness of determination into irresolution: while a delicacy of the sympathetic nerves tended to distract him from any predetermined course, by the diversity of their vibrations, responsive to influences from all quarters, and destructive to unity of purpose.

Of such a one, the *a priori* judgment would be, that he ought to be left to meditate and grow for some time, before being called upon to produce the fruits of action. But add to these mental conditions a vivid imagination, and a high sense of honour, nourished in childhood by the reading of the old knightly romances, and then put the youth in a position in which action is imperative, and you have elements of strife sufficient to reduce that fair kingdom of his to utter anarchy and madness. Yet so little, do we know ourselves, and so different are the symbols with which the imagination works its algebra, from the realities which those symbols represent, that as yet the youth felt no uneasiness, but contemplated his new calling with a glad enthusiasm and some vanity; for all his prospect lay in the glow of the scarlet and the gold. Nor did this excitement receive any check till the day before his departure, on which day I have introduced him to my readers, when, accidently taking up a newspaper of a week old, his eye fell on these words—"*Already crying women are to be met in the streets.*" With this cloud afar on his horizon, which, though no bigger than a man's hand, yet cast a perceptible shadow over his mind, he departed next morning. The coach carried him beyond the consecrated circle of home laws and impulses, out into the great tumult, above which rises ever and anon the cry of Cain, "Am I my brother's keeper?"

Every tragedy of higher order, constructed in Christian times, will correspond more or less to the grand drama of the Bible; wherein the first act opens with a brilliant sunset vision of Paradise, in which childish sense and need are served with all the profusion of the indulgent nurse. But the glory fades off into grey and black, and night settles down upon the heart which, rightly uncontent with the childish, and not having yet learned the childlike, seeks knowledge and manhood as a thing denied by the Maker, and yet to be gained by the creature; so sets forth alone to climb the heavens, and instead of climbing, falls into the abyss. Then follows the long dismal night of feverish efforts and delirious visions, or, it may be, helpless despair; till at length a deeper stratum of the soul is heaved to the surface; and amid the first dawn of morning, the youth says within him, "I have sinned against my *Maker*—I will arise and go to my *Father*." More or less, I say, will Christian tragedy correspond to this—a fall and a rising again; not a rising only, but a victory; not a victory merely, but a triumph. Such, in its way and degree, is my story. I have shown, in one passing scene, the home paradise; now I have to show a scene of a far differing nature.

The young ensign was lying in his tent, weary, but wakeful. All day long the cannon had been bellowing against the walls of the city, which now lay with wide, gaping breach, ready for the morrow's storm, but covered yet with the friendly darkness. His regiment was ordered to be ready with the earliest dawn to march up to the breach. That day, for the first time, there had been blood on his sword—there the sword lay, a spot on the chased hilt still. He had cut down one of the enemy in a skirmish with a sally party of the besieged and the look of the man as he fell, haunted him. He felt, for the time, that he dared not pray to the Father, for the blood of a brother had rushed forth at the stroke of his arm, and there was one fewer of living souls on the earth because he lived thereon. And to-morrow he must lead a troop of men up to that poor disabled town, and turn them loose upon it, not knowing what might follow in the triumph of enraged and victorious foes, who for weeks had been subjected, by the constancy of the place, to the greatest privations. It was true the general had issued his commands against all disorder and pillage; but if the soldiers once yielded to temptation, what might not be done before the officers could reclaim them! All the wretched tales he had read of the sack of cities rushed back on his memory. He shuddered as he lay. Then his conscience began to speak, and to ask what right he had to be there.—Was the war a just one?—He could not tell; for this was a bad time for settling nice questions. But there he was, right or wrong, fighting and shedding blood on God's earth, beneath God's heaven.

Over and over he turned the question in his mind; again and again the spouting blood of his foe, and the death-look in his eye, rose before him; and the youth who at school could never fight with a companion because he was not sure that he was in the right, was alone in the midst of undoubting men of war, amongst whom he was driven helplessly along, upon the waves of a terrible necessity. What wonder that in the midst of these perplexities his courage should fail him! What wonder that the consciousness of fainting should increase the faintness! or that the dread of fear and its consequences should hasten and invigorate its attacks! To crown all, when he dropped into a troubled slumber at length, he found himself hurried, as on a storm of fire, through the streets of the captured town, from all the windows of which looked forth familiar faces, old and young, but distorted from the memory of his boyhood by fear and wild despair. On one spot lay the body of his father, with his face to the earth; and he woke at the cry of horror and rage that burst from his own lips, as he saw the rough, bloody hand of a soldier twisted in the loose hair of his elder sister, and the younger fainting in the arms of a scoundrel belonging to his own regiment. He slept no more. As the grey morning broke, the troops appointed for the attack assembled without sound of trumpet or drum, and were silently formed in fitting order. The young ensign was in his place, weary and wretched after his miserable night. Before him he saw a great, broad-shouldered lieutenant, whose brawny hand seemed almost too large for his sword-hilt, and in any one of whose limbs played more animal life than in the whole body of the pale youth. The firm-set lips of this officer, and the fire of his eye, showed a concentrated resolution, which, by the contrast, increased the misery of the ensign, and seemed, as if the stronger absorbed the weaker, to draw out from him the last fibres of self-possession: the sight of unattainable determination, while it increased the feeling of the arduousness of that which required such determination, threw him into the great gulf which lay between him and it. In this disorder of his nervous and mental condition, with a doubting conscience and a shrinking heart, is it any wonder that the terrors which lay before him at the gap in those bristling walls, should draw near, and, making sudden inroad upon his soul, overwhelm the government of a will worn out by the tortures of an unassured spirit? What share fear contributed to unman him, it was impossible for him, in the dark, confused conflict of differing emotions, to determine; but doubtless a natural shrinking from danger, there being no excitement to deaden its influence, and no hope of victory to encourage to the struggle, seeing victory was dreadful to him as defeat, had its part in the sad result. Many men who have courage, are dependent on ignorance and a low state of the moral feeling for that courage; and a further progress towards the development of the higher nature would, for a time at least, entirely overthrow it. Nor could such loss of courage be rightly designated by the name of cowardice. But, alas! the colonel happened to fix his eyes upon him as he passed along the file; and this completed his confusion. He betrayed such evident symptoms of perturbation, that that officer ordered him under arrest; and the result was, that, chiefly for the sake of example to the army, he was, upon trial by court-martial, expelled from the service, and had his sword broken over his head. Alas for the delicate minded youth! Alas for the home-darling!

Long after, he found at the bottom of his chest the pieces of the broken sword, and remembered that, at the time, he had lifted them from the ground and carried them away. But he could not recall under what impulse he had done so. Perhaps the agony he suffered, passing the bounds of mortal endurance, had opened for him a vista into the eternal, and had shown him, if not the injustice of the sentence passed upon him, yet his freedom from blame, or, endowing him with dim prophetic vision, had given him the assurance that some day the stain would be wiped from his soul, and leave him standing clear before the tribunal of his own honour. Some feeling like this, I say, may have caused him, with a passing gleam of indignant protest, to lift the fragments from the earth, and carry them away; even as the friends of a so-called traitor may bear away his mutilated body from the wheel. But if such was the case, the vision was soon overwhelmed and forgotten in the succeeding anguish. He could not see that, in mercy to his doubting spirit, the question which had agitated his mind almost to madness, and which no results of the impending conflict could have settled for him, was thus quietly set aside for the time; nor that, painful as was the dark, dreadful existence that he was now to pass in self-torment and moaning, it would go by, and leave his spirit clearer far, than if, in his apprehension, it had been stained with further blood-guiltiness, instead of the loss of honour. Years after, when he accidentally learned that on that very morning the whole of his company, with parts of several more, had, or ever they began to mount the breach, been blown to pieces by the explosion of a mine, he cried aloud in bitterness, "Would God that my fear had not been discovered before I reached that spot!" But surely it is better to pass into the next region of life having reaped some assurance, some firmness of character, determination of effort, and consciousness of the worth of life, in the present world; so approaching the future steadily and faithfully, and if in much darkness and ignorance, yet not in the oscillations of moral uncertainty.

Close upon the catastrophe followed a torpor, which lasted he did not know how long, and which wrapped in a thick fog all the succeeding events. For some time he can hardly be said to have had any conscious history. He awoke to life and torture when half-way across the sea towards his native country, where was no home any longer for him. To this point, and no farther, could his thoughts return in after years. But the misery which he then endured is hardly to be understood, save by those of like delicate temperament with himself. All day long he sat silent in his cabin; nor could any effort of the captain, or others on board, induce him to go on deck till night came on, when, under the starlight, he ventured into the open air. The sky soothed him then, he knew not how. For the face of nature is the face of God, and must bear expressions that can influence, though unconsciously to them, the most ignorant and hopeless of His children. Often did he watch the clouds in hope of a storm, his spirit rising and falling as the sky darkened or cleared; he longed, in the necessary selfishness of such suffering, for a tumult of waters to swallow the vessel; and only the recollection of how many lives were involved in its safety besides his own, prevented him from praying to God for lightning and tempest, borne on which he might dash into the haven of the other world. One night, following a sultry calm day, he thought that Mercy had heard his unuttered prayer. The air and sea were intense darkness, till a light as intense for one moment annihilated it, and the succeeding darkness seemed shattered with the sharp reports of the thunder that cracked without reverberation. He who had shrunk from battle with his fellow-men, rushed to the mainmast, threw himself on his knees, and stretched forth his arms in speechless energy of supplication; but the storm passed away overhead, and left him kneeling still by the uninjured mast. At length the vessel reached her port. He hurried on shore to bury himself in the most secret place he could find. *Out of sight* was his first, his only thought. Return to his mother he would not, he could not; and, indeed, his friends never learned his fate, until it had carried him far beyond their reach.

For several weeks he lurked about like a malefactor, in low lodging-houses in narrow streets of the seaport to which the vessel had borne him, heeding no one, and but little shocked at the strange society and conversation with which, though only in bodily presence, he had to mingle. These formed the subjects of reflection in after times; and he came to the conclusion that, though much evil and much misery exist, sufficient to move prayers and tears in those who love their kind, yet there is less of both than those looking down from a more elevated social position upon the weltering heap of humanity, are ready to imagine; especially if they regard it likewise from the pedestal of self-congratulation on which a meagre type of religion has elevated them. But at length his little stock of money was nearly expended, and there was nothing that he could do, or learn to do, in this seaport. He felt impelled to seek manual labour, partly because he thought it more likely he could obtain that sort of employment, without a request for reference as to his character, which would lead to inquiry about his previous history; and partly, perhaps, from an instinctive feeling that hard bodily labour would tend to lessen his inward suffering.

He left the town, therefore, at nightfall of a July day, carrying a little bundle of linen, and the remains of his money, somewhat augmented by the sale of various articles of clothing and convenience, which his change of life rendered superfluous and unsuitable. He directed his course northwards, travelling principally by night—so painfully did he shrink from the gaze even of foot-farers like himself; and sleeping during the day in some hidden nook of wood or thicket, or under the shadow of a great tree in a solitary field. So fine was the season, that for three successive weeks he was able to travel thus without inconvenience, lying down when the sun grew hot in the forenoon, and generally waking when the first faint stars were hesitating in the great darkening heavens that covered and shielded him. For above every cloud, above every storm, rise up, calm, clear, divine, the deep infinite skies; they embrace the tempest even as the sunshine; by their permission it exists within their boundless peace: therefore it cannot hurt, and must pass away, while there they stand as ever, domed up eternally, lasting, strong, and pure.

Several times he attempted to get agricultural employment; but the whiteness of his hands and the tone of his voice not merely suggested unfitness for labour, but generated suspicion as to the character of one who had evidently dropped from a rank so much higher, and was seeking admittance within the natural masonic boundaries and secrets and privileges of another. Disheartened somewhat, but hopeful, he journeyed on. I say hopeful; for the blessed power of life in the universe in fresh air and sunshine absorbed by active exercise, in winds, yea in rain, though it fell but seldom, had begun to work its natural healing, soothing effect, upon his perturbed spirit. And there was room for hope in his new endeavour. As his bodily strength increased, and his health, considerably impaired by inward suffering, improved, the trouble of his soul became more endurable—and in some measure to endure is to conquer and destroy. In proportion as the mind grows in the strength of patience, the disturber of its peace sickens and fades away. At length, one day, a widow lady in a village through which his road led him, gave him a day's work in her garden. He laboured hard and well, notwithstanding his soon-blistered hands, received his wages thankfully, and found a resting-place for the night on the low part of a haystack from which the upper portion had been cut away. Here he ate his supper of bread and cheese, pleased to have found such comfortable quarters, and soon fell fast asleep.

When he awoke, the whole heavens and earth seemed to give a full denial to sin and sorrow. The sun was just mounting over the horizon, looking up the clear cloud-mottled sky. From millions of water-drops hanging on the bending stalks of grass, sparkled his rays in varied refraction, transformed here to a gorgeous burning ruby, there to an emerald, green as the grass, and yonder to a flashing, sunny topaz. The chanting priest-lark had gone up from the low earth, as soon as the heavenly light had begun to enwrap and illumine the folds of its tabernacle; and had entered the high heavens with his offering, whence, unseen, he now dropped on the earth the sprinkled sounds of his overflowing blessedness. The poor youth rose but to kneel, and cry, from a bursting heart, "Hast Thou not, O Father, some care for me? Canst Thou not restore my lost honour? Can anything befall Thy children for which Thou hast no help? Surely, if the face of Thy world lie not, joy and not grief is at the heart of the universe. Is there none for me?"

The highest poetic feeling of which we are now conscious, springs not from the beholding of perfected beauty, but from the mute sympathy which the creation with all its children manifests with us in the groaning and travailing which look for the sonship. Because of our need and aspiration, the snowdrop gives birth in our hearts to a loftier spiritual and poetic feeling, than the rose most complete in form, colour, and odour. The rose is of Paradise—the snowdrop is of the striving, hoping, longing Earth. Perhaps our highest poetry is the expression of our aspirations in the sympathetic forms of visible nature. Nor is this merely a longing for a restored Paradise; for even in the ordinary history of men, no man or woman that has fallen, can be restored to the position formerly held. Such must rise to a yet higher place, whence they can behold their former standing far beneath their feet. They must be restored by the attainment of something better than they ever possessed before, or not at all. If the law be a weariness, we must escape it by taking refuge with the spirit, for not otherwise can we fulfil the law than by being above the law. To escape the overhanging rocks of Sinai, we must climb to its secret top.

"Is thy strait horizon dreary?

Is thy foolish fancy chill?

Change the feet that have grown weary

For the wings that never will."

Thus, like one of the wandering knights searching the wide earth for the Sangreal, did he wander on, searching for his lost honour, or rather (for that he counted gone for ever) seeking unconsciously for the peace of mind which had departed from him, and taken with it, not the joy merely, but almost the possibility, of existence.

At last, when his little store was all but exhausted, he was employed by a market gardener, in the neighbourhood of a large country town, to work in his garden, and sometimes take his vegetables to market. With him he continued for a few weeks, and wished for no change; until, one day driving his cart through the town, he saw approaching him an elderly gentleman, whom he knew at once, by his gait and carriage, to be a military man. Now he had never seen his uncle the retired officer, but it struck him that this might be he; and under the tyranny of his passion for concealment, he fancied that, if it were he, he might recognise him by some family likeness — not considering the improbability of his looking at him. This fancy, with the painful effect which the sight of an officer, even in plain clothes, had upon him, recalling the torture of that frightful day, so overcame him, that he found himself at the other end of an alley before he recollected that he had the horse and cart in charge. This increased his difficulty; for now he dared not return, lest his inquiries after the vehicle, if the horse had strayed from the direct line, should attract attention, and cause interrogations which he would be unable to answer. The fatal want of self-possession seemed again to ruin him. He forsook the town by the nearest way, struck across the country to another line of road, and before he was missed, was miles away, still in a northerly direction.

But although he thus shunned the face of man, especially of any one who reminded him of the past, the loss of his reputation in their eyes was not the cause of his inward grief. That would have been comparatively powerless to disturb him, had he not lost his own respect. He quailed before his own thoughts; he was dishonoured in his own eyes. His perplexity had not yet sufficiently cleared away to allow him to see the extenuating circumstances of the case; not to say the fact that the peculiar mental condition in which he was at the time, removed the case quite out of the class of ordinary instances of cowardice. He condemned himself more severely than any of his judges would have dared; remembering that portion of his mental sensations which had savoured of fear, and forgetting the causes which had produced it. He judged himself a man stained with the foulest blot that could cleave to a soldier's name, a blot which nothing but death, not even death, could efface. But, inwardly condemned and outwardly degraded, his dread of recognition was intense; and feeling that he was in more danger of being discovered where the population was sparser, he resolved to hide himself once more in the midst of poverty; and, with this view, found his way to one of the largest of the manufacturing towns.

He reached it during the strike of a great part of the workmen; so that, though he found some difficulty in procuring employment, as might be expected from his ignorance of machine-labour, he yet was sooner successful than he would otherwise have been. Possessed of a natural aptitude for mechanical operations, he soon became a tolerable workman; and he found that his previous education assisted to the fitting execution of those operations even which were most purely mechanical.

He found also, at first, that the unrelaxing attention requisite for the mastering of the many niceties of his work, of necessity drew his mind somewhat from its brooding over his misfortune, hitherto almost ceaseless. Every now and then, however, a pang would shoot suddenly to his heart, and turn his face pale, even before his consciousness had time to inquire what was the matter. So by degrees, as attention became less necessary, and the nervo-mechanical action of his system increased with use, his thoughts again returned to their old misery. He would wake at night in his poor room, with the feeling that a ghostly nightmare sat on his soul; that a want—a loss—miserable, fearful—was present; that something of his heart was gone from him; and through the darkness he would hear the snap of the breaking sword, and lie for a moment overwhelmed beneath the assurance of the incredible fact. Could it be true that *he* was a coward? that *his* honour was gone, and in its place a stain? that *he* was a thing for men—and worse, for women—to point the finger at, laughing bitter laughter? Never lover or husband could have mourned with the same desolation over the departure of the loved; the girl alone, weeping scorching tears over *her* degradation, could resemble him in his agony, as he lay on his bed, and wept and moaned.

His sufferings had returned with the greater weight, that he was no longer upheld by the "divine air" and the open heavens, whose sunlight now only reached him late in an afternoon, as he stood at his loom, through windows so coated with dust that they looked like frosted glass; showing, as it passed through the air to fall on the dirty floor, how the breath of life was thick with dust of iron and wood, and films of cotton; amidst which his senses were now too much dulled by custom to detect the exhalations from greasy wheels and overtasked human-kind. Nor could he find comfort in the society of his fellow-labourers. True, it was a kind of comfort to have those near him who could not know of his grief; but there was so little in common between them, that any interchange of thought was impossible. At least, so it seemed to him. Yet sometimes his longing for human companionship would drive him out of his dreary room at night, and send him wandering through the lower part of the town, where he would gaze wistfully on the miserable faces that passed him, as if looking for some one—some angel, even there—to speak goodwill to his hungry heart.

Once he entered one of those gin-palaces, which, like the golden gates of hell, entice the miserable to worse misery, and seated himself close to a half-tipsy, good-natured wretch, who made room for him on a bench by the wall. He was comforted even by this proximity to one who would not repel him. But soon the paintings of warlike action—of knights, and horses, and mighty deeds done with battle-axe, and broad-sword, which adorned the—panels all round, drove him forth even from this heaven of the damned; yet not before the impious thought had arisen in his heart, that the brilliantly painted and sculptural roof, with the gilded vine-leaves and bunches of grapes trained up the windows, all lighted with the great shining chandeliers, was only a microcosmic repetition of the bright heavens and the glowing earth, that overhung and surrounded the misery of man. But the memory of how kindly they had comforted and elevated him, at one period of his painful history, not only banished the wicked thought, but brought him more quiet, in the resurrection of a past blessing, than he had known for some time. The period, however, was now at hand when a new grief, followed by a new and more elevated activity, was to do its part towards the closing up of the fountain of bitterness.

Amongst his fellow-labourers, he had for a short time taken some interest in observing a young woman, who had lately joined them. There was nothing remarkable about her, except what at first sight seemed a remarkable plainness. A slight scar over one of her rather prominent eyebrows, increased this impression of plainness. But the first day had not passed, before he began to see that there was something not altogether common in those deep eyes; and the plain look vanished before a closer observation, which also discovered, in the forehead and the lines of the mouth, traces of sorrow or other suffering. There was an expression, too, in the whole face, of fixedness of purpose, without any hardness of determination. Her countenance altogether seemed the index to an interesting mental history. Signs of mental trouble were always an attraction to him; in this case so great, that he overcame his shyness, and spoke to her one evening as they left the works. He often walked home with her after that; as, indeed, was natural, seeing that she occupied an attic in the same poor lodging-house in which he lived himself. The street did not bear the best character; nor, indeed, would the occupations of all the inmates of the house have stood investigation; but so retiring and quiet was this girl, and so seldom did she go abroad after work hours, that he had not discovered till then that she lived in the same street, not to say the same house with himself.

He soon learned her history—a very common one as outward events, but not surely insignificant because common. Her father and mother were both dead, and hence she had to find her livelihood alone, and amidst associations which were always disagreeable, and sometimes painful. Her quick womanly instinct must have discovered that he too had a history; for though, his mental prostration favouring the operation of outward influences, he had greatly approximated in appearance to those amongst whom he laboured, there were yet signs, besides the educated accent of his speech, which would have distinguished him to an observer; but she put no questions to him, nor made any approach towards seeking a return of the confidence she reposed in him. It was a sensible alleviation to his sufferings to hear her kind voice, and look in her gentle face, as they walked home together; and at length the expectation of this pleasure began to present itself, in the midst of the busy, dreary work-hours, as the shadow of a heaven to close up the dismal, uninteresting day.

But one morning he missed her from her place, and a keener pain passed through him than he had felt of late; for he knew that the Plague was abroad, feeding in the low stagnant places of human abode; and he had but too much reason to dread that she might be now struggling in its grasp. He seized the first opportunity of slipping out and hurrying home. He sprang upstairs to her room. He found the door locked, but heard a faint moaning within. To avoid disturbing her, while determined to gain an entrance, he went down for the key of his own door, with which he succeeded in unlocking hers, and so crossed her threshold for the first time. There she lay on her bed, tossing in pain, and beginning to be delirious. Careless of his own life, and feeling that he could not die better than in helping the only friend he had; certain, likewise, of the difficulty of finding a nurse for one in this disease and of her station in life; and sure, likewise, that there could be no question of propriety, either in the circumstances with which they were surrounded, nor in this case of terrible fever almost as hopeless for her as dangerous to him, he instantly began the duties of a nurse, and returned no more to his employment. He had a little money in his possession, for he could not, in the way in which he lived, spend all his wages; so he proceeded to make her as comfortable as he could, with all the pent-up tenderness of a loving heart finding an outlet at length. When a boy at home, he had often taken the place of nurse, and he felt quite capable of performing its duties. Nor was his boyhood far behind yet, although the trials he had come through made it appear an age since he had lost his light heart. So he never left her bedside, except to procure what was necessary for her. She was too ill to oppose any of his measures, or to seek to prohibit his presence. Indeed, by the time he had returned with the first medicine, she was insensible; and she continued so through the whole of the following week, during which time he was constantly with her.

That action produces feeling is as often true as its converse; and it is not surprising that, while he smoothed the pillow for her head, he should have made a nest in his heart for the helpless girl. Slowly and unconsciously he learned to love her. The chasm between his early associations and the circumstances in which he found her, vanished as he drew near to the simple, essential womanhood. His heart saw hers and loved it; and he knew that, the centre once gained, he could, as from the fountain of life, as from the innermost secret of the holy place, the hidden germ of power and possibility, transform the outer intellect and outermost manners as he pleased. With what a thrill of joy, a feeling for a long time unknown to him, and till now never known in this form or with this intensity, the thought arose in his heart that here lay one who some day would love him; that he should have a place of refuge and rest; one to lie in his bosom and not despise him! "For," said he to himself, "I will call forth her soul from where it sleeps, like an unawakened echo, in an unknown cave; and like a child, of whom I once dreamed, that was mine, and to my delight turned in fear from all besides, and clung to me, this soul of hers will run with bewildered, half-sleeping eyes, and tottering steps, but with a cry of joy on its lips, to me as the life-giver. She will cling to me and worship me. Then will I tell her, for she must know all, that I am low and contemptible; that I am an outcast from the world, and that if she receive me, she will be to me as God. And I will fall down at her feet and pray her for comfort, for life, for restoration to myself; and she will throw herself beside me, and weep and love me, I know. And we will go through life together, working hard, but for each other; and when we die, she shall lead me into paradise as the prize her angel-hand found cast on a desert shore, from the storm of winds and waves which I was too weak to resist—and raised, and tended, and saved." Often did such thoughts as these pass through his mind while watching by her bed; alternated, checked, and sometimes destroyed, by the fears which attended her precarious condition, but returning with every apparent betterment or hopeful symptom.

I will not stop to decide the nice question, how far the intention was right, of causing her to love him before she knew his story. If in the whole matter there was too much thought of self, my only apology is the sequel. One day, the ninth from the commencement of her illness, a letter arrived, addressed to her; which he, thinking he might prevent some inconvenience thereby, opened and read, in the confidence of that love which already made her and all belonging to her appear his own. It was from a soldier—*her lover*. It was plain that they had been betrothed before he left for the continent a year ago; but this was the first letter which he had written to her. It breathed changeless love, and hope, and confidence in her. He was so fascinated that he read it through without pause.

Laying it down, he sat pale, motionless, almost inanimate. From the hard-won sunny heights, he was once more cast down into the shadow of death. The second storm of his life began, howling and raging, with yet more awful lulls between. "Is she not *mine*?" he said, in agony. "Do I not feel that she is mine? Who will watch over her as I? Who will kiss her soul to life as I? Shall she be torn away from me, when my soul seems to have dwelt with hers for ever in an eternal house? But have I not a right to her? Have I not given my life for hers? Is he not a soldier, and are there not many chances that he may never return? And it may be that, although they were engaged in word, soul has never touched soul with them; their love has never reached that point where it passes from the mortal to the immortal, the indissoluble: and so, in a sense, she may be yet free. Will he do for her what I will do? Shall this precious heart of hers, in which I see the buds of so many beauties, be left to wither and die?"

But here the voice within him cried out, "Art thou the disposer of destinies? Wilt thou, in a universe where the visible God hath died for the Truth's sake, do evil that a good, which He might neglect or overlook, may be gained? Leave thou her to Him, and do thou right." And he said within himself, "Now is the real trial for my life! Shall I conquer or no?" And his heart awoke and cried, "I will. God forgive me for wronging the poor soldier! A brave man, brave at least, is better for her than I."

A great strength arose within him, and lifted him up to depart. "Surely I may kiss her once," he said. For the crisis was over, and she slept. He stooped towards her face, but before he had reached her lips he saw her eyelids tremble; and he who had longed for the opening of those eyes, as of the gates of heaven, that she might love him, stricken now with fear lest she should love him, fled from her, before the eyelids that hid such strife and such victory from the unconscious maiden had time to unclose. But it was agony—quietly to pack up his bundle of linen in the room below, when he knew she was lying awake above, with her dear, pale face, and living eyes! What remained of his money, except a few shillings, he put up in a scrap of paper, and went out with his bundle in his hand, first to seek a nurse for his friend, and then to go he knew not whither. He met the factory people with whom he had worked, going to dinner, and amongst them a girl who had herself but lately recovered from the fever, and was yet hardly able for work. She was the only friend the sick girl had seemed to have amongst the women at the factory, and she was easily persuaded to go and take charge of her. He put the money in her hand, begging her to use it for the invalid, and promising to send the equivalent of her wages for the time he thought she would have to wait on her. This he easily did by the sale of a ring, which, besides his mother's watch, was the only article of value he had retained. He begged her likewise not to mention his name in the matter; and was foolish enough to expect that she would entirely keep the promise she had made him.

Wandering along the street, purposeless now and bereft, he spied a recruiting party at the door of a public-house; and on coming nearer, found, by one of those strange coincidences which do occur in life, and which have possibly their root in a hidden and wondrous law, that it was a party, perhaps a remnant, of the very regiment in which he had himself served, and in which his misfortune had befallen him. Almost simultaneously with the shock which the sight of the well-known number on the soldiers' knapsacks gave him, arose in his mind the romantic, ideal thought, of enlisting in the ranks of this same regiment, and recovering, as a private soldier and unknown, that honour which as officer he had lost. To this determination, the new necessity in which he now stood for action and change of life, doubtless contributed, though unconsciously. He offered himself to the sergeant; and, notwithstanding that his dress indicated a mode of life unsuitable as the antecedent to a soldier's, his appearance, and the necessity for recruits combined, led to his easy acceptance.

The English armies were employed in expelling the enemy from an invaded and helpless country. Whatever might be the political motives which had induced the Government to this measure, the young man was now able to feel that he could go and fight, individually and for his part, in the cause of liberty. He was free to possess his own motives for joining in the execution of the schemes of those who commanded his commanders.

With a heavy heart, but with more of inward hope and strength than he had ever known before, he marched with his comrades to the seaport and embarked. It seemed to him that because he had done right in his last trial, here was a new glorious chance held out to his hand. True, it was a terrible change to pass from a woman in whom he had hoped to find healing, into the society of rough men, to march with them, *"mitgleichem Tritt und Schritt,"* up to the bristling bayonets or the horrid vacancy of the cannon mouth. But it was the only cure for the evil that consumed his life.

He reached the army in safety, and gave himself, with religious assiduity, to the smallest duties of his new position. No one had a brighter polish on his arms, or whiter belts than he. In the necessary movements, he soon became precise to a degree that attracted the attention of his officers; while his character was remarkable for all the virtues belonging to a perfect soldier.

One day, as he stood sentry, he saw the eyes of his colonel intently fixed on him. He felt his lip quiver, but he compressed and stilled it, and tried to look as unconscious as he could; which effort was assisted by the formal bearing required by his position. Now the colonel, such had been the losses of the regiment, had been promoted from a lieutenancy in the same, and had belonged to it at the time of the ensign's degradation. Indeed, had not the changes in the regiment been so great, he could hardly have escaped so long without discovery. But the poor fellow would have felt that his name was already free of reproach, if he had seen what followed on the close inspection which had awakened his apprehensions, and which, in fact, had convinced the colonel of his identity with the disgraced ensign. With a hasty and less soldierly step than usual the colonel entered his tent, threw himself on his bed and wept like a child. When he rose he was overheard to say these words—and these only escaped his lips: "He is nobler than I."

But this officer showed himself worthy of commanding such men as this private; for right nobly did he understand and meet his feelings. He uttered no word of the discovery he had made, till years afterwards; but it soon began to be remarked that whenever anything arduous, or in any manner distinguished, had to be done, this man was sure to be of the party appointed. In short, as often as he could, the colonel "set him in the forefront of the battle." Passing through all with wonderful escape, he was soon as much noticed for his reckless bravery, as hitherto for his precision in the discharge of duties bringing only commendation and not honour. But his final lustration was at hand.

A great part of the army was hastening, by forced marches, to raise the siege of a town which was already on the point of falling into the hands of the enemy. Forming one of a reconnoitring party, which preceded the main body at some considerable distance, he and his companions came suddenly upon one of the enemy's outposts, occupying a high, and on one side precipitous rock, a short way from the town, which it commanded. Retreat was impossible, for they were already discovered, and the bullets were falling amongst them like the first of a hail-storm. The only possibility of escape remaining for them was a nearly hopeless improbability. It lay in forcing the post on this steep rock; which if they could do before assistance came to the enemy, they might, perhaps, be able to hold out, by means of its defences, till the arrival of the army. Their position was at once understood by all; and, by a sudden, simultaneous impulse, they found themselves halfway up the steep ascent, and in the struggle of a close conflict, without being aware of any order to that effect from their officer. But their courage was of no avail; the advantages of the place were too great; and in a few minutes the whole party was cut to pieces, or stretched helpless on the rock. Our youth had fallen amongst the foremost; for a musket ball had grazed his skull, and laid him insensible.

But consciousness slowly returned, and he succeeded at last in raising himself and looking around him. The place was deserted. A few of his friends, alive, but grievously wounded, lay near him. The rest were dead. It appeared that, learning the proximity of the English forces from this rencontre with part of their advanced guard, and dreading lest the town, which was on the point of surrendering, should after all be snatched from their grasp, the commander of the enemy's forces had ordered an immediate and general assault; and had for this purpose recalled from their outposts the whole of his troops thus stationed, that he might make the attempt with the utmost strength he could accumulate.

As the youth's power of vision returned, he perceived, from the height where he lay, that the town was already in the hands of the enemy. But looking down into the level space immediately below him, he started to his feet at once; for a girl, bare-headed, was fleeing towards the rock, pursued by several soldiers. "Aha!" said he, divining her purpose—the soldiers behind and the rock before her—"I will help you to die!" And he stooped and wrenched from the dead fingers of a sergeant the sword which they clenched by the bloody hilt. A new throb of life pulsed through him to his very finger-tips; and on the brink of the unseen world he stood, with the blood rushing through his veins in a wild dance of excitement. One who lay near him wounded, but recovered afterwards, said that he looked like one inspired. With a keen eye he watched the chase. The girl drew nigh; and rushed up the path near which he was standing. Close on her footsteps came the soldiers, the distance gradually lessening between them.

Not many paces higher up, was a narrower part of the ascent, where the path was confined by great stones, or pieces of rock. Here had been the chief defence in the preceding assault, and in it lay many bodies of his friends. Thither he went and took his stand.

On the girl came, over the dead, with rigid hands and flying feet, the bloodless skin drawn tight on her features, and her eyes awfully large and wild. She did not see him though she bounded past so near that her hair flew in his eyes. "Never mind!" said he, "we shall meet soon." And he stepped into the narrow path just in time to face her pursuers—between her and them. Like the red lightning the bloody sword fell, and a man beneath it. Cling! clang! went the echoes in the rocks—and another man was down; for, in his excitement, he was a destroying angel to the breathless pursuers. His stature rose, his chest dilated; and as the third foe fell dead, the girl was safe; for her body lay a broken, empty, but undesecrated temple, at the foot of the rock. That moment his sword flew in shivers from his grasp. The next instant he fell, pierced to the heart; and his spirit rose triumphant, free, strong, and calm, above the stormy world, which at length lay vanquished beneath him.

THE GRAY WOLF

One evening-twilight in spring, a young English student, who had wandered northwards as far as the outlying fragments of Scotland called the Orkney and Shetland Islands, found himself on a small island of the latter group, caught in a storm of wind and hail, which had come on suddenly. It was in vain to look about for any shelter; for not only did the storm entirely obscure the landscape, but there was nothing around him save a desert moss.

At length, however, as he walked on for mere walking's sake, he found himself on the verge of a cliff, and saw, over the brow of it, a few feet below him, a ledge of rock, where he might find some shelter from the blast, which blew from behind. Letting himself down by his hands, he alighted upon something that crunched beneath his tread, and found the bones of many small animals scattered about in front of a little cave in the rock, offering the refuge he sought. He went in, and sat upon a stone. The storm increased in violence, and as the darkness grew he became uneasy, for he did not relish the thought of spending the night in the cave. He had parted from his companions on the opposite side of the island, and it added to his uneasiness that they must be full of apprehension about him. At last there came a lull in the storm, and the same instant he heard a footfall, stealthy and light as that of a wild beast, upon the bones at the mouth of the cave. He started up in some fear, though the least thought might have satisfied him that there could be no very dangerous animals upon the island. Before he had time to think, however, the face of a woman appeared in the opening. Eagerly the wanderer spoke. She started at the sound of his voice. He could not see her well, because she was turned towards the darkness of the cave.

"Will you tell me how to find my way across the moor to Shielness?" he asked.

"You cannot find it to-night," she answered, in a sweet tone, and with a smile that bewitched him, revealing the whitest of teeth.

"What am I to do, then?"

"My mother will give you shelter, but that is all she has to offer."

The Portent And Other Stories | 181

"And that is far more than I expected a minute ago," he replied. "I shall be most grateful."

She turned in silence and left the cave. The youth followed.

She was barefooted, and her pretty brown feet went catlike over the sharp stones, as she led the way down a rocky path to the shore. Her garments were scanty and torn, and her hair blew tangled in the wind. She seemed about five and twenty, lithe and small. Her long fingers kept clutching and pulling nervously at her skirts as she went. Her face was very gray in complexion, and very worn, but delicately formed, and smooth-skinned. Her thin nostrils were tremulous as eyelids, and her lips, whose curves were faultless, had no colour to give sign of indwelling blood. What her eyes were like he could not see, for she had never lifted the delicate films of her eyelids.

At the foot of the cliff, they came upon a little hut leaning against it, and having for its inner apartment a natural hollow within. Smoke was spreading over the face of the rock, and the grateful odour of food gave hope to the hungry student. His guide opened the door of the cottage; he followed her in, and saw a woman bending over a fire in the middle of the floor. On the fire lay a large fish broiling. The daughter spoke a few words, and the mother turned and welcomed the stranger. She had an old and very wrinkled, but honest face, and looked troubled. She dusted the only chair in the cottage, and placed it for him by the side of the fire, opposite the one window, whence he saw a little patch of yellow sand over which the spent waves spread themselves out listlessly. Under this window there was a bench, upon which the daughter threw herself in an unusual posture, resting her chin upon her hand. A moment after, the youth caught the first glimpse of her blue eyes. They were fixed upon him with a strange look of greed, amounting to craving, but, as if aware that they belied or betrayed her, she dropped them instantly. The moment she veiled them, her face, notwithstanding its colourless complexion, was almost beautiful.

When the fish was ready, the old woman wiped the deal table, steadied it upon the uneven floor, and covered it with a piece of fine table-linen. She then laid the fish on a wooden platter, and invited the guest to help himself. Seeing no other provision, he pulled from his pocket a hunting knife, and divided a portion from the fish, offering it to the mother first.

"Come, my lamb," said the old woman; and the daughter approached the table. But her nostrils and mouth quivered with disgust.

The next moment she turned and hurried from the hut.

"She doesn't like fish," said the old woman, "and I haven't anything else to give her."

"She does not seem in good health," he rejoined.

The woman answered only with a sigh, and they ate their fish with the help of a little rye bread. As they finished their supper, the youth heard the sound as of the pattering of a dog's feet upon the sand close to the door; but ere he had time to look out of the window, the door opened, and the young woman entered. She looked better, perhaps from having just washed her face. She drew a stool to the corner of the fire opposite him. But as she sat down, to his bewilderment, and even horror, the student spied a single drop of blood on her white skin within her torn dress. The woman brought out a jar of whisky, put a rusty old kettle on the fire, and took her place in front of it. As soon as the water boiled, she proceeded to make some toddy in a wooden bowl.

Meantime the youth could not take his eyes off the young woman, so that at length he found himself fascinated, or rather bewitched. She kept her eyes for the most part veiled with the loveliest eyelids fringed with darkest lashes, and he gazed entranced; for the red glow of the little oil-lamp covered all the strangeness of her complexion. But as soon as he met a stolen glance out of those eyes unveiled, his soul shuddered within him. Lovely face and craving eyes alternated fascination and repulsion.

The mother placed the bowl in his hands. He drank sparingly, and passed it to the girl. She lifted it to her lips, and as she tasted—only tasted it—looked at him. He thought the drink must have been drugged and have affected his brain. Her hair smoothed itself back, and drew her forehead backwards with it; while the lower part of her face projected towards the bowl, revealing, ere she sipped, her dazzling teeth in strange prominence. But the same moment the vision vanished; she returned the vessel to her mother, and rising, hurried out of the cottage.

Then the old woman pointed to a bed of heather in one corner with a murmured apology; and the student, wearied both with the fatigues of the day and the strangeness of the night, threw himself upon it, wrapped in his cloak. The moment he lay down, the storm began afresh, and the wind blew so keenly through the crannies of the hut, that it was only by drawing his cloak over his head that he could protect himself from its currents. Unable to sleep, he lay listening to the uproar which grew in violence, till the spray was dashing against the window. At length the door opened, and the young woman came in, made up the fire, drew the bench before it, and lay down in the same strange posture, with her chin propped on her hand and elbow, and her face turned towards the youth. He moved a little; she dropped her head, and lay on her face, with her arms crossed beneath her forehead. The mother had disappeared.

Drowsiness crept over him. A movement of the bench roused him, and he fancied he saw some four-footed creature as tall as a large dog trot quietly out of the door. He was sure he felt a rush of cold wind. Gazing fixedly through the darkness, he thought he saw the eyes of the damsel encountering his, but a glow from the falling together of the remnants of the fire revealed clearly enough that the bench was vacant. Wondering what could have made her go out in such a storm, he fell fast asleep.

In the middle of the night he felt a pain in his shoulder, came broad awake, and saw the gleaming eyes and grinning teeth of some animal close to his face. Its claws were in his shoulder, and its mouth in the act of seeking his throat. Before it had fixed its fangs, however, he had its throat in one hand, and sought his knife with the other. A terrible struggle followed; but regardless of the tearing claws, he found and opened his knife. He had made one futile stab, and was drawing it for a surer, when, with a spring of the whole body, and one wildly contorted effort, the creature twisted its neck from his hold, and with something betwixt a scream and a howl, darted from him. Again he heard the door open; again the wind blew in upon him, and it continued blowing; a sheet of spray dashed across the floor, and over his face. He sprung from his couch and bounded to the door.

It was a wild night—dark, but for the flash of whiteness from the waves as they broke within a few yards of the cottage; the wind was raving, and the rain pouring down the air. A gruesome sound as of mingled weeping and howling came from somewhere in the dark. He turned again into the hut and closed the door, but could find no way of securing it.

The lamp was nearly out, and he could not be certain whether the form of the young woman was upon the bench or not. Overcoming a strong repugnance, he approached it, and put out his hands—there was nothing there. He sat down and waited for the daylight: he dared not sleep any more.

When the day dawned at length, he went out yet again, and looked around. The morning was dim and gusty and gray. The wind had fallen, but the waves were tossing wildly. He wandered up and down the little strand, longing for more light.

At length he heard a movement in the cottage. By and by the voice of the old woman called to him from the door.

"You're up early, sir. I doubt you didn't sleep well."

"Not very well," he answered. "But where is your daughter?"

"She's not awake yet," said the mother. "I'm afraid I have but a poor breakfast for you. But you'll take a dram and a bit of fish. It's all I've got."

Unwilling to hurt her, though hardly in good appetite, he sat down at the table. While they were eating, the daughter came in, but turned her face away and went to the farther end of the hut. When she came forward after a minute or two, the youth saw that her hair was drenched, and her face whiter than before. She looked ill and faint, and when she raised her eyes, all their fierceness had vanished, and sadness had taken its place. Her neck was now covered with a cotton handkerchief. She was modestly attentive to him, and no longer shunned his gaze. He was gradually yielding to the temptation of braving another night in the hut, and seeing what would follow, when the old woman spoke.

"The weather will be broken all day, sir," she said. "You had better be going, or your friends will leave without you."

Ere he could answer, he saw such a beseeching glance on the face of the girl, that he hesitated, confused. Glancing at the mother, he saw the flash of wrath in her face. She rose and approached her daughter, with her hand lifted to strike her. The young woman stooped her head with a cry. He darted round the table to interpose between them. But the mother had caught hold of her; the handkerchief had fallen from her neck; and the youth saw five blue bruises on her lovely throat—the marks of the four fingers and the thumb of a left hand. With a cry of horror he darted from the house, but as he reached the door he turned. His hostess was lying motionless on the floor, and a huge gray wolf came bounding after him.

There was no weapon at hand; and if there had been, his inborn chivalry would never have allowed him to harm a woman even under the guise of a wolf. Instinctively, he set himself firm, leaning a little forward, with half outstretched arms, and hands curved ready to clutch again at the throat upon which he had left those pitiful marks. But the creature as she sprung eluded his grasp, and just as he expected to feel her fangs, he found a woman weeping on his bosom, with her arms around his neck. The next instant, the gray wolf broke from him, and bounded howling up the cliff. Recovering himself as he best might, the youth followed, for it was the only way to the moor above, across which he must now make his way to find his companions.

All at once he heard the sound of a crunching of bones—not as if a creature was eating them, but as if they were ground by the teeth of rage and disappointment; looking up, he saw close above him the mouth of the little cavern in which he had taken refuge the day before. Summoning all his resolution, he passed it slowly and softly. From within came the sounds of a mingled moaning and growling.

Having reached the top, he ran at full speed for some distance across the moor before venturing to look behind him. When at length he did so, he saw, against the sky, the girl standing on the edge of the cliff, wringing her hands. One solitary wail crossed the space between. She made no attempt to follow him, and he reached the opposite shore in safety.

UNCLE CORNELIUS HIS STORY

It was a dull evening in November. A drizzling mist had been falling all day about the old farm. Harry Heywood and his two sisters sat in the house-place, expecting a visit from their uncle, Cornelius Heywood. This uncle lived alone, occupying the first floor above a chemist's shop in the town, and had just enough of money over to buy books that nobody seemed ever to have heard of but himself; for he was a student in all those regions of speculation in which anything to be called knowledge is impossible.

"What a dreary night!" said Kate. "I wish uncle would come and tell us a story."

"A cheerful wish," said Harry. "Uncle Cornie is a lively companion— isn't he? He cant even blunder through a Joe Miller without tacking a moral to it, and then trying to persuade you that the joke of it depends on the moral."

"Here he comes!" said Kate, as three distinct blows with the knob of his walking-stick announced the arrival of Uncle Cornelius. She ran to the door to open it.

The air had been very still all day, but as he entered he seemed to have brought the wind with him, for the first moan of it pressed against rather than shook the casement of the low-ceiled room.

Uncle Cornelius was very tall, and very thin, and very pale, with large gray eyes that looked greatly larger because he wore spectacles of the most delicate hair-steel, with the largest pebble-eyes that ever were seen. He gave them a kindly greeting, but too much in earnest even in shaking hands to smile over it. He sat down in the arm-chair by the chimney corner.

I have been particular in my description of him, in order that my reader may give due weight to his words. I am such a believer in words, that I believe everything depends on who says them. Uncle Cornelius Heywood's story told word for word by Uncle Timothy Warren, would not have been the same story at all. Not one of the listeners would have believed a syllable of it from the lips of round-bodied, red-faced, small-eyed, little Uncle Tim; whereas from Uncle Cornie—disbelieve one of his stories if you could!

One word more concerning him. His interest in everything conjectured or believed relative to the awful borderland of this world and the next, was only equalled by his disgust at the vulgar, unimaginative forms which curiosity about such subjects has assumed in the present day. With a yearning after the unseen like that of a child for the lifting of the curtain of a theatre, he declared that, rather than accept such a spirit-world as the would-be seers of the nineteenth century thought or pretended to reveal,—the prophets of a pauperised, workhouse immortality, invented by a poverty-stricken soul, and a sense so greedy that it would gorge on carrion,—he would rejoice to believe that a man had just as much of a soul as the cabbage of Iamblichus, namely, an aerial double of his body.

"I'm so glad you're come, uncle!" said Kate. "Why wouldn't you come to dinner? We have been so gloomy!"

"Well, Katey, you know I don't admire eating. I never could bear to see a cow tearing up the grass with her long tongue." As he spoke he looked very much like a cow. He had a way of opening his jaws while he kept his lips closely pressed together, that made his cheeks fall in, and his face look awfully long and dismal. "I consider eating," he went on, "such an animal exercise that it ought always to be performed in private. You never saw me dine, Kate."

"Never, uncle; but I have seen you drink;—nothing but water, I must confess."

"Yes that is another affair. According to one eyewitness that is no more than the disembodied can do. I must confess, however, that, although well attested, the story is to me scarcely credible. Fancy a glass of Bavarian beer lifted into the air without a visible hand, turned upside down, and set empty on the table!—and no splash on the floor or anywhere else!"

A solitary gleam of humour shone through the great eyes of the spectacles as he spoke.

"Oh, uncle! how can you believe such nonsense!" said Janet.

"I did not say I believed it—did I? But why not? The story has at least a touch of imagination in it."

"That is a strange reason for believing a thing, uncle," said Harry.

"You might have a worse, Harry. I grant it is not sufficient; but it is better than that commonplace aspect which is the ground of most faith. I believe I did say that the story puzzled me."

"But how can you give it any quarter at all, uncle?"

"It does me no harm. There it is—between the boards of an old German book. There let it remain."

"Well, you will never persuade me to believe such things," said Janet.

"Wait till I ask you, Janet," returned her uncle, gravely. "I have not the slightest desire to convince you. How did we get into this unprofitable current of talk? We will change it at once. How are consols, Harry?"

"Oh, uncle!" said Kate, "we were longing for a story, and just as I thought you were coming to one, off you go to consols!"

"I thought a ghost story at least was coming," said Janet.

"You did your best to stop it, Janet," said Harry.

Janet began an angry retort, but Cornelius interrupted her. "You never heard me tell a ghost story, Janet."

"You have just told one about a drinking ghost, uncle," said Janet—in such a tone that Cornelius replied—

"Well, take that for your story, and let us talk of something else."

Janet apparently saw that she had been rude, and said as sweetly as she might—"Ah! but you didn't make that one, uncle. You got it out of a German book."

"Make it!—Make a ghost story!" repeated Cornelius. "No; that I never did."

"Such things are not to be trifled with, are they?" said Janet.

"I at least have no inclination to trifle with them."

"But, really and truly, uncle," persisted Janet, "you don't believe in such things?"

"Why should I either believe or disbelieve in them? They are not essential to salvation, I presume."

"You must do the one or the other, I suppose."

"I beg your pardon. You suppose wrong. It would take twice the proof I have ever had to make me believe in them; and exactly your prejudice, and allow me to say ignorance, to make me disbelieve in them. Neither is within my reach. I postpone judgment. But you, young people, of course, are wiser, and know all about the question."

"Oh, uncle! I'm so sorry!" said Kate. "I'm sure I did not mean to vex you."

"Not at all, not at all, my dear.—It wasn't you."

"Do you know," Kate went on, anxious to prevent anything unpleasant, for there was something very black perched on Janet's forehead, "I have taken to reading about that kind of thing."

"I beg you will give it up at once. You will bewilder your brains till you are ready to believe anything, if only it be absurd enough. Nay, you may come to find the element of vulgarity essential to belief. I should be sorry to the heart to believe concerning a horse or dog what they tell you nowadys about Shakespeare and Burns. What have you been reading, my girl?"

"Don't be alarmed, uncle. Only some Highland legends, which are too absurd either for my belief or for your theories."

"I don't know that, Kate."

"Why, what could you do with such shapeless creatures as haunt their fords and pools for instance? They are as featureless as the faces of the mountains."

"And so much the more terrible."

"But that does not make it easier to believe in them," said Harry.

"I only said," returned his uncle, "that their shapelessness adds to their horror."

"But you allowed—almost, at least, uncle," said Kate, "that you could find a place in your theories even for those shapeless creatures."

Cornelius sat silent for a moment; then, having first doubled the length of his face, and restored it to its natural condition, said thoughtfully, "I suspect, Katey, if you were to come upon an ichthyosaurus or a pterodactyl asleep in the shubbery, you would hardly expect your report of it to be believed all at once either by Harry or Janet."

"I suppose not, uncle. But I can't see what—"

"Of course such a thing could not happen here and now. But there was a time when and a place where such a thing may have happened. Indeed, in my time, a traveller or two have got pretty soundly disbelieved for reporting what they saw,—the last of an expiring race, which had strayed over the natural verge of its history, coming to life in some neglected swamp, itself a remnant of the slime of Chaos."

"I never heard you talk like that before, uncle," said Harry. "If you go on like that, you'll land me in a swamp, I'm afraid."

"I wasn't talking to you at all, Harry. Kate challenged me to find a place for kelpies, and such like, in the theories she does me the honour of supposing I cultivate."

"Then you think, uncle, that all these stories are only legends which, if you could follow them up, would lead you back to some one of the awful monsters that have since quite disappeared from the earth."

"It is possible those stories may be such legends; but that was not what I intended to lead you to. I gave you that only as something like what I am going to say now. What if,—mind, I only suggest it,—what if the direful creatures, whose report lingers in these tales, should have an origin far older still? What if they were the remnants of a vanishing period of the earth's history long antecedent to the birth of mastodon and iguanodon; a stage, namely, when the world, as we call it, had not yet become quite visible, was not yet so far finished as to part from the invisible world that was its mother, and which, on its part, had not then become quite invisible—was only almost such; and when, as a credible consequence, strange shapes of those now invisible regions, Gorgons and Chimaeras dire, might be expected to gloom out occasionally from the awful Fauna of an ever-generating world upon that one which was being born of it. Hence, the life-periods of a world being long and slow, some of these huge, unformed bulks of half-created matter might, somehow, like the megatherium of later times,—a baby creation to them,—roll at age-long intervals, clothed in a mighty terror of shapelessness into the half-recognition of human beings, whose consternation at the uncertain vision were barrier enough to prevent all further knowledge of its substance."

"I begin to have some notion of your meaning, uncle," said Kate.

"But then," said Janet, "all that must be over by this time. That world has been invisible now for many years."

"Ever since you were born, I suppose, Janet. The changes of a world are not to be measured by the changes of its generations."

"Oh, but, uncle, there can't be any such things. You know that as well as I do."

"Yes, just as well, and no better."

"There can't be any ghosts now. Nobody believes such things."

"Oh, as to ghosts, that is quite another thing. I did not know you were talking with reference to them. It is no wonder if one can get nothing sensible out of you, Janet, when your discrimination is no greater than to lump everything marvellous, kelpies, ghosts, vampires, doubles, witches, fairies, nightmares, and I don't know what all, under the one head of ghosts; and we haven't been saying a word about them. If one were to disprove to you the existence of the afreets of Eastern tales, you would consider the whole argument concerning the reappearance of the departed upset. I congratulate you on your powers of analysis and induction, Miss Janet. But it matters very little whether we believe in ghosts, as you say, or not, provided we believe that we are ghosts—that within this body, which so many people are ready to consider their own very selves, their lies a ghostly embryo, at least, which has an inner side to it God only can see, which says I concerning itself, and which will soon have to know whether or not it can appear to those whom it has left behind, and thus solve the question of ghosts for itself, at least."

"Then you do believe in ghosts, uncle?" said Janet, in a tone that certainly was not respectful.

"Surely I said nothing of the sort, Janet. The man most convinced that he had himself had such an interview as you hint at, would find—ought to find it impossible to convince any one else of it."

"You are quite out of my depth, uncle," said Harry. "Surely any honest man ought to be believed?"

"Honesty is not all, by any means, that is necessary to being believed. It is impossible to convey a conviction of anything. All you can do is to convey a conviction that you are convinced. Of course, what satisfied you might satisfy another; but, till you can present him with the sources of your conviction, you cannot present him with the conviction—and perhaps not even then."

"You can tell him all about, it, can't you?"

"Is telling a man about a ghost, affording him the source of your conviction? Is it the same as a ghost appearing to him? Really, Harry!—You cannot even convey the impression a dream has made upon you."

"But isn't that just because it is only a dream?"

"Not at all. The impression may be deeper and clearer on your mind than any fact of the next morning will make. You will forget the next day altogether, but the impression of the dream will remain through all the following whirl and storm of what you call facts. Now a conviction may be likened to a deep impression on the judgment or the reason, or both. No one can feel it but the person who is convinced. It cannot be conveyed."

"I fancy that is just what those who believe in spirit-rapping would say."

"There are the true and false of convictions, as of everything else. I mean that a man may take that for a conviction in his own mind which is not a conviction, but only resembles one. But those to whom you refer profess to appeal to facts. It is on the ground of those facts, and with the more earnestness the more reason they can give for receiving them as facts, that I refuse all their deductions with abhorrence. I mean that, if what they say is true, the thinker must reject with contempt the claim to anything like revelation therein."

"Then you do not believe in ghosts, after all?" said Kate, in a tone of surprise.

"I did not say so, my dear. Will you be reasonable, or will you not?"

"Dear uncle, do tell us what you really think."

"I have been telling you what I think ever since I came, Katey; and you won't take in a word I say."

"I have been taking in every word, uncle, and trying hard to understand it as well.—Did you ever see a ghost, uncle?"

Cornelius Heywood was silent. He shut his lips and opened his jaws till his cheeks almost met in the vacuum. A strange expression crossed the strange countenance, and the great eyes of his spectacles looked as if, at the very moment, they were seeing something no other spectacles could see. Then his jaws closed with a snap, his countenance brightened, a flash of humour came through the goggle eyes of pebble, and, at length, he actually smiled as he said—"Really, Katey, you must take me for a simpleton!"

"How, uncle?"

"To think, if I had ever seen a ghost, I would confess the fact before a set of creatures like you—all spinning your webs like so many spiders to catch and devour old Daddy Longlegs."

By this time Harry had grown quite grave. "Indeed, I am very sorry, uncle," he said, "if I have deserved such a rebuke."

"No, no, my boy," said Cornelius; "I did not mean it more than half. If I had meant it, I would not have said it. If you really would like—" Here he paused.

"Indeed we should, uncle," said Kate, earnestly. "You should have heard what we were saying just before you came in."

"All you were saying, Katey?"

"Yes," answered Kate, thoughtfully. "The worst we said was that you could not tell a story without—well, we did say tacking a moral to it."

"Well, well! I mustn't push it. A man has no right to know what people say about him. It unfits him for occupying his real position amongst them. He, least of all, has anything to do with it. If his friends won't defend him, he can't defend himself. Besides, what people say is so often untrue!—I don't mean to others, but to themselves. Their hearts are more honest than their mouths. But Janet doesn't want a strange story, I am sure."

Janet certainly was not one to have chosen for a listener to such a tale. Her eyes were so small that no satisfaction could possibly come of it. "Oh! I don't mind, uncle," she said, with half-affected indifference, as she searched in her box for silk to mend her gloves.

"You are not very encouraging, I must say," returned her uncle, making another cow-face.

"I will go away, if you like," said Janet, pretending to rise.

"No, never mind," said her uncle hastily. "If you don't want me to tell it, I want you to hear it; and, before I have done, that may have come to the same thing perhaps."

"Then you really are going to tell us a ghost story!" said Kate, drawing her chair nearer to her uncle's; and then, finding this did not satisfy her sense of propinquity to the source of the expected pleasure, drawing a stool from the corner, and seating herself almost on the hearth-rug at his knee.

"I did not say so," returned Cornelius, once more. "I said I would tell you a strange story. You may call it a ghost story if you like; I do not pretend to determine what it is. I confess it will look like one, though."

After so many delays, Uncle Cornelius now plunged almost hurriedly into his narration.

"In the year 1820," he said, "in the month of August, I fell in love." Here the girls glanced at each other. The idea of Uncle Cornie in love, and in the very same century in which they were now listening to the confession, was too astonishing to pass without ocular remark; but, if he observed it, he took no notice of it; he did not even pause. "In the month of September, I was refused. Consequently, in the month of October, I was ready to fall in love again. Take particular care of yourself, Harry, for a whole month, at least, after your first disappointment; for you will never be more likely to do a foolish thing. Please yourself after the second. If you are silly then, you may take what you get, for you will deserve it—except it be good fortune."

"Did you do a foolish thing then, uncle?" asked Harry, demurely.

"I did, as you will see; for I fell in love again."

"I don't see anything so very foolish in that."

"I have repented it since, though. Don't interrupt me again, please. In the middle of October, then, in the year 1820, in the evening, I was walking across Russell Square, on my way home from the British Museum, where I had been reading all day. You see I have a full intention of being precise, Janet."

"I'm sure I don't know why you make the remark to me, uncle," said Janet, with an involuntary toss of her head. Her uncle only went on with his narrative.

"I begin at the very beginning of my story," he said; "for I want to be particular as to everything that can appear to have had anything to do with what came afterwards. I had been reading, I say, all the morning in the British Museum; and, as I walked, I took off my spectacles to ease my eyes. I need not tell you that I am short-sighted now, for that you know well enough. But I must tell you that I was short-sighted then, and helpless enough without my spectacles, although I was not quite so much so as I am now;—for I find it all nonsense about short-sighted eyes improving with age. Well, I was walking along the south side of Russell Square, with my spectacles in my hand, and feeling a little bewildered in consequence—for it was quite the dusk of the evening, and short-sighted people require more light than others. I was feeling, in fact, almost blind. I had got more than half-way to the other side, when, from the crossing that cuts off the corner in the direction of Montagu Place, just as I was about to turn towards it, an old lady stepped upon the kerbstone of the pavement, looked at me for a moment, and passed—an occurrence not very remarkable, certainly. But the lady was remarkable, and so was her dress. I am not good at observing, and I am still worse at describing dress, therefore I can only say that hers reminded me of an old picture—that is, I had never seen anything like it, except in old pictures. She had no bonnet, and looked as if she had walked straight out of an ancient drawing-room in her evening attire. Of her face I shall say nothing now. The next instant I met a man on the crossing, who stopped and addressed me. So short-sighted was I that, although I recognised his voice as one I ought to know, I could not identify him until I had put on my spectacles, which I did instinctively in the act of returning his greeting. At the same moment I glanced over my shoulder after the old lady. She was nowhere to be seen.

"'What are you looking at?' asked James Hetheridge.

"'I was looking after that old lady,' I answered, 'but I can't see her.'

"'What old lady?' said Hetheridge, with just a touch of impatience.

"'You must have seen her,' I returned. 'You were not more than three yards behind her.'

"'Where is she then?'

"'She must have gone down one of the areas, I think. But she looked a lady, though an old-fashioned one.'

"'Have you been dining?' asked James, in a tone of doubtful inquiry.

"'No,' I replied, not suspecting the insinuation; 'I have only just come from the Museum.'

"'Then I advise you to call on your medical man before you go home.'

"'Medical man!' I returned; 'I have no medical man. What do you mean? I never was better in my life.'

"'I mean that there was no old lady. It was an illusion, and that indicates something wrong. Besides, you did not know me when I spoke to you.'

"'That is nothing," I returned. 'I had just taken off my spectacles, and without them I shouldn't know my own father.'

"'How was it you saw the old lady, then?'

"The affair was growing serious under my friend's cross-questioning. I did not at all like the idea of his supposing me subject to hallucinations.

So I answered, with a laugh, 'Ah! to be sure, that explains it. I am so blind without my spectacles, that I shouldn't know an old lady from a big dog.'

"'There was no big dog,' said Hetheridge, shaking his head, as the fact for the first time dawned upon me that, although I had seen the old lady clearly enough to make a sketch of her, even to the features of her care-worn, eager old face, I had not been able to recognise the well-known countenance of James Hetheridge.

"'That's what comes of reading till the optic nerve is weakened," he went on. 'You will cause yourself serious injury if you do not pull up in time. I'll tell you what; I'm going home next week—will you go with me?'

"'You are very kind,' I answered, not altogether rejecting the proposal, for I felt that a little change to the country would be pleasant, and I was quite my own master. For I had unfortunately means equal to my wants, and had no occasion to follow any profession—not a very desirable thing for a young man, I can tell you, Master Harry. I need not keep you over the commonplaces of pressing and yielding. It is enough to say that he pressed and that I yielded. The day was fixed for our departure together; but something or other, I forget what, occurred, to make him advance the date, and it was resolved that I should follow later in the month.

"It was a drizzly afternoon in the beginning of the last week of October when I left the town of Bradford in a post-chaise to drive to Lewton Grange, the property of my friend's father. I had hardly left the town, and the twilight had only begun to deepen, when, glancing from one of the windows of the chaise, I fancied I saw, between me and the hedge, the dim figure of a horse keeping pace with us. I thought, in the first interval of unreason, that it was a shadow from my own horse, but reminded myself the next moment that there could be no shadow where there was no light. When I looked again, I was at the first glance convinced that my eyes had deceived me. At the second, I believed once more that a shadowy something, with the movements of a horse in harness, was keeping pace with us. I turned away again with some discomfort, and not till we had reached an open moorland road, whence a little watery light was visible on the horizon, could I summon up courage enough to look out once more. Certainly then there was nothing to be seen, and I persuaded myself that it had been all a fancy, and lighted a cigar. With my feet on the cushions before me, I had soon lifted myself on the clouds of tobacco far above all the terrors of the night, and believed them banished for ever. But, my cigar coming to an end just as we turned into the avenue that led up to the Grange, I found myself once more glancing nervously out of the window. The moment the trees were about me, there was, if not a shadowy horse out there by the side of the chaise, yet certainly more than half that conviction in here in my consciousness. When I saw my friend, however, standing on the doorstep, dark against the glow of the hall fire, I forgot all about it; and I need not add that I did not make it a subject of conversation when I entered, for I was well aware that it was essential to a man's reputation that his senses should be accurate, though his heart might without prejudice swarm with shadows, and his judgment be a very stable of hobbies.

"I was kindly received. Mrs. Hetheridge had been dead for some years, and Laetitia, the eldest of the family, was at the head of the household. She had two sisters, little more than girls. The father was a burly, yet gentlemanlike Yorkshire squire, who ate well, drank well, looked radiant, and hunted twice a week. In this pastime his son joined him when in the humour, which happened scarcely so often. I, who had never crossed a horse in my life, took his apology for not being able to mount me very coolly, assuring him that I would rather loiter about with a book than be in at the death of the best-hunted fox in Yorkshire.

"I very soon found myself at home with the Hetheridges; and very soon again I began to find myself not so much at home; for Miss Hetheridge—Laetitia as I soon ventured to call her—was fascinating. I have told you, Katey, that there was an empty place in my heart. Look to the door then, Katey. That was what made me so ready to fall in love with Laetitia. Her figure was graceful, and I think, even now, her face would have been beautiful but for a certain contraction of the skin over the nostrils, suggesting an invisible thumb and forefinger pinching them, which repelled me, although I did not then know what it indicated. I had not been with her one evening before the impression it made on me had vanished, and that so entirely that I could hardly recall the perception of the peculiarity which had occasioned it. Her observation was remarkably keen, and her judgment generally correct. She had great confidence in it herself; nor was she devoid of sympathy with some of the forms of human imagination, only they never seemed to possess for her any relation to practical life. That was to be ordered by the judgment alone. I do not mean she ever said so. I am only giving the conclusions I came to afterwards. It is not necessary that you should have any more thorough acquaintance with her mental character. One point in her moral nature, of special consequence to my narrative, will show itself by and by.

"I did all I could to make myself agreeable to her, and the more I succeeded the more delightful she became in my eyes. We walked in the garden and grounds together; we read, or rather I read and she listened;— read poetry, Katey—sometimes till we could not read any more for certain haziness and huskiness which look now, I am afraid, considerably more absurd than they really were, or even ought to look. In short, I considered myself thoroughly in love with her."

"And wasn't she in love with you, uncle?"

"Don't interrupt me, child. I don't know. I hoped so then. I hope the contrary now. She liked me I am sure. That is not much to say. Liking is very pleasant and very cheap. Love is as rare as a star."

"I thought the stars were anything but rare, uncle."

"That's because you never went out to find one for yourself, Katey. They would prove a few miles apart then."

"But it would be big enough when I did find it."

"Right, my dear. That is the way with love.—Laetitia was a good housekeeper. Everything was punctual as clockwork. I use the word advisedly. If her father, who was punctual to one date,—the dinner-hour,— made any remark to the contrary as he took up the carving-knife, Laetitia would instantly send one of her sisters to question the old clock in the hall, and report the time to half a minute. It was sure to be found that, if there was a mistake, the mistake was in the clock. But although it was certainly a virtue to have her household in such perfect order, it was not a virtue to be impatient with every infringement of its rules on the part of others. She was very severe, for instance, upon her two younger sisters if, the moment after the second bell had rung, they were not seated at the dinner-table, washed and aproned. Order was a very idol with her. Hence the house was too tidy for any sense of comfort. If you left an open book on the table, you would, on returning to the room a moment after, find it put aside. What the furniture of the drawing-room was like, I never saw; for not even on Christmas Day, which was the last day I spent there, was it uncovered. Everything in it was kept in bibs and pinafores. Even the carpet was covered with a cold and slippery sheet of brown holland. Mr. Hetheridge never entered that room, and therein was wise. James remonstrated once. She answered him quite kindly, even playfully, but no change followed. What was worse, she made very wretched tea. Her father never took tea; neither did James. I was rather fond of it, but I soon gave it up. Everything her father partook of was first-rate. Everything else was somewhat poverty-stricken. My pleasure in Laetitia's society prevented me from making practical deductions from such trifles."

"I shouldn't have thought you knew anything about eating, uncle," said Janet.

"The less a man eats, the more he likes to have it good, Janet. In short,—there can be no harm in saying it now,—Laetitia was so far from being like the name of her baptism,—and most names are so good that they are worth thinking about; no children are named after bad ideas,—Laetitia was so far unlike hers as to be stingy—an abominable fault. But, I repeat, the notion of such a fact was far from me then. And now for my story.

"The first of November was a very lovely day, quite one of the 'halcyon days' of 'St. Martin's summer.' I was sitting in a little arbour I had just discovered, with a book in my hand,—not reading, however, but day-dreaming,—when, lifting my eyes from the ground, I was startled to see, through a thin shrub in front of the arbour, what seemed the form of an old lady seated, apparently reading from a book on her knee. The sight instantly recalled the old lady of Russell Square. I started to my feet, and then, clear of the intervening bush, saw only a great stone such as abounded on the moors in the neighbourhood, with a lump of quartz set on the top of it. Some childish taste had put it there for an ornament. Smiling at my own folly, I sat down again, and reopened my book. After reading for a while, I glanced up again, and once more started to my feet, overcome by the fancy that there verily sat the old lady reading. You will say it indicated an excited condition of the brain. Possibly; but I was, as far as I can recall, quite collected and reasonable. I was almost vexed this second time, and sat down once more to my book. Still, every time I looked up, I was startled afresh. I doubt, however, if the trifle is worth mentioning, or has any significance even in relation to what followed.

"After dinner I strolled out by myself, leaving father and son over their claret. I did not drink wine; and from the lawn I could see the windows of the library, whither Laetitia commonly retired from the dinner-table. It was a very lovely soft night. There was no moon, but the stars looked wider awake than usual. Dew was falling, but the grass was not yet wet, and I wandered about on it for half an hour. The stillness was somehow strange. It had a wonderful feeling in it as if something were expected—as if the quietness were the mould in which some event or other was about to be cast.

"Even then I was a reader of certain sorts of recondite lore. Suddenly I remembered that this was the eve of All Souls. This was the night on which the dead came out of their graves to visit their old homes. 'Poor dead!' I thought with myself; 'have you any place to call a home now? If you have, surely you will not wander back here, where all that you called home has either vanished or given itself to others, to be their home now and yours no more! What an awful doom the old fancy has allotted you! To dwell in your graves all the year, and creep out, this one night, to enter at the midnight door, left open for welcome! A poor welcome truly!—just an open door, a clean-swept floor, and a fire to warm your rain-sodden limbs! The household asleep, and the house-place swarming with the ghosts of ancient times,—the miser, the spendthrift, the profligate, the coquette,—for the good ghosts sleep, and are troubled with no waking like yours! Not one man, sleepless like yourselves, to question you, and be answered after the fashion of the old nursery rhyme—

'*What makes your eyes so holed?*'
'*I've lain so long among the mould.*'
'*What makes your feet so broad?*'
'*I've walked more than ever I rode!*'

"'Yet who can tell?' I went on to myself. 'It may be your hell to return thus. It may be that only on this one night of all the year you can show yourselves to him who can see you, but that the place where you were wicked is the Hades to which you are doomed for ages.' I thought and thought till I began to feel the air alive about me, and was enveloped in the vapours that dim the eyes of those who strain them for one peep through the dull mica windows that will not open on the world of ghosts. At length I cast my fancies away, and fled from them to the library, where the bodily presence of Laetitia made the world of ghosts appear shadowy indeed.

"'What a reality there is about a bodily presence!' I said to myself, as I took my chamber-candle in my hand. 'But what is there more real in a body?' I said again, as I crossed the hall. 'Surely nothing,' I went on, as I ascended the broad staircase to my room. 'The body must vanish. If there be a spirit, that will remain. A body can but vanish. A ghost can appear.'

"I woke in the morning with a sense of such discomfort as made me spring out of bed at once. My foot lighted upon my spectacles. How they came to be on the floor I could not tell, for I never took them off when I went to bed. When I lifted them I found they were in two pieces; the bridge was broken. This was awkward. I was so utterly helpless without them! Indeed, before I could lay my hand on my hair-brush I had to peer through one eye of the parted pair. When I looked at my watch after I was dressed, I found I had risen an hour earlier than usual. I groped my way downstairs to spend the hour before breakfast in the library.

"No sooner was I seated with a book than I heard the voice of Laetitia scolding the butler, in no very gentle tones, for leaving the garden door open all night. The moment I heard this, the strange occurrences I am about to relate began to dawn upon my memory. The door had been open the night long between All Saints and All Souls. In the middle of that night I awoke suddenly. I knew it was not the morning by the sensations I had, for the night feels altogether different from the morning. It was quite dark. My heart was beating violently, and I either hardly could or hardly dared breathe. A nameless terror was upon me, and my sense of hearing was, apparently by the force of its expectation, unnaturally roused and keen. There it was—a slight noise in the room!—slight, but clear, and with an unknown significance about it! It was awful to think it would come again. I do believe it was only one of those creaks in the timbers which announce the torpid, age-long, sinking flow of every house back to the dust—a motion to which the flow of the glacier is as a torrent, but which is no less inevitable and sure. Day and night it ceases not; but only in the night, when house and heart are still, do we hear it. No wonder it should sound fearful! for are we not the immortal dwellers in ever-crumbling clay? The clay is so near us, and yet not of us, that its every movement starts a fresh dismay. For what will its final ruin disclose? When it falls from about us, where shall we find that we have existed all the time?

"My skin tingled with the bursting of the moisture from its pores. Something was in the room beside me. A confused, indescribable sense of utter loneliness, and yet awful presence, was upon me, mingled with a dreary, hopeless desolation, as of burnt-out love and aimless life. All at once I found myself sitting up. The terror that a cold hand might be laid upon me, or a cold breath blow on me, or a corpse-like face bend down through the darkness over me, had broken my bonds!—I would meet half-way whatever might be approaching. The moment that my will burst into action the terror began to ebb.

"The room in which I slept was a large one, perfectly dreary with tidiness. I did not know till afterwards that it was Laetitia's room, which she had given up to me rather than prepare another. The furniture, all but one article, was modern and commonplace. I could not help remarking to myself afterwards how utterly void the room was of the nameless charm of feminine occupancy. I had seen nothing to wake a suspicion of its being a lady's room. The article I have excepted was an ancient bureau, elaborate and ornate, which stood on one side of the large bow window. The very morning before, I had seen a bunch of keys hanging from the upper part of it, and had peeped in. Finding however, that the pigeon-holes were full of papers, I closed it at once. I should have been glad to use it, but clearly it was not for me. At that bureau the figure of a woman was now seated in the posture of one writing. A strange dim light was around her, but whence it proceeded I never thought of inquiring. As if I, too, had stepped over the bourne, and was a ghost myself, all fear was now gone. I got out of bed, and softly crossed the room to where she was seated. 'If she should be beautiful!' I thought—for I had often dreamed of a beautiful ghost that made love to me. The figure did not move. She was looking at a faded brown paper. 'Some old love-letter,' I thought, and stepped nearer. So cool was I now, that I actually peeped over her shoulder. With mingled surprise and dismay I found that the dim page over which she bent was that of an old account-book. Ancient household records, in rusty ink, held up to the glimpses of the waning moon, which shone through the parting in the curtains, their entries of shillings and pence!—Of pounds there was not one. No doubt pounds and farthings are much the same in the world of thought—the true spirit-world; but in the ghost-world this eagerness over shillings and pence must mean something awful! I To think that coins which had since been worn smooth in other pockets and purses, which had gone back to the Mint, and been melted down, to come out again and yet again with the heads of new kings and queens,—that dinners, eaten by men and women and children whose bodies had since been eaten by the worms,— that polish for the floors, inches of whose thickness had since been worn away,—that the hundred nameless trifles of a life utterly vanished, should be perplexing, annoying, and worst of all, interesting the soul of a ghost who had been in Hades for centuries! The writing was very old-fashioned, and the words were contracted. I could read nothing but the moneys and one single entry—'Corinths, Vs.'

"Currants for a Christmas pudding, most likely!—Ah, poor lady! the pudding and not the Christmas was her care; not the delight of the children over it, but the beggarly pence which it cost. And she cannot get it out of her head, although her brain was 'powdered all as thin as flour' ages ago in the mortar of Death. 'Alas, poor ghost!' It needs no treasured hoard left behind, no floor stained with the blood of the murdered child, no wickedly hidden parchment of landed rights! An old account-book is enough for the hell of the housekeeping gentlewoman!

"She never lifted her face, or seemed to know that I stood behind her. I left her, and went into the bow window, where I could see her face. I was right. It was the same old lady I had met in Russell Square, walking in front of James Hetheridge. Her withered lips went moving as if they would have uttered words had the breath been commissioned thither; her brow was contracted over her thin nose; and once and again her shining forefinger went up to her temple as if she were pondering some deep problem of humanity. How long I stood gazing at her I do not know, but at last I withdrew to my bed, and left her struggling to solve that which she could never solve thus. It was the symbolic problem of her own life, and she had failed to read it. I remember nothing more. She may be sitting there still, solving at the insolvable.

"I should have felt no inclination, with the broad sun of the squire's face, the keen eyes of James, and the beauty of Laetitia before me at the breakfast table, to say a word about what I had seen, even if I had not been afraid of the doubt concerning my sanity which the story would certainly awaken. What with the memories of the night and the want of my spectacles, I passed a very dreary day, dreading the return of the night, for, cool as I had been in her presence, I could not regard the possible reappearance of the ghost with equanimity. But when the night did come, I slept soundly till the morning.

"The next day, not being able to read with comfort, I went wandering about the place, and at length began to fit the outside and inside of the house together. It was a large and rambling edifice, parts of it very old, parts comparatively modern. I first found my own window, which looked out of the back. Below this window, on one side, there was a door. I wondered whither it led, but found it locked. At the moment James approached from the stables. 'Where does this door lead?' I asked him. 'I will get the key,' he answered. 'It is rather a queer old place. We used to like it when we were children.' 'There's a stair, you see,' he said, as he threw the door open. 'It leads up over the kitchen.' I followed him up the stair. 'There's a door into your room,' he said, 'but it's always locked now.—And here's Grannie's room, as they call it, though why, I have not the least idea,' he added, as he pushed open the door of an old-fashioned parlour, smelling very musty. A few old books lay on a side table. A china bowl stood beside them, with some shrivelled, scentless rose-leaves in the bottom of it. The cloth that covered the table was riddled by moths, and the spider-legged chairs were covered with dust.

"A conviction seized me that the old bureau must have belonged to this room, and I soon found the place where I judged it must have stood. But the same moment I caught sight of a portrait on the wall above the spot I had fixed upon. 'By Jove!' I cried, involuntarily, 'that's the very old lady I met in Russell Square!'

"'Nonsense!' said James. 'Old-fashioned ladies are like babies—they all look the same. That's a very old portrait.'

"'So I see,' I answered. 'It is like a Zucchero.'

"'I don't know whose it is," he answered hurriedly, and I thought he looked a little queer.

"'Is she one of the family?' I asked.

"'They say so; but who or what she was, I don't know. You must ask Letty," he answered.

"'The more I look at it,' I said, 'the more I am convinced it is the same old lady.'

"'Well,' he returned with a laugh, 'my old nurse used to say she was rather restless. But it's all nonsense.'

"'That bureau in my room looks about the same date as this furniture,' I remarked.

"'It used to stand just there,' he answered, pointing to the space under the picture. 'Well I remember with what awe we used to regard it; for they said the old lady kept her accounts at it still. We never dared touch the bundles of yellow papers in the pigeon-holes. I remember thinking Letty a very heroine once when she touched one of them with the tip of her forefinger. She had got yet more courageous by the time she had it moved into her own room.'

"'Then that is your sister's room I am occupying?' I said.

"'Yes.'

"'I am ashamed of keeping her out of it.'

"'Oh! she'll do well enough.'

"'If I were she though,' I added, 'I would send that bureau back to its own place.'

"'What do you mean, Heywood? Do you believe every old wife's tale that ever was told?'

"'She may get a fright some day—that's all!' I replied.

"He smiled with such an evident mixture of pity and contempt that for the moment I almost disliked him; and feeling certain that Laetitia would receive any such hint in a somewhat similar manner, I did not feel inclined to offer her any advice with regard to the bureau.

"Little occurred during the rest of my visit worthy of remark. Somehow or other I did not make much progress with Laetitia. I believe I had begun to see into her character a little, and therefore did not get deeper in love as the days went on. I know I became less absorbed in her society, although I was still anxious to make myself agreeable to her—or perhaps, more properly, to give her a favourable impression of me. I do not know whether she perceived any difference in my behaviour, but I remember that I began again to remark the pinched look of her nose, and to be a little annoyed with her for always putting aside my book. At the same time, I daresay I was provoking, for I never was given to tidiness myself.

"At length Christmas Day arrived. After breakfast, the squire, James, and the two girls arranged to walk to church. Laetitia was not in the room at the moment. I excused myself on the ground of a headache, for I had had a bad night. When they left, I went up to my room, threw myself on the bed, and was soon fast asleep.

"How long I slept I do not know, but I woke again with that indescribable yet well-known sense of not being alone. The feeling was scarcely less terrible in the daylight than it had been in the darkness. With the same sudden effort as before, I sat up in the bed. There was the figure at the open bureau, in precisely the same position as on the former occasion. But I could not see it so distinctly. I rose as gently as I could, and approached it, after the first physical terror. I am not a coward. Just as I got near enough to see the account book open on the folding cover of the bureau, she started up, and, turning, revealed the face of Laetitia. She blushed crimson.

"'I beg your pardon, Mr. Heywood,' she said in great confusion; 'I thought you had gone to church with the rest.'

"'I had lain down with a headache, and gone to sleep,' I replied. 'But,— forgive me, Miss Hetheridge,' I added, for my mind was full of the dreadful coincidence,—'don't you think you would have been better at church than balancing your accounts on Christmas Day?'

"'The better day the better deed,' she said, with a somewhat offended air, and turned to walk from the room.

"'Excuse me, Laetitia,' I resumed, very seriously, 'but I want to tell you something.'

"She looked conscious. It never crossed me, that perhaps she fancied I was going to make a confession. Far other things were then in my mind. For I thought how awful it was, if she too, like the ancestral ghost, should have to do an age-long penance of haunting that bureau and those horrid figures, and I had suddenly resolved to tell her the whole story. She listened with varying complexion and face half turned aside. When I had ended, which I fear I did with something of a personal appeal, she lifted her head and looked me in the face, with just a slight curl on her thin lip, and answered me. 'If I had wanted a sermon, Mr. Heywood, I should have gone to church for it. As for the ghost, I am sorry for you.' So saying she walked out of the room.

"The rest of the day I did not find very merry. I pleaded my headache as an excuse for going to bed early. How I hated the room now! Next morning, immediately after breakfast, I took my leave of Lewton Grange."

"And lost a good wife, perhaps, for the sake of a ghost, uncle!" said Janet.

"If I lost a wife at all, it was a stingy one. I should have been ashamed of her all my life long."

"Better than a spendthrift," said Janet.

"How do you know that?" returned her uncle. "All the difference I see is, that the extravagant ruins the rich, and the stingy robs the poor."

"But perhaps she repented, uncle," said Kate.

"I don't think she did, Katey. Look here."

Uncle Cornelius drew from the breast pocket of his coat a black-edged letter.

"I have kept up my friendship with her brother," he said. "All he knows about the matter is, that either we had a quarrel, or she refused me;—he is not sure which. I must say for Laetitia, that she was no tattler. Well, here's a letter I had from James this very morning. I will read it to you.

"'MY DEAR MR. HEYWOOD,—We have had a terrible \shock this morning. Letty did not come down to breakfast, and Lizzie went to see if she was ill. We heard her scream, and, rushing up, there was poor Letty, sitting at the old bureau, quite dead. She had fallen forward on the desk, and her housekeeping-book was crumpled up under her. She had been so all night long, we suppose, for she was not undressed, and was quite cold. The doctors say it was disease of the heart.'

"There!" said Uncle Cornie, folding up the letter.

"Do you think the ghost had anything to do with it, uncle?" asked Kate, almost under her breath.

"How should I know, my dear? Possibly."

"It's very sad," said Janet; "but I don't see the good of it all. If the ghost had come to tell that she had hidden away money in some secret place in the old bureau, one would see why she had been permitted to come back. But what was the good of those accounts after they were over and done with? I don't believe in the ghost."

"Ah, Janet, Janet! but those wretched accounts were not over and done with, you see. That is the misery of it."

Uncle Cornelius rose without another word, bade them good-night, and walked out into the wind.